In the Shadows of Bliss

In the Shadows of Bliss

Alisa Lynn

Labyrinth Publishing

RALEIGH, NORTH
CAROLINA

In the Shadows of Bliss
By Alisa Lynn

Labyrinth Publishing
P.O. Box 19243
Raleigh, NC 27619

Editorial services: Paula R. Bryant/ASarah Publications, www.paularbryant.com
Cover design: Precise Marketing Solutions, www.precisemarketingsolutions.net
Special thanks to Joyce Nicole Photography and Kenneth Gardner.

ISBN 978-0-9890199-0-3
Library of Congress Control Number: 2013933197

*The ending of a soul's time on Earth is but the beginning
of its most vicarious escapade!*

───

*For my soul mate and the love of my life…
You are my passion and inspiration.*

───

For my father, John, Sr.

and

For Melva and Naomi

*…whose souls gloriously soar in another realm
while awaiting that which is yet to come.*

I give my heartfelt thanks to:

My Heavenly Father
…for the opportunity to experience this life,
the vision of this story, and the many talents and blessings
that He has so graciously granted me

My endearing family

My extraordinary village of support:
Dad, Ashley, Dorion, Zynde, Deidre, Kyla, John, Jr., Michelle,
Marcia, Cathy, Silena, Carlos, Percy, Rose,
Jackie, Linda, Brenda, Tamecca and Allen
…for their tenacious love, unyielding devotion,
enlightening collaboration and unwavering encouragement

Rev. Dr. Julius Carroll and Rev. Charlene Limenih
…for their spiritual guidance in this endeavor

My editor, Paula, and my marketing representative, Johnny
…for the blessed alliance that we've established and the
professional manner in which they have led me through this process

Table of Contents

Prologue

He slowly moved his eyes around the room, searching through the shadows, unable to remember where he was or what was going on around him. His mind struggled to focus. He wasn't afraid, though his vision was blurred from awakening abruptly in the darkness.

He realized that just before opening his eyes he was vividly aware of a calming presence in the room. Someone, something, had been speaking gently to him in a whisper. He could still feel the warm, tingling breath on his ear...and he was being warned about something. It was confusing. Had he been dreaming? It felt too real for that.

The angel Carlonian was there, though the young man only sensed a surreal, yet caring and familiar presence near him. To this soul, the room seemed to be cloaked with this presence, wrapping him in a warm embrace.

Chapter 1

BLISS

Bliss: complete happiness; a state of spiritual joy;
a place of rare beauty; a distant realm
located between Heaven and Earth.

ar above Earth's atmosphere, above the galaxies and the universe, there is another world known simply as…Bliss.

Drenched in the golden rays of Heaven's bright light, Bliss is a shimmering sphere of silver clouds floating above the black sea of space. Ignited by flecks of shiny, metallic confetti swirling around the silver clouds, Bliss is a magnificent sight to see. It is a perfected world filled with rich splendor and unparalleled beauty. Having an atmosphere much like Earth, yet somehow inexplicably different, Bliss is a realm of deep blue skies, dazzlingly radiant nights, crystal-clear, crisp waters, lush grasses, magnificent mountain ranges and picturesque valleys. Without the spoils of mankind, it is truly a pristine world.

Bliss is filled with thousands and thousands of souls who are sent there in spiritual form by the Heavenly Father. They live there for thirty-three years. While in Bliss, the souls are weightless, allowing them to soar in the clouds along with the multitudes of angels who come and go throughout the vast lands and raging oceans.

In this exceptionally unique society, angels befriend souls. They listen to them, share insightful knowledge with them and give them guidance in worship and praise. Yet these relationships are equally gratifying. Some of the angels once lived as mortals on Earth and empathize with the souls as they awkwardly anticipate the unknown. After their time in Bliss, each soul is transformed into a mortal form and moves on to experience life on Earth.

All are happy and enthusiastic in this spirit-filled world. They live each day to the fullest with praise and adoration for their Creator and

1

with endless celebrations of life. Together, the angels and souls sing trium-phantly, filling the clouds of Bliss with unrivaled rhapsody.

Eventually, each soul is paired with a mate. The two souls join, becoming one, and discover the contentment of perfect companionship until their time in Bliss comes to an end. This is the story of one of those souls. A soul named Wesley.

During his thirty-three years there, Wesley enjoyed his uncomplicated life in the only world he had ever known; but he knew, as every soul did, that Bliss was only a stopover. He would soon become a mortal being and be granted his opportunity to travel to Earth. This process was known as the Changeover.

He was unaware of what awaited him in his earthly life to come.

．．．．．．．．．．．．．．．

Bliss is a world of logic and order. As Wesley grew in age he realized that he was learning a great deal about himself, as well as others. He knew that his personal mission while in Bliss was to learn all that he could dur-ing his time there. His interactions with souls and angels would become invaluable life lessons for living in harmony with others. He had also been told by an angel that life was an endless line of infinity, and that his first thirty-three years were only a small part of that line. Wesley wondered if the next phase of his existence would be another brief interruption in the long, infinite line or if it would turn out to be his life eternally.

Although he was coming to know himself well as an inhabitant of Bliss, Wesley wasn't aware of the traits that had been selected for him to carry when he left there on his next journey. Later, in his life to come, Wes-ley would find that his confidence, compassion and charisma would draw others to him. He had been blessed with a kind heart that would lead him out of his way to help others, especially the underdog in any situation. He would also possess his own clear-cut, unyielding sense of justice. Wesley would be straightforward and brutally honest. He would be hard-work-ing, hard-nosed and intimidating, though he wouldn't try to be. It would simply be who he was. Wesley would do everything with a sense of pre-cise, constructed purpose, and in spite of his basic need to help others, he would be a skeptic: trusting few, but uncharacteristically giving what he had to anyone in need.

These attributes were already forming in him. Although he respected and revered the angels and listened to them, he debated them on nearly every issue and felt that he had all the answers. These personal traits would continue to be a contradiction in Wesley, one that would result in a persistent inner struggle throughout his time as a human being on Earth.

Then one glorious day Wesley turned thirty-three years old and his time in Bliss came to an end. His Changeover would happen that day.

Wesley wasn't happy or sad about it; he was just curious and anxious about getting started. His only concern was for another there, the one whom he had come to recognize as his soul's mate, his other half. Her name was Arie.

Arie's spirit was warm and caring, yet she was feisty and witty. This often challenged Wesley's mind and soul to the core of his being. It seemed their souls were nestled tightly together; they were virtually attached…yet a subtle, comfortable independence lingered within their relationship. Perfection. It seemed to Wesley that they had been perfectly matched throughout his life, though he knew that wasn't true because Arie had not been in Bliss for thirty-three years as he had. Amazingly, he couldn't even remember their first meeting. It was as though it had never happened and Arie had been ever-present in his life. The two souls were paired flawlessly. Arie was strong where Wesley was weak and his strengths compensated for her weaknesses.

As he prepared to leave Bliss, Wesley remembered a celebration they had recently attended. Arie was known for her captivating voice and was asked to participate in the program by singing a song. She was flattered and decided to present an original song of her own. For weeks, Arie worked tirelessly to prepare for the program. She practiced the song over and over again, adjusted the words, changed the key, and fretted over it until the melody and words sounded exactly how she had envisioned them. Satisfied that it was just right, she and Wesley visited the celebration site early on the day of the event so she would have time to practice there.

They arrived to a flurry of excited energy that literally filled the air. The organizer came to greet them, explaining that Arie's song would be the highlight of the program. It wasn't until that moment Arie realized: *She would be the main focus of the evening.* Wesley picked up on her apprehension immediately. He could visibly see the proud contentment she felt about her song just seconds earlier drain from her entire being. Struggling with contradicting thoughts, Arie wanted to practice more, make her song even better—but time wouldn't allow it. She pondered whether she should have chosen a different song, convincing herself that had she known she would be the main focus of the celebration, she wouldn't have picked an original song. The organizer was stunned by Arie's reluctant reaction. She had heard her beautiful voice and loved it, completely.

Perplexed by Arie's apparent hesitation, she asked, "Is something wrong?"

"No, b-but I'll need to go make a few adjustments," Arie stammered.

"Okay, but please be back early so we can make sure everything is just right and on time for the evening."

"I will."

The organizer scurried away, shooting a quick look toward Wesley, obviously concerned.

When they were safely alone Arie blurted, "I should never have agreed to sing; I shouldn't have prepared an original piece...maybe I could go and practice another song. Come on, let's hurry."

"Stop doing this to yourself, Arie," Wesley reassured, "Everyone will love your song. It's incredible."

"Of course, *you* would say that."

"I'm only saying it because it's true."

"How can I sing here tonight and watch them analyzing my song while they watch me...while they're listening to my words? What if they don't like it?"

"They are going to like it! There's no way they can't like it. It's brilliant."

"Again..." she said cynically, "*You* would say that."

Wesley decided to play into it, "Okay, so if they don't like it, so what?"

"What! It's not that simple, Wesley. If they don't like my song, then what will they think of me?" she protested.

"What are you talking about? It's just a song. It's not *you*."

"But they'll be saying, 'Who does she think she is to sing her own song? She isn't even a real singer.'"

Wesley was amazed. He had to set this right. "You have a beautiful voice, Arie. You are a real singer *because* you sing!" He moved closer. "You have to stop caring so much about what others think. You have to start defining who and what you are by what *you* think."

"That's easy for you to say," she shot back. "Look at who you are."

"What do you mean, who I am?"

"You do everything right, everyone thinks so! No one ever thinks you don't. It's like they want you around and can't wait for you to be with them...including me."

"I don't do everything completely right; I just don't care if anyone thinks I didn't do something right, because it doesn't matter to me what they think." He spread his arms wide as he turned around, canvassing the beautiful plateau that was the setting of their celebration. "You can't see that it's not so much about what you sing; it's about that they asked you to sing in this beautiful place because they want to hear you sing. You're right about one thing: Everyone may not like what you sing, but everyone isn't going to dislike it, either. If you are happy with your song, it should be enough."

"Well, I thought I was happy with it until I found out that *my song* is the main part of the program and that everyone will be waiting to hear it all evening. Now I'm not sure if this is what I should have prepared to sing."

Wesley attempted to nip her uncertainty in the bud. "Stop doubting yourself and your choices!"

"I can't help it, I don't know why. I'm not sure I want to come tonight... let's just leave and not show up."

"Arie! You are coming tonight and I'm coming with you. I'll be listening to your incredible voice singing your wonderful song, and I will be so proud of you." He smiled a brilliant smile.

Reluctantly, Arie went to the event with Wesley that evening, Wesley expecting nothing less than to be the center of all of the attention and admiration with Arie. Everything turned out just as he had said, and he completely enjoyed every moment of the jovial spotlight. Arie, on the other hand, though she sang enchantingly as usual, immediately rushed to Wesley's side afterwards. She uncomfortably weathered the remainder of the long, painful night, worrying that each compliment was in fact a smartly camouflaged criticism of her performance, and ultimately, of her very being.

Wesley came back to himself, and to the reality that he was about to leave Bliss. Yes, leaving Arie alone there to continue struggling with her insecurities was bittersweet. He was saddened that it wasn't Arie's time to changeover as well. Wesley loved her deeply; he was sure of it. He couldn't imagine that she wouldn't be with him as he went through the Changeover, or that she would later experience the Changeover alone, without him. He felt certain that whatever his next phase would be, he would be able to get settled into that life and await her arrival there. He thought they'd ultimately be together again, because they were devoted and committed to each other for all eternity, whatever eternity turned out to be.

As he left Arie, the realization that he had no idea when he would see her again settled in. He felt a peculiar separation within himself. He was no longer whole. A fiercely startling emotion gripped him, causing him deep inner pain...something he'd never known before. Wesley hesitated, and for the first time in his life, questioned his impending journey. Then hesitation was replaced with fear. Though Wesley had routinely questioned everything in his world, he had never been afraid to meet anything head-on. He was accustomed to seizing every challenge, unafraid of the unknown. But suddenly, he was skeptical as he stood on the brink of what he had anticipated for thirty-three years...because he was changing over without the one whom he had come to believe was his soul's other half.

Wesley's faith was tested that day as his journey began. Filled with a contradiction of heartrending hesitation and agitated joy, he said his goodbyes to all and began making his way to the garden which would lead him to the Transfer Station.

Chapter 2

REFLECTION

*T*he Transfer Station was a dazzling, magnificent building set high on a mountain overlooking all of Bliss, or so it seemed. As Wesley started his approach he noticed that the colossal peak was covered with long, thick, radiant grass in every possible hue of green. Then he paused and stood in amazement, admiring the vibrant flowers he knew were indigenous to different climates flourishing throughout what was actually a magnificent garden. The trees were gigantic and of endless varieties, bearing bountiful, luscious blooms and fruit. Then Wesley noticed a wide, glistening path. It wrapped evenly around and around the mountain, from the bottom all the way up, and appeared to enter the building at the top.

When Wesley reached the bottom of the mountain, he noticed there wasn't another living soul in sight. He stopped, looking upward, realizing he was completely alone. He could no longer see the building at the top. However, what he could see was a beautiful paradise beckoning him to continue his journey.

He moved onto the path and was instantly wrapped in a blanket of heavenly peace and tranquility. Suddenly…quietly, like a gentle mist on a summer morning, the unexplainable calm erased all fear and hesitation. Wesley slowly entered the garden, taking notice of each and every rock, leaf and flower. He inhaled deeply, enjoying the soft, warm breeze—so light and fragrant with pleasing aromas of jasmine, honeysuckle and lavender—as he walked on the brilliant path through the thick, breathtaking foliage. He marveled at how he had never noticed such things before. Completely overwhelmed with feelings of gratitude, Wesley stopped for awhile to meditate in the midst of this paradise.

Soon Wesley resumed his journey, only to hear the incredibly melodic sounds of what seemed to be nearly a thousand birds singing in beautiful, syncopated harmony. He could hardly contain his composure again. He passed a small pond and admired the stunning, multi-colored fish swimming in the sparkling water. He still hadn't seen anyone else, but now it really didn't matter. He realized that he was completely surrounded by lovely animals. All of them were unique, with varying colors and remarkable eyes: cats and dogs of all varieties; beautiful insects; brightly-colored frogs and enormous mice covered in spectacular, lush fur. Suddenly a deer appeared, and then raccoons, followed closely by a fox...and then out of nowhere a giant, gentle bear emerged.

None of the animals acknowledged Wesley's presence, and curiously, he felt no fear whatsoever being in the midst of them. As time went on more animals appeared along the path, including an enormous lion tenderly sharing water with a majestic lamb. All of these amazing creatures were living together, peacefully, harmoniously, in this mystifying mountain garden.

Wesley had no idea how long he had been traveling and couldn't see where the path was going; he just continued to follow it as it curved, rose and descended along the landscape. Along the way his peaceful mindset began to be replaced with introspective thoughts. He began to think about everything: His life thus far, and especially his problem with trust and control. He wondered how he could trust, who he could trust, and why would he trust? After all, he felt he had been given all of the tools he needed to handle his own life. Why should he rely on anyone else when he could reason things out for himself? The fact that he was in the garden now proved he had been chosen by God to enter this place and move on to the next phase. He had successfully navigated his way through Bliss for thirty-three years. Having reached this day, he was moving on to the next phase of his life into infinity—and he would navigate his way through that phase, whatever that may be.

Wesley also thought about how he was compelled to help others when they were making obvious mistakes. They needed his advice and he felt that he was chosen to show them the way, the right way, the sensible way, to do things. It actually angered him to think about how many others he knew had handled certain situations. The decisions they made were absurd, even when the solution was completely clear. Wesley was sure there would be definitive answers to these perplexing thoughts in the next phase, or at least he hoped so.

Wesley's thoughts began to subside and were replaced with excitement as he happily glided on for what seemed like days or even weeks through the garden. He lost all track of time. There was only daylight on this mountain path, so he was able to see and experience everything. He never slept, and remarkably, never got tired. As Wesley moved farther along, he became overjoyed. It was an unexplainable, completely engulfing sense of delight! He had never known such a feeling of absolute satisfaction. There were no troubling thoughts now, no regrets, no anticipation—all of that had passed. Now there was just total contentment. Wesley took his time, ambling along the path, soaking it all in, praying to never forget any of it, most importantly, how he felt right at that moment.

The path led him beneath crystal-clear, plummeting waterfalls and mile after mile of pure, peaceful serenity. There was no rush and no time clock…no expectations of him whatsoever. Cloaked in an armor of fascination, he sauntered onward, taking the time to stop and marvel at the awesome magnificence of God's creativity and the realization that God had fashioned it all for those He loved.

When Wesley finally reached the top of the mountain forty days had passed, but he was blissfully unaware of it. He only knew that since he had begun this journey, he had not wanted it to end. He had been ecstatically happy while making his way through the magnificent garden. Now that he had reached his destination he immediately felt vulnerable. The garden path had been so tranquil and reflective, and now his arrival at the Transfer Station jolted him back to the reality of his journey. Suddenly, out of nowhere, FEAR returned. For Wesley, the reality of the unknown now loomed immediately ahead. It was standing right in front of him.

The Transfer Station was unlike anything Wesley could have ever imagined. As he stood at the end of the path he marveled at its existence and was overwhelmed with its intensity. Perched on the highest peak in Bliss, it overlooked the world he'd known from one side of the building, while the other side overlooked a vast sea of darkness speckled with shiny, bright lights. The Transfer Station was a colossal formation of incomparable grandeur. Built in earthly fashion, it resembled a majestic castle. It was constructed of the precious metals of Earth and its exterior walls were crafted of pure gold, giving the castle a brilliant, lustrous sheen. There were diamond, opal and zircon embellishments defining its circular towers, which stood on every side, reflecting the luminous heavenly sunlight. Adorned with endless precious gems and stones of rare beauty, the castle stood flickering to distant mountains and valleys, amazing all that approached, beckoning them to enter its grounds and continue their destined journeys. Wesley's fear melted away as he stood in awe at the wondrous sight before him.

God's glorious angels filled the sky, and though Wesley hadn't seen another soul since before he entered the garden, hundreds (or could it have been thousands?) of others just like him filled the grassy, meadow-like grounds of the castle. *Where had they come from?* Instantly, all of these other souls appeared, who had apparently traveled through the garden and were there to encounter the same thing that he was. Wesley marveled at the miraculous character and magnificence of God as the angels' harmonic voices filled the atmosphere with praise and adoration, singing the most beautiful songs he had ever heard. He was filled with an excitement he could barely contain as he joined the triumphant crowd moving through the vast pasture toward the imminent castle.

When at last Wesley reached the entrance to the castle he was ushered into an enormous foyer along with the other souls. Delight overcame him as he relished the exquisite décor of his surroundings. This round, massive space had soaring walls that were covered with incandescent platinum panels encrusted with sparkling emeralds. Gigantic, intricately-carved archways speckled with sapphires and rubies led from the foyer, fanning out in every direction. This magnificent entrance hall continually filled and emptied with anxious souls as they came and were directed to specific archways by angels, who welcomed and gently guided them. There were no random placements; it was evident that a very meticulous plan was being followed. God's plan.

Wesley was shepherded with a group of other souls through one of the extraordinary archways into a tunnel of dazzling aquamarine. The group moved quickly and quietly through the tunnel's space as though swimming through a channel of weightless water. Then the passageway opened into a courtyard filled with the lovely, sweet aroma of yellow roses in full bloom and park-like marble benches sprinkled throughout. As he emerged from the tunnel, Wesley sensed that something was very different. He suddenly felt heavy, as though he were anchored to the ground. He was still able to move around, but not as effortlessly as he always had. Filled with confusion and curiosity, he awkwardly made his way to a nearby bench and plunged his newly-acquired mass onto it. An angel approached and explained that he had lost his weightlessness in the process of preparation for his next phase of life.

The angel led Wesley to a room with no walls that had a spectacular, unobstructed view, and left him alone with his thoughts. Now he was on the other side of the building looking out into the dark, empty sea of lights that he had noticed just before entering this marvelous place. He was far above the galaxies. Looking up, he saw a bright, vibrant blue sky stretching upward without limits. When he looked down he saw only darkness, something he had never seen before reaching the Transfer Station. It intrigued him. He closely examined the darkness with an edgy anticipation.

Another angel came to him and introduced himself. His name was Carlonian. He explained to Wesley that this was the portal designated for his transfer to Earth, and that he was there to take part in this process with him. Wesley was relieved to meet the angel and hear that he wouldn't be alone. Carlonian smiled in an effort to comfort Wesley's mounting anxiety.

"What's happening now?" Wesley mumbled.

He wondered how he could suddenly be alone with Carlonian. *Where were all of the other souls he had just seen?* He knew there were thousands of others there.

"Don't worry or be afraid, Wesley. You will soon reach the next phase, the place where you will find out who you are and learn so much more about life."

"I'm not afraid anymore," Wesley confided. "I just want to know what to expect, so I can get ready to handle this."

"You are already ready to handle what is ahead. Just trust in the Lord, He will not forsake you."

"I know that!" Wesley snapped, and then caught himself. "But I always pride myself on being prepared for any situation, so I can do my best and always be the best."

"Being the best is not what your journey is about, Wesley. Relax and you will see that this opportunity is one that you will grow from."

"Why do I need to learn or grow? I've been learning all my life, now I'm ready to get on with it. I want to move on to this phase, all the more close to eternal life with God, right? You know, Infinity."

"Yes, I do know. It's not time for that yet. The place where you are going is a place of challenges and there are many pitfalls. It will be challenging like you have never been challenged."

"Okay. I'm ready...for all of it...for any challenge put before me."

Carlonian continued, "The difference in the place you are going and your life here in Bliss, is that you will be given the right to choose."

"Choose what?"

"Mainly, whether or not you choose eternal life with God."

"Of course, I do. I already know that."

"I told you, there will be pitfalls. The world you are entering is a world of deception. It is ruled by another whose purpose is to distract you from the truth and the existence of God and eternal life. You will not remember your life here. Your soul will arrive in the world known as Earth, and you will begin as a baby. That vessel will carry you through your mortal life."

"I'm expected to accomplish something as this baby?"

"You will grow from a baby into a child and eventually become an adult, if you are to exist there for that long. Some souls go to Earth for a short stay as a baby or a small child, and some are there until long after adulthood. Each soul's journey is different, and each is pre-determined based on what that soul's purpose is for that phase of life. Some go to learn, some go to teach, some do both."

"I don't understand. Will I be learning or teaching?"

"Only God knows that, because only God truly knows your soul. One day you will unquestionably know your own soul, and you will choose. That choice will determine your continued existence. Many are derailed in this phase. I pray that you will not be one of them and that you will be reunited here for eternity with our Heavenly Father, all of the angels, and all of the souls of those that you have loved here in Bliss. You will also come to love many on Earth who are in your future."

"Will you be on Earth with me?"

"I will be with you, but you will not be aware of my presence. You may suspect at times that I or someone like me is there, or you may not be convinced that I even exist. It is hard to say what a soul will believe while on Earth. There are many factors that will take place once you arrive there to shape the beliefs that you will grow with. Only time will determine this. That is all for now. Go in peace."

Chapter 3

EARTH

*C*arlonian watched as Wesley was transferred to Earth and born into *the next phase of his life. He would be the son of an unwed mother who was living in a place called New York City in 1943. The second phase of Wesley's journey had begun.*

Lorraine Mae Lewis now had four children, all of them by different fathers, and she had not been married to any of them. When Wesley was born Lorraine's three older children were living with relatives. She kept Wesley with her until he was six months old, and then she took him to her parents' farm in the beautiful countryside of North Carolina…just outside the little town of Belhaven.

She visited with her parents, Thomas and Lois Lewis, for nearly a week before disappearing during the night, leaving little Wesley behind. At first, Wesley's grandfather had been angry, but his grandmother was delighted. Though a new baby required a lot of work and brought many sleepless nights, Lois knew the baby would also bring buckets of joy into the house. So Wesley lived with his grandparents on the little farm and became the center of their lives.

None of Lorraine's children had lived with their mother for very long. Wesley's two brothers and one sister had been shifted around, either living with relatives or in foster homes. Most of the time, the other three children were separated because no one wanted to take all three at the same time. Of all the children, Wesley's life had been the most stable.

When Wesley was 4 years old, his mother showed up for a visit. She brought Chris, one of her other children, with her. Wesley was overjoyed to know that he had a big brother, and was even more excited to hear about his other brother and sister. He wanted them to come and live with him on the farm. He was happy when he overheard his grandfather telling his mother that they could all come home to live.

"Lorraine, your kids need a stable home. If you come live here, you can bring them all. There's plenty of room, and it would make your momma real happy."

"You know you don't want me here, Daddy," she said sarcastically.

"Lorraine, I'm just tired of watchin you run all over the place like you're crazy or somethin. You come here four years ago and left your baby, and we don't hear nothin from you til now."

"Listen, Daddy, I don't want to live on no farm ever again. I'm sorry I left Wesley here, but I knew I couldn't take good care of him."

"Well, why didn't you just ask us? Why'd you have to sneak off in the night like that? Makes us feel like a couple a fools."

"I'll just take him back with me, Daddy. I don't want you and Momma to feel like I was just usin you."

"No! No, Lorraine, don't go upsettin his life now. I don't like the way you did it, but that boy's life is here. This is all he knows and he means the world to us."

"I know, but ya'll are gettin older and I know I need to be takin care of my own children."

"So is Chris livin with you now? Are you takin care of him? Is that why you're here, so you can get all your kids together?"

"No, Daddy, Chris' daddy is sick. He's been stayin with his daddy, and so I just have him with me for awhile. I'm takin him back to Queens before school starts back up in the fall."

Thomas couldn't hold back his concern any longer. "Honey, you know I love you, but you have to slow down, stop livin that fast life up there in New York City. Raising children is a rewardin thing."

He paused, letting his words sink in. They sat in silence for a few minutes. Wesley's grandmother saw Wesley listening and whisked him into the house to help her with dinner.

"Where are Elizabeth and John livin? How are they? Do you even know about your children, Lorraine?" He was annoyed just thinking about it.

"Okay, Daddy, that's enough of this conversation. I came to see Wesley and to visit you and Momma. Can we just leave it at that?"

She realized that her voice had raised and quickly looked at her father, who was stunned at her disrespect.

"What I'm tryin to say, Daddy," she continued in a soft voice, "…is that Momma's in the house fryin us some chicken. She's so happy to see me and Chris, and so is Wesley. Can't we just have a good time today? I don't want to talk about anything else right now."

"Go on, girl," he mumbled as he walked away toward the barn, "Go on in the house."

· · · · · · · · · · · · · · ·

Lorraine and Chris spent the night and were gone when Wesley woke up the next morning. He had enjoyed their visit, but it didn't matter much to him that they had left—he loved his life there on the farm with Grandpap and Grandy. He did hope that his mother had left to go get his other brother and his sister and bring them back, so they could all live together on the farm.

Wesley lived with his grandparents until he was 6 years old. These early years were unhurried, uncomplicated and carefree, though he virtually had no interaction with his many cousins who lived nearby. One of his aunts, Aunt Clara, was cruel to him. Wesley had overheard her arguing with his grandparents about who his father was. She said she couldn't understand why they would take Wesley in like they had, in view of the conflicts she was having with Wesley's mother and father. He didn't understand any of it, and it didn't seem to affect him directly, so he dismissed it.

Wesley was the only child on the farm during those years and was the apple of his Grandpap's eye. He went everywhere with his grandfather and learned a lot from him. They loved each other tremendously. Grandy also spent a lot of time with Wesley teaching him many practical things, including how to bake.

Every morning after breakfast Wesley became his Grandpap's shadow. They went to the barn together, and then to the fields together; they even napped together. As Wesley grew, his Grandpap began to teach him things out in the fields and gave him daily chores and responsibilities, which he did well and with great pride.

"Wesley, did you get the eggs for breakfast?" Grandpap kindly asked his 6-year-old sidekick.

"Yes, Grandpap," Wesley proudly announced. "They're in the basket waitin for Grandy to cook em."

Life was pleasant and uneventful until one day Wesley's mother came back again. He was in his room practicing his letters when he heard loud noises in the front yard. He ran down the hall to the front room window and watched as his Grandpap and mother stood shouting at each other. Grandy saw Wesley watching and hurried him off to the kitchen. A few minutes later his mother stomped into the house, went into Wesley's room and gathered all of his clothes.

Then the unthinkable happened; the moment that changed Wesley's life forever. As the terrible scene unfolded it froze in his psyche, so it seemed everything was happening in slow motion. He would never forget that horrifying feeling when his mother burst into the kitchen, destroying his peaceful sense of contentment: the safe cocoon that his grandparents had so naturally provided for him.

As Lorraine pulled Wesley from the house into the waiting car that one of her sisters was driving, he cried out violently and reached for his Grandpap—who stood proudly, but defeated, watching with moist eyes as they pulled away. In this same manner, Wesley's mother gathered all four of her children and moved them away with her to New York City.

Never one to accept handouts, Lorraine refused to live in the projects. Instead, she found an old, run-down rooming house in a somewhat better neighborhood in Brooklyn, where she rented a large room. The family of five lived there: Wesley, his mother Lorraine, his sister Elizabeth (whom he called Liz), and his two brothers, John (who everyone except his mother called JoJo) and Chris. They had one bed, two cots, a chair, a small couch and some shelves for their stuff.

The community bathroom was down the hall; they all despised that the most. *Everybody in the house knew what you were doing and when you had to do it.* There was absolutely no privacy. Wesley vowed he'd one day have all the privacy he wanted, like it was back on the farm. They also shared the kitchen. Their family got one cabinet for their food. No one was supposed to touch anything that wasn't theirs. It was the rooming house's honor system. It didn't take much imagination to know what was going to happen. Their cabinet was always empty because their mother was never there. They were regularly taken advantage of by the other tenants.

Six Years Later...

The four kids had been and were now on their own. Wesley, the youngest, was 12 years old. Liz was the oldest at 15 and had a job after school bagging groceries at the nearby grocery store. Liz worked hard because she detested the life that they were living and wanted to get out at all costs. Most of the time, she skipped school so she could work and get extra money. Her mother didn't know about that part.

Liz was determined. Wesley could hardly remember ever seeing her smile. He'd think, *If only she'd smile she'd be the prettiest girl in the world.* Liz had the looks, alright. She was tall and slender, and she never seemed to gain weight. Her silky hair cascaded down her back, from the Sioux influence on their mother's side of the family, only she had curls instead of the usual straight hair of their ancestors. In spite of her beauty, Liz usually had a look of urgency on her face, as if she was going somewhere and might be late. Wesley looked up to her. He thought she could do anything, maybe even that she'd be the first woman President or something like that. Now that would really be something.

John "JoJo" was the second oldest. He was average in size, but athletically built and a force to be reckoned with. He stayed in trouble all the time. He ditched school too, but he wasn't working; he was just hanging out with his boys, and they got into and (usually) out of everything. Now and then they'd get caught in their mischief, and his mother would have to leave whichever job she was on and catch the bus... to the store he was accused of stealing from, JoJo's school, or occasionally the police station. He was only 14, but was already known by the police. Wesley couldn't understand why JoJo kept doing the things he did. It was like he wanted a one-way ticket for a dead-end trip that he was bent on making happen.

Whenever the phone rang down the hall and someone yelled that it was for them, Wesley cringed a little. He'd imagine JoJo lying in an alley dead or being sent off to prison forever. He had already spent many nights in juvenile detention. When he was at home, he was either talking to Liz or sleeping. JoJo and Liz got along great; she was the only person he really trusted. He would do anything for her. Once a guy tripped her at school and JoJo beat him so badly that he was hospitalized.

Chris, on the other hand, had a fear of the streets. He had a small build and was very thin. He avoided getting in a fight at all costs, sometimes going a mile or so out of his way while walking home to avoid any possibility. He went to school every day, studied hard, and got the best grades. He was a little cocky about it, too. Chris did so well with language that his sixth grade English teacher recommended him for special programs. He liked to write stories and wrote about everything, winning many awards. That year he wrote a story that was published in the local newspaper. The editor promised him that if he went to college and graduated, he would give Chris a job. Chris was ecstatic about this offer and even more motivated to keep his steady drive going. He wanted no part of the streets and told everyone that one day he would be "somebody." Chris had plans to go to college, but whenever he talked about it in the neighborhood they laughed at him, except when JoJo was around. JoJo wouldn't let anyone laugh at any of them. Their jokes didn't bother Chris anyway; he kept on dreaming his dream and moving toward it, getting honor role grades and all kinds of crazy awards that none of them had ever heard of.

Wesley, one could say, was a combination of them all. Tall, even stately for his age, he wanted to get out of the neighborhood just like Liz did… and he had a ruthless determination when he set his mind on something. Wesley wanted to have a *real home* one day—but he just couldn't study like Chris. He knew he'd never make it out that way. Hanging out with the guys like JoJo did was definitely not for him. That situation would just end up as a prison term. And Wesley saw how Liz worked herself to death bagging groceries every day, staying late to clean the store and restock the shelves. The manager would order her around like she was nothing, paid her less than minimum wage, and acted like he was waiting for her to make the smallest mistake to get rid of her.

Their mother worked all the time; they hardly saw her. She did domestic work all day and went straight to her other job, sewing at night, usually getting back home around midnight after riding two buses across town.

"Liz, everybody in?" she would ask wearily every night as she dragged herself inside, anticipating bad news.

"Everybody cept JoJo, Momma," was Liz's usual answer.

"Oh, Lawd. When did you last see him, girl?"

"This morning fore school. He ain't been back since then."

One night she made her way over to the cot that Chris and Wesley shared. She watched them sleeping peacefully at separate ends. Chris so focused and determined, yet with a ruthless core. And Wesley, her baby boy, her youngest, with a beautiful heart, so caring and loyal. She worried about him, but knew that to strengthen him for the world, she would have to make some very difficult decisions.

Oh, how she longed for the deep sleep that the young, unburdened enjoyed: deep, restful sleep. The kind where you don't feel like the whole world is on your shoulders; where the decisions you either make or don't make could break you, and where the lives of other people are relying on you for everything. The weight of four children was sometimes more than Lorraine thought she could bear, but she loved them all. She was trying, the best way that she knew how, to love and provide for them.

She plopped down in the ragged blue, upholstered armchair by the window, the one place in her world that was her private space. The children all recognized this and never intruded when she went to sit there and gaze through the glass. Her thoughts turned inward that night as she reflected on her life. *How had things ever come to this?* She had been filled with the excitement of youth when she left the farm at 19 years of age, where she had lived so many years with her family. She excitedly left the beautiful North Carolina countryside to explore life in the "Big City."

Lorraine had been an alluring young woman with beautiful, smooth skin, strikingly contrasting, sharp facial features and silky, thick jet black hair. Her laugh was loud, contagious and constant. She had an easy way about her, enjoying life and the people that it brought into hers. She readily fell in love and offered herself completely to her suitor: mind, body and soul, without reservation.

To her disappointment, none of the four men she had given her heart to had reciprocated her affection, and each had left behind a child. There were no professions of love, no promises, and no financial help. She had done what she thought was best by sending her children to live with other family members, all of whom she felt would give them better lives.

Following a particularly painful heartbreak Lorraine decided to give up on men, pull her family together in one place, and take care of her responsibilities. But look at how things had been going. She never dreamed it would be so hard. She never had any time or money to have fun anymore, not that it mattered much to her now. She had certainly had plenty of fun in the past. What bothered her most was that she couldn't provide well for her children, and she could see that life for them was really hard. She couldn't bring herself to call on her family for help, especially her father, whom she hadn't spoken to since the day she had taken Wesley from the farm.

She was losing John to the streets, and she didn't know what was going on with the others. She was too tired all the time to even try to find out. One of her sisters had taken a job with a family in Ohio. She lived with them and was making very good money. She told Lorraine that in the wealthy community where she worked and lived, there were many other families looking for live-in housekeepers. Lorraine was sure she could find a position there, too. The amount of money her sister made was unbelievable, but she didn't have any children, so it was easy for her to make a move like that. Still, it was an intriguing thought.

Lorraine decided that she would push through the fatigue each night so she could spend time with Liz, and wake the boys earlier some mornings so she could talk to them more frequently. *What better time than the present?* she thought...*while Liz is here, right now.* She turned from the window.

"Liz," she called out.

But Liz had quietly slipped into the bed she shared with her mother and drifted off to sleep. As she watched Liz sleeping, she reasoned to herself that because Liz could rest well she must not have disturbing thoughts that would keep her awake. Maybe things weren't so bad. She smiled and decided to wait up for John so she could talk to him. While she was waiting, she thought she'd make a cup of tea. She went down to the kitchen and found that their shelf was empty. They didn't have anything and payday was a week away. Anxiety returned.

JoJo tiptoed into the room at 4:10 in the morning. Lorraine was sitting at the window, waiting. She had dozed off, but woke instantly when she heard the key in the door.

"John," she whispered as she walked toward him, motioning for him to go back into the hallway.

"Momma? What you doin awake?"

"Go on, walk downstairs, I want to talk to you."

"Why, Momma?"

She walked past him and down the steps to what was once a living room and now served as a lobby of sorts. One floor lamp stood in a corner and was always left on at night. The dull light cast a yellow glow over a long, paint-chipped brown counter with mailboxes behind it and a pay phone on the wall. There were folding chairs around two walls, and one large table sat in the center of the room with chairs around it. Lorraine sat at one end of the table and watched John as he paced the floor like a caged animal.

"You watchin out for Liz and the boys, or you just gettin into more trouble?" she calmly asked.

"Momma, I'm jus tryin to help us all survive. Look..." He opened his coat and pulled out a bag. "I got us some peanut butter and some bread so they can eat today when they wake up. And for you, Momma, here's some tea bags."

Lorraine wanted to smile and cry at the same time. She thought, *If only the circumstances were different, he would be, too.*

"John, you're a good son and brother, but you have to stop this. I know you stole it or did somethin illegal to get money to buy it. You gonna get caught, then what? Then what are the boys and Liz gonna do?"

"I can't stand to see them hungry, Momma."

"I know John, and I'm lookin, tryin to find better work. Things gonna change."

"Well, Momma, til they do, I gotta do what I can to help."

"Then get a job like Liz, that kind of help is the kind I need."

"I can't do nothin like Liz can. I ain't never been that smart that anybody gonna give me a job, Momma. I got to use my head to help."

"Son, can't you see your luck is not gonna hold out? You will get caught…YOU WILL GET CAUGHT."

"I can't think about that, I know what I'm doin. Come on, Momma, go rest before you go back to work."

"No, it's too late. I got to get ready for work now. I'm gonna try to see if there's work at my second job, takin out trash or cleanin up; there has to be somethin. You just stop all this foolishness and let me see what I can do, John! You hear me?"

"Come on, Momma, let's go upstairs."

Chapter 4

LIFE

*L*ife went on and Wesley decided that he had to do things his way. The only problem was he hadn't figured out exactly what that was yet. He was a loner. It never bothered him if only Chris was there when he came home, or if no one was there at all. His mom usually left 50¢ on the dresser for his and Chris' dinner, JoJo took care of himself, and Liz did her own thing by eating at the store or with her boyfriend. Most days Wesley and Chris walked to White Castle and had three burgers, a donut and a coke each.

"Do you think we'll ever move out of the roomin house?" Wesley asked Chris on the way to White Castle one evening.

"Mom says that we will, but she's been saying that as long as I can remember. I'm planning to get a scholarship to college; then I won't have to live there anymore. I'll be able to get myself out."

"What about me?" Wesley was stunned.

"What about you, Baby Brother? I've been wondering that, too. What about you? When are you going to start planning a life for yourself and doing something about it?"

"What do you mean?"

"I mean, I found out that I am smart, really smart, and being smart in school gets me a lot of attention. The teachers and counselors love it when you make good grades and they go out of their way to help you, even if you are from the ghetto. I think they like it better if you are. It makes them feel like they're helping the poor underprivileged. So I decided that I was going to make the best grades I can and get them to help me get up and out. I'm going to be a writer, a famous one."

"Well, I don't get good grades," Wesley confided. "School is hard and I hate it."

"You have to find out what you do well, a strength that you have, and then use that to get where you want to be in life, Wes. You can do it, too. You can have a good life, a better one than we have now. I'll help you."

19

"What about Momma? Are you gonna help her when you get out of college and get famous?"

"Wesley, Mom doesn't want my help. She won't even ask her own father to help her. She's happy doing what she does. If she weren't, she would have tried harder to make a better life for all of us or asked our fathers for some help. We'd probably be better off living with them!"

Wesley stopped in his tracks. "How can you say that?" he shouted. "She's just had some really hard luck."

"That's for sure," Chris laughed.

"Wow, Chris, you're not suppose to be like that. We're a family. We're suppose to be there for each other, help each other."

"Look Wesley, I told you, I'll help you. It's always you and me anyway. Liz just goes to work then hangs around with that thug boyfriend of hers… what's his name again?"

"Cim, and he's pretty cool."

"Whatever you say," he scoffed, "…and JoJo, he's never leaving the hood. He's like Mom: bad breaks because of bad decisions. I'm not like them. It's clear I took after my father. I keep in touch with him. He's got a good life and he wants to be in my life. I sure want to be in his."

"I wish I could meet my father."

"I know you do, Wesley, but maybe you should get in touch with Grandpap. I bet he'd help you. I hear Mom talking to her sisters; they say he thought you were something special and wanted to keep you on the farm. Liz calls him sometimes. She keeps him up on us, and he's sent money to Liz behind Mom's back when things were really bad here. He can't blame the way Mom is on you or any of us. I'm going to visit him one day; Liz says so, too."

He felt bad for Wesley and decided to change the subject. "Come on, little brother, let's go inside and eat our delicious dinner then go back home and play a game of dominoes. You're really good at that," he said, smiling, "You always win."

Once again, they enjoyed their White Castle ritual. Wesley thought all that independence and going out to eat every day was great. He was feeling pretty good about it until one day at school when he was bragging about his evening routine and how lucky he was, and became the laughing stock of the whole class. He didn't know that most kids went home to their families, did their homework and sat down to dinner together. *How dare they laugh at me and my family,* Wesley fumed to himself. But he couldn't help wondering if they were right. *Were he and his family a bunch of freaks, living like they did in one room with no dining room of their own to share a meal together?* He skipped school for a week before he could face those kids again, which only put him farther behind in school. Finally he decided, *Forget em, that's their life, this is mine.*

. . . .

Nothing changed much for two years, and then life as they had known it began to fall apart. Wesley came home from school as usual to find Liz there packing her clothes...and she was happy. It was one of the few times he saw her smile. She was even singing.

"Where you goin, Liz?"

"Wes, always remember, you can come to me anytime. You don't have to live this way anymore." She cheerfully declared.

"What do you mean?"

Before she could answer the door swung open and their mother rushed in. She pushed Wesley out of the way and shoved Liz on the bed. Then she started slapping her and crying and yelling at her. Liz just took it for a moment, and then she seemed to come to her senses and lurched up, grabbing for her mother's arms.

"Stop hittin me, get off me!" Liz shouted.

"How could you be so stupid?" Lorraine screamed as she struggled with Liz. "You're so young, you could've had anything, been anything, done anything with your life!"

"Momma, I *am* being what I want to be."

"No!" Lorraine cried out, sobbing almost uncontrollably. "It's over for you. Your choices are over now, don't you understand? You are becomin me! You're pregnant and that no good piece of man ain't gonna stand by you."

"Momma, yes he is...Cimarron wants me and he wants our baby. This is my dream, Momma. I'm gonna be a mother, and I'll be a good one."

"Do you think I didn't think that, too? Look at our life here in this room."

"Momma, this is gonna work. Me and Cimarron love each other and—"

"Cimarron, *humph*...what kind a name is that anyway? I know about it, it's a street name, that's what it is. His handle out there in the street, Mr. Cool Cimarron!! Can't you see he ain't nothin but a drug dealer or a pimp? I see him out there one, two o'clock in the morning hangin on the corner, turnin everybody out. Is it drugs, or is he pimpin the women? Don't matter which. No, you can't do it better, not wit that fool, and you can't go, so just stop packin. You'll have the baby and bring it back here, and we'll all have to help you."

"Momma, I am not stayin here with you."

"Liz, you are only 17; you ain't no adult yet. You'll do what I say."

"No, I won't either. I'm gonna marry Cimarron."

"What? Girl, that boy ain't gonna marry you."

"Oh yes, yes he is! He tol me to pack my stuff and he's comin to get me."

"Well, he's wastin a trip over here."

"Momma, I am gonna marry him. If you don't sign the paper we'll just go to a state where I don't need you to sign."

"You got it all figured out, don't you, girl?" Lorraine sat down in her chair and began to cry again. Wesley slid down the wall in the corner and waited.

Liz finished packing, ignoring everyone. All of her stuff fit into two brown paper grocery sacks. Then she held out the paper for her mother to sign, but Lorraine turned away and stared out the window. Cimarron came to the door.

"Hey, baby, you ready girl? We bout to get real."

"Momma," Liz pleaded. "Please sign it."

Her mother turned and snatched the paper from her. She slammed it on the bedside table, signed it and walked down the hall to the bathroom, closing the door behind her.

Suddenly, Liz was gone. She and Cimarron got married and got their own room in another rooming house around the way. Liz still worked at the grocery store and stopped going to school. She worked and worked and worked whenever the store was open. Wesley found reasons to go buy something, just so he could see her. JoJo had a hard time with it; he missed Liz so much. Their mother had forbidden any of them from going to see her. JoJo stayed away for awhile, but eventually started going to see her all the time. There was no way their mother would know anyway; she was always at work. Before long, Wesley started going over there regularly as well.

Chapter 5

DESERTION

Cimarron seemed to be taking good care of Liz. She was happier than they had ever seen her. Cim also worked hard, but none of the boys knew what he did. They suspected that he was doing illegal stuff after what their mother had said the day Liz left, but they never questioned either Cim or Liz about it. Wesley hoped everything would be okay for Liz. She and Cim were working together, saving money for a better future. Liz believed they both had the same dream and would reach it together one day.

At first, all was well. Cim got home around 9:00 every night and ate dinner with Liz in their room. Then he would go back out to take care of his business, and Liz said that was okay with her, because he'd always come home first to make sure home was tight. Liz would get home from the grocery store at 7:00, so she had plenty of time to cook dinner and carry it up to their room. She wanted to be all that her mother wasn't. She had a husband now and their child was on the way. Her new little family meant the world to her.

Being the oldest child, Liz had been through hell and back as far as she was concerned. When she was younger she had been shifted from place to place while her mother was trying to figure out her own life. Her father was not in the picture at all; matter of fact, she didn't even know him. Liz had lived with relatives, friends and so-called friends, and had been in two foster homes. Yes, her little family had to work out. Most people had roots to grow from when they were brought into the world. As far as she was concerned, Cim, her brothers, and the little life that was growing inside her were all the roots she had or needed.

After a few months, Liz and Cim moved to a small studio apartment with its own kitchen and bathroom a little farther away on Ralph Avenue. The boys were excited for her. It was good to see them doing well. Wesley thought it was great that they wouldn't have to worry about anyone busting in on them in the bathroom or stealing their food from the kitchen

23

shelf anymore. *Wow, they had it made. They were on their way out of this neighborhood…it was only the first step.* He just knew it.

JoJo, Chris and Wesley went over to help move the boxes from the rooming house to their new home. When Wesley walked up the three flights of steps and into the apartment he was amazed that they were going to have all of that space for just for the two of them. There was a room when you walked in the door; that was the living room. It had a big window facing the street and the sun shined brightly into the room, giving it a lift without any help at all. The kitchen opened into the living room. You could see the whole thing. It was painted bright yellow, which went so well with the naturally-lit living room. All of the other walls in the apartment were dull beige, so the kitchen stood out and looked great. There was a half-wall with a space for their bed on the other side of the kitchen and a little hallway that led to a small bathroom. Wesley wished he were moving there with Liz; to him, it seemed like a castle. Cim was able to get some nice furniture, even though it was secondhand. They had a couch and a chair in the living room and a table in the kitchen with three chairs, so they could sit down and eat dinner like a real family. They had a big bed, and even a dresser.

. . . .

After Liz and Cim got settled into their new place Wesley didn't see Liz for awhile. His mother had fallen into a very deep depression. She hardly talked to the boys when she was there; instead, she either sat in her chair staring out the window or was on the pay phone down in the lobby. One day she came home after her day job and took Chris and Wesley to eat at a fancy diner. They were excited to go. Wesley was sure something wonderful was about to happen that would change all of the negativity Chris felt about their mother.

The diner was quite nice, better than any place Wesley had ever been to eat. It wasn't one of the grimy ones they usually went to when their mother had something to celebrate. The ones with filthy floors, greasy food and waitresses wearing dirty uniforms. This one was clean and shiny with red and white striped booths and miniature jukeboxes on each table. The people were friendly, even smiling when they seated them and took their orders.

"Chris, Wesley, this is a celebration. Order whatever you want to eat. I brought you here because I have some wonderful news to tell you."

"That's great, Momma," Wesley gushed with a wide smile as he elbowed Chris.

Chris ignored him and ordered the most expensive steak on the menu.

"What is your news, Mom?" Chris asked evenly.

"I got a new job that pays very good money."

Wesley couldn't believe it. "A NEW JOB?" he nearly shouted. He was so happy, he couldn't contain himself. *Here it was…their time had finally come. They were going to be okay, get a real home, have a real life, like other kids did.* He couldn't believe it. Wesley slid out of the booth, rushed to his mother's side and hugged her, burying his face in her neck, breathing in her comforting scent of lavender.

"Wesley, everything's gonna be okay."

"I know it will, Momma. Now it's great, right?"

"Yes, Wesley, but go sit back down beside Chris…there's more I have to tell you."

"Okay." Wesley was excited to hear what was coming next.

"The job is not here in New York. Remember when I told you about that good job your Aunt Jean got in Cleveland, Ohio, and how she's doin so good, makin all that good money? Huh? You guys remember, don't you?"

"Yes, I remember," Chris responded. "You want us to leave New York and go to Ohio?" he quipped, rolling his eyes.

"No Chris, not yet. See, cause the job is a live-in job. I will be livin with a family there and they only have a place for me to live for right now so—"

"So *you're* goin and not us?" Wesley was dumbfounded.

"Just for a little while, Wesley; see, I have to go ahead and work for a little while, save up some money and find us an apartment there. Then I'm gonna to send for both of you."

"How long is that gonna take and where we gonna be?" Wesley frantically asked.

"Don't worry, that's all taken care of. I paid the rent on the room for two months, cause the family I'm going to be workin for sent me enough money to take care of things for you."

"You already did that?" Wesley couldn't believe what he was hearing. "When are you leavin?"

"Well, I'll be leavin tomorrow evening. I have to go right away since they gave me money before I started. But don't worry; before you know it, I'll be sendin for you."

"How are we supposed to eat?" Chris asked blandly as their food was arriving.

"I got enough money to leave with you for food. You've been on your own for a long time anyway. Ya'll both are survivors like me. You won't even know I'm gone."

Chris was unimpressed. "Okay, sounds like you took care of everything. Pass the steak sauce, please."

Chris began eating his food. He was finished with the conversation and was already planning to call his father. Wesley was devastated and couldn't eat. It was all he could do to hold back the tears and get through the evening.

Their mother left the next day while they were at school. She decided that saying goodbye to them would be too emotional, especially for Wesley, so she wrote them a note telling them that she'd call soon after she got settled.

Chris' father came for him right away and took him to his house in Queens to live there with him and Chris' grandparents. Only JoJo and Wesley remained at the boarding house.

Chapter 6

INJUSTICE

*L*ife was good for Liz until just about the time that she was in her eighth month of pregnancy. One day at the grocery store where she worked several drunk men went in looking for a specific item. Two of them had open cans of beer. They were loud and belligerent.

Liz was busy mopping an aisle where a jar of juice had broken. The men walked down the aisle and through the mess, tracking the sticky liquid all over the floor. Politely, Liz asked them to watch their step to avoid spreading the glass and liquid any farther. They deliberately backtracked through it, stomping their feet, laughing and spilling beer everywhere.

Liz dropped the mop and ran to the manager's office, telling him what was happening in the store. To her utter amazement, he immediately jumped to their defense, saying the customer was always right. Then he led Liz back to the aisle to get things straightened out. The men were still there pretending to skate and had smeared the juice and the beer throughout the aisle. Liz stood with her arms folded, sure to be supported by her boss for once, but Mr. Harrington was speechless for what seemed to be an eternity.

"What's going on here?" He finally demanded.

"This little knocked-up wench threw that bottle down on the floor when she saw us coming down this aisle and told us to get out of here," one of the men lied.

"Mr. Harrington, that isn't true," Liz protested.

"Are you calling us liars?" Another of them exploded.

"Yes, I am. That's exactly what you are!" Liz shouted back.

"Liz, how dare you speak to my customers that way," Mr. Harrington scolded.

"Yeah, girl, you better lissen to your boss. Who you think you are, speakin to us customers like that?" he slurred, "I ain't never shoppin here agin, and neither will anybody else once I get through."

"No, wait sir. The girl is wrong..." Mr. Harrington turned to Liz. "Liz, I think you owe these men an apology."

"Mr. Harrington, I told you what they did. They owe me an apology."

"Liz, if you want to continue to work here, you will not treat my customers this way. Apologize…" he demanded sternly.

"Mr. Harrington, I've worked here for five years and you're gonna take their word over mine?"

"Look at this so-called manager. He ain't got no control in his own store. He's gonna listen to this little knocked-up teenager over his customers. Guess we know who's been hittin what," one of the men laughed.

A crowd had formed. BJ, Liz's co-worker of five years whom she ate lunch with and confided in watched from a distance, offering no support. She hung her head and scurried off to complete an unnecessary task.

"No…no, you've got it all wrong," Mr. Harrington pleaded with the men. "She's nothing more than a smart-mouthed bagger who can consider this chapter of her life over."

He turned to Liz. "Take off that apron and go get your things. You're fired."

"But Mr. Harrington, you know I need this job."

"Well, you should have thought about that before you decided to treat my customers so disrespectfully."

"All right now, that's more like it," one of the men boasted.

Liz couldn't believe it. *This was completely unfair!* She was outraged and humiliated. Numbly, she got her things and left the grocery store, hurrying to the boarding house looking for JoJo—but he wasn't there. Only Wesley was home. So she sat in the chair by the window, crying. When Wesley asked her what was wrong she cried even harder. He got her a glass of water from downstairs, and she told him what had happened. He wished he could have beaten Mr. Harrington into submission.

After awhile Liz said she'd better go so she could get dinner ready for Cim. Then she noticed the closet door was open and none of their mother's things were in it. Wesley had to tell her: *Their mother was gone.* She had left two weeks before to take a live-in job in Cleveland, Ohio. He explained that she planned to send for both he and Chris, but Chris had gone to live with his father. When she called, he would let her know that she only had to send for him.

Liz wrote JoJo a note, packed Wesley's stuff in one brown paper sack, and they left the boarding house for the last time.

"Wes, don't think about goin to Ohio to live with Momma anymore. We're on our own now. You'll stay with us."

"Liz, I told you—"

"Wesley, if she sends for you, fine; but don't count on that now. Right now, you have to go to school and plan to make somethin of your own life. Understand?"

"Liz, do you still talk to Grandpap?"

She was startled by his question. "Who told you that I talk to him at all?"

"Chris. He said you call him sometimes and that he has sent money to help us. Is that true?"

"Yes, Wes, but you can't let Momma know. She would kill me. She acts like she hates him."

"I sure would like to go back there to live again. A long time ago he loved me and so did Grandy…do you think they still do?"

"Oh, yes. Grandpap still loves us all; he always will. But…Wesley… Grandy died a little while ago and Grandpap is so sad. He got sick, and so right now somebody is takin care of him. I thought when Momma heard that her mother died we would all go to North Carolina to see him. But when Momma got the phone call, she just hung up the phone and walked away. She never said anything about it. She just went in the bathroom. I could hear her cryin."

Wesley was heartbroken. He followed Liz to her apartment, his new home, in complete silence.

Being at Liz and Cimarron's apartment was hard for Wesley to get used to, though it was cool sleeping in the living room on the couch. But he had been used to being on his own and by himself for so long it was strange to have this new life. Now Liz was acting like a mother to him, making sure he got up on time, ate breakfast, and that he went to school every day. She was constantly checking up on him. Sometimes he went to school and sometimes he didn't. He made that decision daily. If he felt like going, he did, and if he didn't, he didn't go. JoJo couldn't hang with the newfound family lifestyle, so after the two months their mother had paid for ran out, he found somewhere else to live and stopped by regularly to check on them.

· · · · · · · · · · · · · ·

Wesley didn't get into trouble much; he usually hung out somewhere, doing nothing. He liked watching the guys practicing karate at a place in the old neighborhood. Sometimes they would let him come in and mess around with them. He picked up a few of their techniques, deciding that he'd check into that karate stuff later when he had the money. Other days he went to the gym and watched boxing. The park was also a great place to watch people, and some days he'd sit there and draw things. It didn't take much to entertain him.

Occasionally, he got harassed by some of the guys in the neighborhood gangs. For the most part, it was nothing he couldn't tolerate. Usually he didn't have to worry about it because JoJo always had his back, and nobody wanted to tangle with him. But when he wandered into other neighborhoods he had to consider the consequences.

After Wesley had been living with Liz and Cim for a few months, a letter came from their mother addressed to Liz. It went on and on about the new life that she was living. She said that the family she worked for and lived with had young children, which meant that she would not have weekends off like she thought. Since we had all settled into life so easily without her, she had decided not to get her own apartment in Ohio, and thought that everything should stay the way it was for now: Wesley with Liz, Chris with his father, and JoJo on his own.

There it was…she said it. Finally. Liz had been right all along. Living in the shadows of her life was going to be Wesley's reality until he made a life for himself.

Wesley started to notice that Cim and Liz were arguing every day and hoped that it wasn't because he was there. Money was tight and Liz couldn't get a job since she was so pregnant. Due any day now, all of the pressure was on Cim, and his business wasn't going well. Added to this, Wesley was another mouth to feed. But Cim never complained about him, at least not that he knew of. He just complained about everything else.

Cim stopped coming home at dinnertime and started staying out later and later. When he got home, their arguments would last into the early hours of the morning. The first time he stayed out all night, Liz had false labor. Wesley rode the bus with her to the hospital, only for them to be sent back home. After that, things got better for awhile. Cim got worried about Liz and stayed close to home. He was there for the next two false labors, and even for when the baby was finally born a week later. It was a girl. They named her Tina. For awhile, a very short while, Liz, Cim, baby Tina and Wes were happy.

The baby's irregular sleeping pattern bothered Cim, so before long he was staying out later and later, and then all night, more often. Liz was beside herself with rage. When he would come home, they would argue and sometimes even physically fight. Wesley thought about jumping into it to save his sister, but actually, Cim was getting the worst of it. Liz could always take care of herself. Then they would make up, again and again. By the time Tina was 4 months old, Liz was pregnant.

Wesley had always thought Cim's business wasn't a good one; then they found out that not only was he selling drugs, he was using them. The using began to outweigh the selling and before long, Cim was hooked, using more of his product than he was selling. No money had been saved, Liz still wasn't working, and life became nearly unbearable in their once peaceful little home.

The bills weren't getting paid and they had hardly any food, so Liz applied for welfare; something that she had vowed never to do. They were able to get emergency food and supplies based on her saying that Cim had deserted them. In reality, that was a "little white lie." Cim was still with them physically sometimes, but he didn't have a legitimate job. What he did earn, he only shared partially with the family so he could continue to party. He didn't help around the house; he was usually high or hung over while he was there, and he spent most nights out in the streets with whomever, doing whatever. Cim was on a fast track to disaster and Liz was trapped there with one baby and another on the way, saddled with a 15-year-old on the brink of who knows what. But Liz was a trooper. She didn't complain.

Liz still made Wesley go to school. She was already sorry that she didn't go that route herself. She clung to the hope that Wes would get out of that difficult life and believed that finishing school was necessary for him to do it—so she stayed on his case. Wesley hated school. He felt completely inadequate there. No matter how hard he tried, he just couldn't make good grades. Now he was in the ninth grade and had no interest in what they were doing in most of his classes. He didn't understand much of anything they were talking about, and it didn't seem to him that the things he was knocking his head against a wall to learn would make a difference in his life anyway. Why bother when he only seemed to get an endless stream of D's and F's? He started cutting classes in spite of Liz's threats, or rages when she found out. But hanging out in the streets brought another obstacle to deal with: gangs.

JoJo had gotten into serious trouble and been caught. He was doing time in a juvenile facility. Now Wesley was truly in the streets on his own. The way things worked, you either joined a gang and hung out with your boys for protection or you were always pursued, which usually ended with a beating on some level. Wesley had to make a choice to either go to school every day or join a gang. He chose a gang.

Chapter 7

CHOICE

*W*esley slowly moved his eyes around the room, searching through the shadows, unable to remember where he was or what was going on around him. His mind struggled to focus. He wasn't afraid, though his vision was blurred from awakening abruptly in the darkness.

He realized that just before opening his eyes he was vividly aware of a calming presence in the room. Someone, something, had been speaking gently to him in a whisper. He could still feel the warm, tingling breath on his ear…and he was being warned about something. It was confusing. Had he been dreaming? It felt too real for that.

The angel Carlonian was there, though Wesley only sensed the surreal, yet caring and familiar presence near him. To him, the room seemed to be cloaked with this presence, wrapping him in a warm embrace.

He lay awake in the early morning light wondering why he felt there could be a presence of something unseen there in the room, good or bad. He had heard about people believing in God and being led by God or angels or something, but that religion stuff was definitely not for him. *Just look at my life,* he thought, *God is not interested in me or my family. We have it too hard and we're survivors; we do for ourselves. We don't wait around for God or angels to reach out and rescue us. God is for people who come from another kind of life.* So Wesley concentrated on his choice to join a gang and tried to shake the feeling that someone or something had come to guide or even warn him about his decision.

After all, Wesley reasoned, *gangs aren't all that bad.* To him, their priority was to hang out and protect their territory. Hanging out could mean many things. It could mean walking the streets of the neighborhood day and night checking on things, making sure that other gangs didn't disrespect yours by coming into your neighborhood uninvited. It could mean playing ball or messing around with girls, or whatever else the guys wanted to do on their turf. He knew gangs made routine stops at stores, houses, basketball courts, wherever, in their territory, and that wasn't a bad thing. The way he saw it, being in a gang would bring a different kind of respect for him in their hood, even from older folks. *Gangs don't usually cause much trouble,* he mused. *Every now and then they might get into a minor situation with the law, but for the most part, they're pretty orderly.* Wesley wasn't concerned about possible fights with other gangs; they happened, but rarely resulted in somebody being seriously injured or dying. Things like that only happened by accident. The purpose of most fights was to maintain territory or to save face if one of their boys was disrespected. No biggie.

Wesley joined his neighborhood's gang and started getting in and out of trouble, due in large part to his association with it. Liz was outraged. She didn't understand the necessity of Wesley aligning himself with a gang. She couldn't grasp the difference in being female, versus male, in the hood with no alliances. She wanted Wesley to stand his own ground and be his own person and stop getting into trouble. She stood her ground. She was constantly in Wesley's face about the gang. The funny part about it was, Wesley didn't enjoy being in the gang or have much loyalty to it. The association was simply a means to an end until he could get out of the neighborhood.

Things got worse between Liz and Cim, and Liz's threats to kick Cim out of her life became a daily exchange. Wesley hated being there and began to run with the gang more and more, which resulted in bigger trouble. At first, there were small scuffles and disorderly behavior, and then a few bogus accusations of more serious offenses like breaking and entering. Eventually, at 17 years old, Wesley landed in a youth detention center.

Liz, who now had three children and was still with Cim, still living on welfare, had been keeping in touch with their mother. When Wesley went away she called her. One day almost a year later when Wesley was almost 18, Lorraine showed up and visited him at the center. He thought she was there to rescue him from his miserable life, that she had finally come back to take him with her. Wesley was so happy to see her—but soon found out otherwise.

"Wesley, of all of my children, you are the one that I thought would make somethin of your life, and not end up in here. This is John's route."

"I thought you were gonna send for me, Momma. I waited, even though everyone said you wouldn't, but I believed you."

"Things change, son. After I got there, I knew that was not a world you could live in, so I thought the best place for you was with Liz."

Perplexed, Wesley asked, "Are you here because you changed your mind?"

"No, I came to see you because you're bout to be viewed as a man, Wesley. You have to stop all this mess and straighten up, or you gonna end up like your brother, John. He's out of jail, but watch, he's gonna go back and go back and go back, til one day they just gonna keep him and never let him out."

She took Wesley's hand and squeezed it. Then she smiled and said, "I love you, son. You come visit me when you get your life together, when you become a man. You still got some growin up to do."

Just as suddenly as she came, she was gone. Wesley remained in the center until he turned 18. On the day he was released he remembered his mother's words, "Come see me when you get your life together." He knew that his life certainly wasn't together and realized more than ever that he could only depend on himself and Liz. He headed back to Liz's place, vowing to help her build a life for them all.

. . . .

While Wesley was in the detention center a year had passed and things hadn't changed much. Cim had gone crazy on drugs and was working the streets 24/7. He didn't stay at their apartment anymore, which suited Liz just fine. He was still using and had a string of ladies working the streets for him. Cim did have a way with women, many of whom despised Liz and were all too happy to stick it to her by sleeping with Cim and turning tricks for him: putting money in his pocket. They just couldn't see how by sticking it to Liz they were really hurting themselves.

Liz was at the end of her rope with Cim and was trying to come up with a way to get out of the neighborhood and provide a decent life for her three children. Baby Girl Tina (as they called her) was now 4 years old; Andre, 3, and Tyrell, 8 months. Liz's welfare caseworker told her that there were good government jobs Liz could get, but she would have to have a high school diploma or GED to qualify. Liz had never finished high school, though she had always made good grades, so she decided to get her GED. For weeks, she studied everything that she could get her hands on at the library while Wesley helped out by watching the kids. She passed the test on her first try, and then started applying for jobs. Relentless in her quest to find better employment, she was up, dressed and out of the house by 7:00 every morning and returned late evening.

Liz was happy again, and that made Wesley happy. She was convinced that she would be called any day for one of the jobs she had applied for. Her plan was to work all the hours she could, save every dime, and move herself, the kids and Wesley to a better area away from all the grime of the hood—away from Cim and all of his mayhem. *Let the women and the streets have him,* she decided. For so long, she had been wrong about him. True, she had loved that man, *But look at him now,* she realized, *he was a loser and she was not going down with him.* Wesley being there was just what she needed to make it out. She trusted him to take care of the kids while she was actively working her plan to save them all from a nothing life.

Momma had been right about JoJo. He was back in prison, and this time for a long haul. He had gotten out of jail and come by to help Liz, but was soon in a huge mess with one of his foolproof crimes, guaranteed to make them rich. When it backfired John became a statistic who would be spending most of his life in jail. Wesley was sad for his brother. He looked up to JoJo, and now the thought of him being incarcerated infuriated him.

Chris lived in another world. He had gone with a one-way ticket, never looking back, and gotten a scholarship to college. He didn't call Liz about his graduation or college plans. None of them knew what school he went to or what state it was in. Chris never visited, called or wrote. His father gave no information and hardly talked to them if they called about Chris. Sadly, Chris didn't exist in their lives, at least not then. Liz and Wes were too consumed with the problems at hand to feel bitterness toward him. For all they knew, they might never see or hear from him again…and at that moment in the space they were living, Chris didn't matter at all.

One night when Liz was at home Wesley decided to go out and check in with the gang to see what was going on with everyone. He hadn't seen or heard from any of them while he was locked up or since he had returned. He walked the familiar path through the streets and alleyways of the neighborhood and squeezed in through a window of the small, abandoned house they had claimed as their spot.

It happened to be a night when they were in an uproar because one of them had been disrespected by another gang for no apparent reason. Wesley arrived as they were assembling to head over to the other gang's turf and get it straight. He instantly knew he had made a mistake stopping by. For him, going to see them was just something to do after being cooped up with his niece and nephews for weeks. When the guys saw him, they pulled him into the madness. Before he knew it, he was in a car with a group of them headed to another neighborhood, shrouded with a sense of dread he couldn't shake.

When their three cars arrived across town the other gang was waiting, pipes, sticks and bottles in hand. Things jumped off so fast that Wesley didn't have time to think. As soon as the cars stopped, there was nothing to do but get out into the insanity and fight. It was the most violent gang fight Wesley had ever seen. Some of the boards the other gang was using had nails sticking through them; there were chains and bats, and he even saw a screwdriver. The fight seemed to go on for an eternity before he heard a siren in the distance.

Wesley's goal was to stay alive; he certainly didn't want to hurt anybody. After all, he had the poor misfortune of walking back into this mess on the wrong night. As the police sirens got nearer both gangs scattered. Wesley had just started running when he felt himself trip and fall on his face. As he turned over, a huge man pounced on him and began punching his face, head and sides with both fists. He could barely move, the guy was all over him. Wesley could hear the sirens closing in on them, but couldn't get free from the beating. The guy was screaming and crying while he was beating Wesley with all his might.

Finally, three policemen pulled him off of Wesley and subdued him. It took all of them to get him under control. Wesley was covered in blood and could barely stand up on his own. The cops grabbed him and put on the handcuffs.

Wesley looked around and saw pure pandemonium. Two of the three cars they had come in were gone, as were most of the members of both gangs. Many of the wounded were left behind, and those were the ones who would make it to jail that night.

In the middle of the street there was one limp, lifeless body. A broken piece of mirror was protruding from his chest. The guy was clearly dead. The big guy who had been beating Wesley turned out to be his brother and he had tried to take it all out on him. He could only imagine how he would have felt if that had been JoJo. But now, all he could think of was Liz's plans for their lives and that things were starting to work out. Suddenly, he was filled with the realization that he had blown it all for all of them. How could he face his sister, who had been there for him no matter what? There he was, right back in trouble, because he had made one bad decision.

The next morning when Wesley was taken for arraignment, he was worried about whether Liz was going to show up or not, and if she did, how she would feel toward him. When he called her the night before, she listened and hung up without a word. He also realized that he was now 18 years old and had a juvenile record, so he expected the worst outcome.

Liz was in the courtroom when he got there. He was glad that she had come, even though she was giving him dirty looks. The kids were there with her. Wesley wanted more than anything to erase the past 24 hours, so he could be hanging out with the kids again. When his name was called the judge looked at him and shook his head.

"Mr. Lewis," the judged roared. "I'm looking over this mess of a life of yours here, and now you were involved in a man losing his life last night. I guess you have nothing to say about that, right?

"Well….uh…Not really, sir."

"Sir? Did I hear you correctly? Did you address me as sir?" the judge's voiced thundered throughout the courtroom.

"Yes, uh, sir."

"Humph, so where is your family, Mr. Lewis?"

"Uh, my sister is here, sir."

"Who is your sister?"

Liz stood up and said, "I am, your Honor."

The judge paused to look toward Liz, and then turned back to Wesley.

"So, tell me what do you have to say for yourself, Mr. Lewis?"

"I made a mistake sir, uhmmm, I was helpin my sister and I got bored and—"

"MISTAKE!!!" the judge exploded. "A man lost his life and all you can say is MISTAKE?"

"No sir, I don't mean to disrespect that man or his family. The mistake I made was goin to hang out with my boys last night. I had been away and—"

"Oh, I know you had been away. I have your whole life right here on this piece of paper and I can fill in the blank spaces. It would seem that you didn't learn a thing in the detention center. You got out and stayed out of trouble for a whole month or so, now here you are and a man is dead."

"I know how this looks, sir, but I didn't kill that man. I've been helpin my sister with the kids, and I had been with them all day for weeks, and I didn't go nowhere at night...I just picked the wrong night to go out...I was just goin to check everybody out last night, and all the stuff was already happenin...I got all caught up in it...I didn't even know where we were goin...that wasn't my fight...I didn't know nothin about that fight...I was just all of a sudden in the middle of it. I sure didn't mean for anybody to get hurt...and I am sorry...I am so sorry that I have messed it all up for us, for me and for my sister and my family..." Wesley was crying as he turned to look at Liz. "And I know I messed it all up for the kids and a better life for us all...I'm sorry Liz, please Liz, I'm sorry, forgive me. Just don't hate me, you're all I have," he pleaded across the courtroom.

Liz couldn't hold back the tears. She stood up and reached out toward Wes in a way that let him know, she did forgive him. She was still, and would always, be there for him.

The judge looked at Wesley and at Liz, and then at those three little innocent children. The courtroom was still as he contemplated the possibilities for this young man's life. It hit home. He was at a turning point in his own life and had a number of personal issues with his only son, many of which were spilling into the courtroom that day. He took a deep breath and continued.

"I've decided that I'm going to give you a choice!" he boldly declared.

Wes's heart skipped a beat; he just knew that he would be going to a real jail this time...but now the judge talking about choices.

"Yes, Mr. Lewis," the judge said. "I'm going to give you a CHOICE today. You see, for some unknown reason, I think that you have some degree of potential. So instead of simply sentencing you to a stint in jail, I will make jail ONE of two options for you. The other option is for you to join the Army. The Army has made a difference in many lives. Now, what do you think about that?" he challenged Wesley.

What do I think of that? he pondered. Well, actually, he had never thought of the Army at all, one way or the other. *Hmmm, the Army.* Wesley suddenly remembered all of the commercials he had seen and laughed at.

Army...Jail...Army...Jail. He turned to look at Liz, who was still standing and had both hands clasped as though hope was alive. Wesley turned back to the judge and simply thanked him. He was processed out of the legal system and driven to a recruitment office.

Chapter 8

REBELLION

A few days later Liz and the kids came to see Wesley before he shipped out to Fort Gordon, Georgia for boot camp. He could see through Liz's excitement for him, to the disappointment she had for herself and the kids. With Wesley gone, there was no one to watch the kids, so her plan to begin work was off. The cost of day care for three children was not an option for Liz; once again, she felt trapped in her life.

Wesley promised to send money to help her make it out, but she didn't plan on that as an option. She was back to depending on herself and finding a way on her own. Always a survivor, she hadn't given up. She was regrouping mentally, viewing this setback as another hurdle to overcome. Wesley felt like a heel. He watched her going through the motions of being there for him, as always, while wishing he could do something, anything, to change her new reality.

"I really did it this time, got myself in a mess and took you down with me. I'm sorry, Liz," Wesley lamented, "If I could just go back to that day…"

"Okay, but you can't. It is what it is. But you got a shot here, this Army thing. It ain't bad for you. I called Grandpap and told him you were gonna be down his way."

"What he say?"

"He was proud. He's doin real good now: Got his strength back and livin good. He said to tell you that now you're a grown man and can make your own decisions. He hopes he'll be seein you sometime soon."

"I'm gonna go see him after I get out of this mess I got myself into. We can all go; maybe we can move there."

"Wesley, this ain't no mess. I told you, this is a shot. You can make this turn out good for you."

"And what about you and the kids? What's this gonna do for you and them?"

"Don't worry about me, I'm gonna be alright…just need a new plan. I'm gonna figure it out." She hugged him and shoved him away. "Now, go on baby boy, and do your thing."

Wesley really viewed Liz as his mother and never stopped seeking her approval. So when she told him to go to boot camp and be the best he could be, he knew that he'd be able to work things out in his own way. He told them goodbye, kissed the kids and hugged Liz again, holding onto her for as long as she would let him. He wasn't ready to move forward into the next phase of his life.

As Wesley was sworn in he looked across the room to Liz, his only supporter. She stood tall and proud and blew him a kiss as he boarded the bus. Wesley thought of their mother. She had checked in and out of his life by telephone for years. The wealthy family she worked for had taken care of all of her needs and had come to appreciate and love her. She was raising their children, who thought of her as a member of their family. She traveled with the family on vacations, caring for their children as her own. The life she was living, though as a servant, left her wanting for nothing. Though Wesley's sense of loyalty never permitted him to feel resentment toward her, he wondered if he would ever see her again.

When he arrived at boot camp Wesley wondered how he ever thought joining the Army was the lesser of two evils. It turned out to be worse than he expected. Wesley didn't like his Sergeant talking to him like he was nobody and dictating his every move. *Was he crazy? How could he think that he could talk to you like you were nothing and expect you to give him your best effort?* That wasn't how Wesley was wired, and the more he was ridden by his superiors the more he rebelled. After the third week of basic training he was on the way to becoming dishonorably discharged, and that didn't bother him because he wanted out. He had decided that he'd made a mistake thinking he could put up with this abuse.

Wesley hated the Sergeant and Sergeant Creed didn't think much of him, either. He predicted that Wesley would be the kind of soldier he was: smart-mouthed, confrontational and doing just enough to get by while trying to figure out a way to get out of the Army. It wasn't that Wesley was lazy or couldn't do what was expected of him; it was that he didn't want to. He was trying to get back to the apartment with Liz and the kids. He felt responsible for messing things up and believed that if he could just get back to the City, they could continue with their plan to get out of the hood. Surely, the court couldn't hold him responsible if the Army kicked him out.

One Sunday afternoon, Sergeant Creed sent for him. Wesley reported to his office, though he didn't want to, but it turned out that he had visitors. His Grandpap and Uncle Bill were there to see him. Wesley hadn't seen them since he was 6 years old when his mother had taken him away from the country farm where his grandfather lived. He still adored and respected his Grandpap.

Wesley had not had an easy time with his mother's large family of twelve siblings and their offspring. Many of them had not accepted him and mistreated him badly when he was young because of his father, though he had never met him. He still remembered, as if it had happened last week, when his Grandpap and Grandy gave him a party for his fifth birthday. He was so excited as Grandy baked his favorite cake and he and his Grandpap decorated the dining room with balloons and brightly colored paper. When everything was ready, Wesley sat waiting at the head of the table for the arrival of his cousins. To his disappointment, only Uncle Bill showed up on time. As the afternoon slowly passed, no one else came. Wesley sat, waiting—not letting anyone cut the cake or sing "Happy Birthday." He moved to the window and watched the long dirt road for their cars until the sun went down.

Wesley hadn't forgotten that day; he hadn't been able to shake that devastating wound. Grandpap was furious with the others. He took up for Wesley, like he always had, protecting and defending him from them. That was just one of many reasons Wesley loved living on the farm. He later learned that Grandpap had threatened to report his mother and have her declared unfit. It was then that she gathered her four children from their various situations and moved them all to the New York City rooming house.

Now, here they were at the Army base, Grandpap and Uncle Bill, just to see him. He was so happy that he could hardly contain himself. For a moment, he thought that his wish had come true: that he was leaving and they had come to take him home to the farm. He hoped that Liz and the kids were already there waiting, and that they would all be together.

"Grandpap!" Wesley practically screamed as he grabbed onto him and squeezed him tightly.

But his grandfather pulled away and glared at him through cold, disapproving eyes. Wesley was shocked and confused. He was sure that his Grandpap loved him and would be happy to see him again. It had been a long time since that horrible day twelve years ago.

Uncle Bill took Wesley by the arm and motioned for them to walk. Grandpap followed them outside where the three of them walked in silence.

"Wesley," Uncle Bill began. "Liz called your grandfather and told him that you're not doin what you're suppose to be doin here. What's that all about?"

"Oh...well, I decided that I...really don't want to do this, cause see, when I was in court the ju—"

"SILENCE!!!" Grandpap commanded, startling both Wesley and Uncle Bill.

As Wesley turned around to face him, his Grandpap backhanded him across his face. Wesley stumbled backward and gawked in disbelief. Then Uncle Bill and his Grandpap commenced to give him the beating of his life. These were the two men Wesley looked up to and respected more than anyone else in this world, and out of respect for them he refused to defend himself. Besides his brothers, these were the only men in the world that he loved—and they had come to the boot camp that day to give him a lesson he wouldn't forget. They had both been devout soldiers and believed in serving their country and serving it well. Grandpap had fought in World War I.

"They're talkin discharge, Wesley...dishonorable discharge!" Then Grandpap reminded him that he had been born with two strikes against him. Number one—he was a half breed (though his mixed features were a little less obvious than Liz's), and Number two—he was poor. They were there that day to prevent him from creating Number three. They told him that they would see him dead in the ground before they'd allow him to be dishonorably discharged from the United States Armed Forces.

"YOU decided that you don't want to do this?" his Grandpap continued in calm, yet stern and commanding voice. "Well, Wesley, that isn't your choice. It is time for you to put all of the foolishness aside. You are here and you have a job to do. You've been given a chance to turn your life around and be a man. If you run from this place, you'll be runnin right back to the streets and a life of prediction. You had challenges growin up, and it hasn't been easy, but that life has prepared you for this one and what is yet to come. You're a member of this country and you have been given an opportunity to serve and defend it. That is an honor, and I expect nothin less from you than your very best."

He turned away from Wesley and leaned on a nearby bench.

"Wesley," he continued, "Give me flowers while I'm livin, son; don't wait til I'm dead."

They walked away and left Wesley lying on the ground. *What did that mean?* he wondered. He was dazed and shocked at the method they used to reach him: the length they had gone to, to convince him that he had been reading the situation wrong. Apparently, there was more at stake here. Wesley realized that his next move may determine the rest of his life. He reasoned that the best way he could help his sister was to see this thing through. Now he was ready to move forward into his next phase. It was then he decided to be a soldier.

Chapter 9

PRIDE

*A*nd become a soldier he did. Wesley not only worked at becoming a good soldier, he became a great, in fact, even an exceptional soldier. Once Wesley decided that soldiering was his calling, he applied himself like he had tried to in school before. The difference was he got incredible results. He had never been on a schedule with an expectation of performance. He liked it. The tougher the schedule, the more he applied himself.

Wesley discovered, as he had early in his life on the farm, that he liked the hard work, the achievement and the results which led to rewards. His first was a marksman medal. He regretted that he hadn't applied himself sooner, because his competitive ego was bruised by the overall superior stats of another soldier in his platoon. Though Wesley excelled in every phase, Private Brent Watkins overshadowed his efforts with his strong, consistent ranking throughout the previous weeks. Wesley pressed on, finishing strong and breaking many records. His performance was nearly unmatched. But Private Brent Watkins was no slouch. At first, he was a nuisance, his stats matching and occasionally topping Wesley's. Eventually, his persistence began to annoy Wesley, who was determined to be the best. The competition between them was vigorous. Their struggles were explosions of exciting opposition. They met each other head-on, unwaveringly approaching the other's challenge. The contests between them were so electrically charged that the other soldiers began to place bets on which one would prevail.

Soon their contests weren't limited to the training field, but extended to include every area of day-to-day life on and off the base. If one saw Wesley talking to a young lady, she would become Brent's newest interest and vice versa. It all came to a head one evening when a desirable young lady, in whom both of them had expressed interest, was at a club they all frequented on the weekend, The Peach Tree.

Both Wesley and Brent were there in separate areas of the club celebrating Friday, a week closer to completing Basic. Tamara Garrison was enjoying a cocktail at the lively bar. She was a tall, quick witted, stunning Jamaican woman with a beautiful complexion, a short, curly cut and a dazzling smile. She wore a low-cut silk blouse and a short skirt that showcased her long, shapely legs as she slightly twirled on the bar stool, captivating every man that caught her beauty in motion.

It was apparent that Tamara was enjoying the attention. Her sultry, frequent laugh was loud and inviting. She was surrounded by soldiers who were out for fun, and at that moment, its name was Tamara. Brent was the first to notice her and quickly made his way through the crowd. As he approached, she took control of the encounter.

"Well, well, Mr. Watkins. Good evening," She said cooingly in her alluring Jamaican accent.

"Hey, hey, now...and don't you look beautiful," Brent complimented.

"Well, thank you, mon. What brings you to—" Before she could finish, one of the soldiers she had been talking with rudely interrupted.

"Tammy baby, what's this all about? You were talking to me, remember?"

"And right now she's not," Brent stated calmly, making direct eye contact with the soldier.

"Hold up, man, that ain't right. I'm sitting here talkin to her...how you gonna just come up and act like I'm not even here?"

"It's cool, man, but the lady spoke to me. Besides, it's up to her to decide who she wants to talk to."

"That's right, so now you spoke and we can get back to our conversation, right baby?" He edged closer to her.

"Okay, look, mon, he's a friend of mine, so..." Tamara's words trailed off as she flashed a quick, beautiful smile.

"Oh, it's like that, huh?" he spat.

"That's not cool, man, this LADY can talk to whoever she wants to talk to," Brent interjected, becoming more agitated.

"These women are all the same. You're not gonna make me look like no fool. I bought you a drink, you better give me all of your attention while you drinking it, fool."

"No fool here, have your drink back!" She threw it in his face.

The soldier grabbed Tamara's arm, yanking her off the barstool. The crowd quickly pushed back from the three of them. Brent tried to free Tamara from the soldier's grip while trying not to hurt her, but the guy wouldn't release his grip and began to twist her arm. Brent landed a punch while trying to free Tamara, but he still wouldn't let go. He kept holding her tightly.

Suddenly, Wesley was there on the other side of the soldier and punched his side, causing him to let go of Tamara's arm. But then in one quick move he turned and threw a punch Wesley's direction. Wesley dodged and in rapid succession outmaneuvered him with a series of fast-paced physical exchanges. The room exploded, turning chaotic; it was a shoving, pushing, pulling, and punching free-for-all. Wesley and the guy were in the midst of a one-sided fight, ending with the soldier unconscious on the floor of the bar. Everyone ran from the club, while Wesley, Brent and Tamara jumped in a taxi and headed to another popular bar. Amused by the turn of events and laughing the whole way, the three of them had the time of their lives barhopping out on the town. It was obvious that both men were interested in Tamara, but out of mutual respect for each other they both backed off.

Wesley and Brent recognized and appreciated each other's strengths. This eventually resulted in a plan to dupe their fellow soldiers out of their money by fixing their competitions and splitting the funds. They worked out together and pushed each other to even higher levels of performance while filling their bank accounts. This was the beginning of an amazing friendship that would last for years.

Wesley was resourceful, coming up with crazy ideas that bordered on the ridiculous, but turned into well-paying schemes. His confidence soared as each escapade succeeded. Eventually, he found an untapped market of providing other soldiers with things they wanted, like special foods, gifts and cigarettes. But nothing illegal for Wesley; he would not end up like JoJo. As time passed, he and Brent began taking orders for difficult-to-find items like designer clothing, imported leathers, jewelry, and pretty much anything else that demanded a premium price.

They were businessmen, virtual masterminds when it came to making money, and genius' at multiplying it. They had found something that worked well. Wesley and Brent made so much extra cash that Wesley increased the monthly amount he sent to Liz. It was enough to cover day care and she was able to finally get a job.

By the end of boot camp, Wesley had been promoted to Private First Class (PFC). Grandpap and Liz came to the base for the graduation ceremony. Wesley could see his accomplishments shining on Grandpap and Liz's faces, and that was all the reward he needed. They were proud of him, which gave him an incredible sense of well-being. After the ceremony, he found them in the crowd and picked Liz up, squeezing her tightly.

"I'm so glad to see you!" he exclaimed, smiling brightly.

"Likewise, Baby Brother," Liz smiled. "I can see you have been one busy man."

"That's right, my girl," Grandpap added. "This is the little determined engine I remember. You have done us proud, son."

Wesley took them to lunch off base before they headed back to the farm. Liz had taken the kids down to the farm; it was their first visit and they loved it. Wesley was thrilled. They had stayed there with Uncle Bill while Liz and Grandpap drove over for the ceremony. Liz also told Wesley she had been saving as much of the money he sent her as possible, in preparation to move. Cim had come around a few times trying to get back with her, but she didn't fall for it. She had a one-track mind, and that was to get out of her old life and find a place to live in a better neighborhood. The government job hadn't come through and she was working as a cashier, but she didn't let that stop her.

Tina was in kindergarten, and Liz was anxious to move to a better place so she could go to a good school. Andre would be old enough for kindergarten next year, but Tyrell had a ways to go before he wouldn't need day care. The money Wesley sent helped a lot, but Liz still wasn't financially ready for the move. She had made a comfortable home for herself and the kids at their apartment, and they had plenty of food to eat, all thanks to Wesley. Liz loved him so much that she stood looking at him, forcing herself to hold back the tears. Though they were tears of joy, she knew Wesley would swear something was wrong and wouldn't be satisfied until he fixed it.

The next phase of training for Wesley and Brent would be Advanced Infantry Training, AIT. There was no question that they were the best in their company. Wesley was on top of the world. For the first time in his life HE WAS THE MAN and it felt great!

Later that night, Wesley and Brent went out to celebrate, wearing pride and unparalleled confidence. Every pore of Wesley's body exuded this, like a sweet perfume, hypnotizing anyone who came in contact with him. His now muscular frame, draped with his impressive, immaculate uniform, pulled admiring glances from every direction. That night, wherever he and Brent went they drew attention. Both men were attractive in their own right. They were out on the town, emotionally high on a job well done.

Everywhere they went, they were shown to the best tables and waitresses rushed to serve them. A nod of Wesley's head brought him the attention that he had longed for throughout his life. Now women were beginning to see him, not look past him for the man in charge. Wesley Lewis was that man.

Not one to have casual sexual encounters, Wesley was a different person that night. He was excited and felt desirable. For the first time he knew that he could pick and choose whoever he wanted to be with, rather than waiting to see if anyone would choose him—like it was back in the days at the gang hangout.

The women that night were ripe for the taking. They were numerous, gorgeous and voluptuous, all trying to catch the eye of a recently graduated soldier with pockets full of money to buy drinks. Wesley gladly discovered that a man in uniform had astonishing drawing powers. He sat back and took it all in, enjoying the female attention.

Then he saw who he wanted to be with that night. She sat across the room, commanding a good amount of attention in her own right. This woman was stately. It was evident that she was enjoying herself as she confidently laughed and interacted with those around her. He admired her wavy light brown hair and buttery skin, which only increased her overall appeal. Usually, beautiful girls never gave Wesley a chance so he rarely tried...but tonight was different. Everything was a go. Then it happened. She was looking around the room as if waiting for someone to join her. Wesley made eye contact, and she returned it. Their eyes held each other's for longer than what felt comfortable. As Wesley got up and moved toward her through the crowd, her eyes stayed with him.

"May I join you?" he asked. She was stunning.

"Please..." She motioned to the stool beside her.

"Would you like a drink?"

"Yes...please, a Tom Collins."

He ordered her drink from the bartender and continued.

"What's your name?"

"They call me Kim."

"I'm Wesley Lewis and you are one beautiful lady, Kim. Would you like to dance?"

"Absolutely."

A slow song was playing. They made their way onto the dance floor. Wesley pulled her closer than he had ever dared to hold a woman he'd just met, and like clay in the hand of an artist, Kim swayed to his every movement. Their bodies fit comfortably. The dark lighting and slow, sensual music were stimulating, especially accented by the influence of the alcohol and the smell of her perfume. Wesley was enjoying his first orchestrated seduction.

Wesley thought that he would never feel the way he did that night. He never imagined that he would want to just have sex for the heck of it. He thought that he would always want it to be with someone special, that he would want one special person. But that's not what he wanted from Kim. She was an attractive, desirable female with an incredible body that he wanted to enjoy that night and that night only. He felt invincible and wanted to be with a beautiful woman, a perfect ending to eight rigid weeks of training: a night of celebration.

And that is what happened. Wesley showed Kim a wonderful night. He planned to enjoy himself and he wanted her to enjoy herself, too; so he treated her like a queen, showering her with affectionate attention. They left the club together, two beautiful people, the envy of both men and women, and went to a chic restaurant for an elaborate meal of delectable seafood. They were served several delicious courses and fine imported wine.

Wesley slipped away and found a vendor on a corner selling flowers, leftovers from the day of graduations. He had them sent to the luxurious hotel suite where they had agreed they would spend the night together. He also sent champagne, chocolates and strawberries. He had heard that strawberries brought out the flavor of the champagne.

When Kim saw the preparations that Wesley had made, she melted. She couldn't believe that she had been so lucky to meet this fine man who had it going on. It was a night neither of them would forget. They had an enjoyable evening, enjoying each other completely.

In the morning Kim continued to delight in the suite, ordering room service and planning her future with Wesley. She knew hanging out at the club would pay off one day, and now it had. She had hit the jackpot. She hoped she was pregnant, but if not, it was okay because she knew she had really put it on him that night. He was hers; she was sure of that. She would follow him anywhere.

It was also a night of pure pleasure for Wesley, but it ended there for him. However, it did serve as a coming-of-age of sorts. He realized who he really was: a man on the threshold of a world he had been unaware of. He could design it to fit his own personal desires. All he had to do was figure out what his desires were and work hard to achieve them.

Chapter 10

ACCOMPLISHMENT

Wesley and Brent continued to Advanced Infantry Training together at Fort Benning, Georgia. They were inseparable. If you saw one and not the other, he was nearby. Wesley had never had a friend like Brent in his life. He had heard about friendships like this and saw guys in school have each other's back, but he had never experienced it. Even while in the gang back home, he hadn't felt an alliance with another person like he did with Brent. Their relationship went beyond friendship; they genuinely liked each other, and where one had a weakness the other compensated. The feeling was vaguely familiar, though he brushed it off, just enjoying the close camaraderie of his pal.

One day on base while he and Brent were sitting outside cleaning their guns Wesley asked, "Hey B, do you ever think about destiny, man?"

"What you talkin bout, man? My destiny is wherever I am at any given moment," Brent joked.

"Nah, man, I'm serious. Sometimes I think about why you meet who you meet, when you meet them. Like, what if I had started Basic before or after you? We wouldn't have met...so, you think we would've met at another time in life or what?"

"Man, Wes, there you go with that deep mess again. If we hadn't met in Basic, then guess what; we wouldn't have met." He chuckled, giving Wes a hard time.

"No, see B, I think you're wrong bout that. I think there's some kind of higher power that decided we were suppose to meet and be friends. Not just any kind of friends, but deep friends. Like man, I got your back all the way. You know you can depend on that."

"Yeah, man, I know I can. And Wes, man, you know I got yours, too, but God has both of us."

"God?"

"Yeah...God!"

"I don't know about that, but it's like I have this funny feelin sometimes,

48

that there's somebody else I'm suppose to meet here…in this life. It almost feels like there's a piece of me I'm looking for."

"Oh, come on, man. No, don't tell me…" Brent was laughing now. "Your other half, right?" He fell on the grass and started rolling around. "Right, man; you know, she'll complete you, right?"

"Dude, hey, come on now. It's not like that. It's just…see man…oh, forget it, man."

Wesley took his gun and went into the barracks, leaving Brent calling behind him.

"Wait, mister man, mister man…come back! You could be my love forever."

. . . .

It didn't take long for them to get their business set up and running at Fort Benning. They learned that they had acquired a reputation from Fort Gordon that had traveled to Fort Benning with them. Wesley was happy that he would be able to keep sending money home to Liz.

Both men proved themselves to be exceptional again as they completed AIT, finishing at the top of their class. They were both decorated for their accomplishments and moved on together to the next phase of training, which was the United States Army Airborne School, also known as Jump School. Though the training proved to be more rigorous, both Wesley and Brent pulled deeper from the core to achieve their usual standard of excellence. Jump School was divided into three weeks: Ground Week, Tower Week and Jump Week. Ground Week was instrumental in that the proper use of parachutes was stressed. To move forward successfully, individuals had to complete all physical training and master the proper use of the lateral drift apparatus, as well as parachute landing falls from a 34-foot tower. Tower Week introduced the "mass exit concept," which was the proper technique for a group to exit an aircraft together, ending with a 250-foot tower jump. Finally, during Jump Week each of them was required to make five parachute jumps from aircraft, at least one of which was at night. During the three-week course they both met and exceeded the expected range.

After Jump School, Wesley and Brent were given a thirty-day leave, which was long overdue. It had been nearly six months since Wesley had left New York and he was excited to see Liz and the kids. On the way to the bus station, he stopped and bought gifts. The boys were easy: toy trucks. Then he saw a pretty little doll baby with a tag that said "Tina Ballerina." He couldn't believe his find. Tina would feel so special. Several weeks before, he had bought Liz a royal blue, 100% silk shawl that was hand embroidered with golden threads from a specialty shop in town. It felt so soft and smooth; he could envision it wrapped around Liz's slim shoulders. Wesley was sure it was of fine quality, and something she would never buy for herself.

The bus ride to New York City took two days. As the bus pulled through the Holland Tunnel and plunged into the heart of Manhattan, Wesley could hardly contain himself. Now that he was back in the City, a different type of excitement began brewing within him. This was the place he had known for most of his life. He gazed out the window as the bus passed familiar places. He saw corners where he had nearly lost his freedom while cruising with a pack of wild kids during his days in the gang. When he left the City, he was a good-for-nothing kid headed toward a nothing life. Now he was returning as a man with a future.

When Wesley began making his way from the bus station to the subway he noticed that he was being watched, even stared at, by just about everyone. Some pointed at him and whispered. It took a small girl, who saluted him while passing by with her mother, for him to realize that all of the attention was the recognition of being a soldier in the United States Armed Forces. Most people in New York City rarely saw a soldier, especially one dressed sharply in a well-fitting uniform. And so, without even noticing, Wesley began walking a little taller, stretching to his full 6 feet, 4 inches: shoulders back, head held high, as he continued his strut with a wide smile and a happy heart in the City that was once his home.

Though Liz still lived in Brooklyn, she no longer lived in the old neighborhood. This one was a little less grimy, but Wesley still felt he had to look over his shoulder there. He hoped that he'd be able to send more money to Liz than he had been, to help her move the family to a better neighborhood. The apartment building was run-down, but it still didn't compare to where they had come from. Liz's apartment was on the fourth floor and there was an elevator that worked. When he walked into the place he couldn't believe the wonderful home that Liz had made for herself and the kids. There was a living room, dining room, a separate kitchen, two bedrooms and a bathroom. Liz had painted the whole apartment bright yellow by herself, and every room was furnished comfortably with nice secondhand furnishings. There were pictures on the walls, rugs on the floors and all kinds of homey little touches that Wesley marveled at: like a framed picture of he and Liz, live plants, and real flowers in a vase. The dining room table was set for five with mismatched dishes, glasses and silverware, and it smelled like something wonderful was cooking. Wesley didn't expect this and was overcome with emotion.

When they sat down for their meal all of the children waited while Liz said a blessing over the food. *What was that about?* Wesley hadn't ever said one word over his food other than, "Let's eat." He had noticed Brent and some of the other soldiers stopping to pray before eating, but he didn't consider doing it or asking anyone why they did. He decided to save that conversation for later with Liz, after the kids went to bed.

The meal was fantastic. Liz had been planning for Wesley's visit and wanted it to be special, so she had prepared baked ham with pineapple, fried chicken, candied sweet potatoes, their mother's special macaroni and cheese (that they used to get on Christmas Day), collard greens, home-made biscuits with gravy, and peach cobbler with real whipped cream. It was a feast for sure. Wesley ate so much that his whole body ached as he made his way to the couch in the front room.

Tina climbed in his lap. "Uncle Wes, what you got in that bag?"

"Oh, well—let's just see here…" He pulled the bag close to his feet as 4-year-old Andre rushed over to see.

When he pulled the doll from the bag, Tina squealed, hugging her uncle with delight.

"What about me?" Andre craned his neck to look in the bag.

"Little man, come on." Wesley pulled him closer as he took one of the trucks from the bag. Baby Tyrell toddled over to investigate, and Wesley went ahead and pulled the other truck out for him. They all hugged Wesley again and again, and Tina began pecking him on the cheek over and over and over.

"You're the best uncle in the world!" Tina shrieked.

"Yeah, the best unca!" Andre shouted. The two of them took their toys, and the baby's, and ran off to the boys' room to play, with baby Tyrell right behind them.

Wesley watched them and smiled. They had a good life. Liz was a great mother, he could tell that. Her children were happy and carefree. Liz came in and sat in the chair, putting her feet up on the table.

"Whew, the kitchen is cleaned up. Okay, so you know I love you baby bro, cause that meal was a whole lotta cookin and cleanin up after."

"Oh, yes ma'am, I do know that without a doubt. Girl, you put your foot in that food…*mmmmm good*. I don't think I could eat for days."

Liz grinned broadly. She was happy that her brother was there and that he was doing well.

"Have you heard from anybody lately, sis? You know, JoJo, Chris, Momma?"

"Well, Wes, you know Momma's doin fine livin with them people in Ohio. She got it good. She sends me a little somethin every now and then. Says she comin to visit."

"Oh, okay, that's good."

"Chris done up and disappeared out of our life completely. I really thought that after he went to college he would get over himself, and then get back in touch with us. Well, nooooo, I guess he just wants to forget that we even exist. So, I am through worryin about him."

"Man, that is sad…our own brother, Liz. I got a friend now that is a real brother to me. It's not like it was with Chris or JoJo. Well, it's kind of like JoJo, cuz we are really there for each other; but we're more equal, where JoJo was more like a protector, you know?"

"I do. He sure loves us all. JoJo writes and he always asks about you and Chris. I keep him up-to-date on you. He's proud of you. I don't go see him, though. I just don't want to see him behind bars. He don't want me to anyway, and especially not the kids. He says when he gets out this time, he ain't never goin back. So I just pray for him."

"Yeah, I noticed that prayin thing you did at dinner! What's that all about?" Wesley crossed his arms and waited.

"What you mean? I pray to God, Wesley. I have always believed in God. I thought we all did."

"Well, I can't say I do or I don't. I don't know Him."

"Wesley, you went to church sometime, didn't you?" She asked, confused.

"No, I never did. I was suppose to go, but I didn't. I just acted like it when Momma told us to go."

"Well, I want you to go with me and the kids on one of the Sundays while you're here. I found a nice church that I like a lot, and I think you'll like it, too. The Pastor talks real easy and it makes me feel good. Church is kind of like a gas station; I go there every Sunday to get filled up for the week."

"Sure, I'll go once, but I'm not promisin you anything about startin to believe in all of that stuff."

Wesley had a great time in New York. He was careful to stay away from their old life and didn't visit the old neighborhoods. He was a different person now, a man with means, so when he went out to enjoy himself, he ventured into places he had never been before: like jazz clubs in the Village and Manhattan. He also decided that it was time for him to visit his mother. The last time he saw her, he was troubled and angry. He realized now it was partly because he wanted her to rescue him from himself and show him love. It was also partly because he was afraid of a future filled with failure. But he had met the future head-on and became a soldier with a promising career. After a week of spending time with Liz and the kids, he caught a bus to Cleveland, Ohio.

Lorraine was nervous about Wesley's visit. She thought that he wouldn't understand what she had done; the choices she had made. She took the day off and drove to the bus station in her 2-year-old car, a gift from the Kingstons, the family she worked for. She sat anxiously waiting in the parking lot, smoking a cigarette. Lorraine recognized Wesley right away; his looks startled her. The resemblance between him and his father had grown stronger as Wesley had matured. Oh, was he handsome! He walked with a slight swagger, smiling brilliantly when he spotted her and headed toward the car, his radiant gray eyes twinkling in the bright, cold sunlight. Lorraine got out of the car to greet him. As he hugged her, the faint smell of lavender brought torrential waves of memories and suppressed emotions he had chosen to forget. A lump in his throat kept him from speaking as he released his mother and walked to the other side of the car.

They drove in silence for awhile and suddenly arrived at a restaurant with valet parking. A reservation had been made by his mother's employer, so they were seated at one of the more preferred private tables; the bill to be taken care of as well.

"Order whatever you'd like, Wesley."

Suddenly he was a teenager again, sitting in the diner with Chris waiting for news he wished he'd never heard.

"Thank you, Mother, I will. You're looking well. How have you been?"

"Well, the work is hard, but it keeps me busy. The Kingston's have three children, and I do just about everything for them. Mr. Kingston travels about two to three weeks out of every month and Mrs. Kingston is never at home, with all of her charity work and luncheons and so on; so, raising those children is just about all up to me. Even when we travel, I have to go so I can keep them all in check. It really is wonderful, though. I've been to some places I never thought I would go, and I do like Ohio and being near your Aunt Jean. We do everything together whenever we get some time to ourselves."

She stopped to puff on her cigarette and laugh briefly at her giddiness.

Wesley looked at his mother as she continued to nervously chatter on about insignificant things. She looked wonderful. He had never seen her dressed so well. She had worn a little make up and her hair was beautifully styled. She spoke openly and free, and smiled often while talking.

At first Wesley was a little annoyed by her disregard for her own children, but as they casually dined in the elegant four-star restaurant on a lazy Saturday afternoon—and he began to remember the love that he carefully protected within his heart for her—he realized that he could never resent his mother. He was happy for her. She was living a life that none of her children could give her. She had brought them into this life, and after all, if he hadn't had the hardships that he had encountered thus far, he wouldn't be the person that he was today. He would not have been able to achieve what he had in the military thus far, and he wouldn't be looking forward to the challenges that were yet to come.

So Wesley sat back and humored his mother, giving her his undivided attention throughout her long, unhurried stories, expressing patient appreciation and occasional animated remarks. His visit was an enlightening experience that he wholeheartedly enjoyed. He would cherish the memory of her, just as she was that day.

Chapter 11

CONTEMPLATION

*W*esley spent the rest of his leave back in New York with Liz and the kids. On the last Sunday of his visit, he kept his word and went with them to church.

The church building was small, but inviting. It was perched on a busy corner in Brooklyn, adorned with shrubbery and a long brick sidewalk, which led to the red, wooden double-doors. Inside, it was warm and welcoming. The ushers greeted them, vigorously shaking Wesley's hand, hoping to make him feel at home. The atmosphere was a little strange for Wesley, but pleasant.

There were too many people crowded inside the quaint little building, all strutting their Sunday attire. A fierce competition was going on, especially among the ladies. Some of them gave Wesley sideway glances and furtive winks, their devious flirtations clear as they passed by with their husbands and children. Wesley wasn't interested; he was appalled. He recognized the church as a sacred place, though it was apparent that many there didn't. Wesley, Liz and the kids sat in the fifth row. He had worn his uniform at Liz's request and they were the center of attention. Wesley sat straight and tall, facing forward, willing himself to focus on the reason he was there. He wanted to listen, to hear something he had never heard before. He secretly wanted to believe in something greater than himself. Though he had vowed total independence, he envied those with strong faith and wanted to know about God.

The vaulted ceiling of the church was filled to capacity with the bright magnificence of God's glorious angels. Carlonian was among them. He had read Wesley's heart and knew that his transformation was inevitable; this made him happy. Of course, neither Wesley nor any other person in the church was aware of the presence of their guardian angels—but the angels were there looking on and taking great pleasure as they joined to praise and worship the Most High.

The Pastor noticed Wesley in his uniform and asked him to stand. The congregation applauded, and he thanked him for his service to the country. The service began. There were readings from the Bible, songs from the hymnal, announcements from the ladies, and lots of prayers going up every few minutes. Finally, the Pastor stepped up to the pulpit to deliver his sermon.

Wesley centered himself and tried hard to focus on each word that the Pastor was saying. When he introduced a Bible verse, something in a "book" called Mark, he noticed that Liz opened her Bible and followed along.

Carlonian drew near and hovered above them.

Wesley heard the Pastor talk about Jesus gathering disciples to follow Him. A picture of his platoon in formation entered Wesley's mind as he thought about them following each other during boot camp. His thoughts drifted off to the memory of those eight weeks…then suddenly he heard the Pastor's voice rise, pulling him back to the sanctuary.

Again, Wesley tried to listen, to catch up, but he had missed a few key points and didn't know what was going on. He struggled within, forcing his mind to grasp each word the Pastor was speaking, and after a few minutes he was able to reconnect. The Pastor continued, talking about how the disciples had dropped their nets, left everything and believed in Jesus unconditionally by following Him to become fishers of men.

"To follow Jesus is not an easy thing," he declared. "It is, in fact, a difficult challenge. It requires you to make a decision to fully accept and trust in God as your Lord and Savior, and to come before Him for the forgiveness of your sins. Conforming your life to truly, and I mean truly, believe and accept His will is not an easy state-of-mind to achieve." Then he echoed dramatically, "Changing your state-of-mind is necessary, and not everyone is willing to make that change." He paused for effect.

"Releasing the reins that you think you are in control of is a commitment within itself to follow Him. Is His expectation too high a price to pay for eternal life in a world free of the confusion we now experience in our normal day-to-day lives?" He continued, "Can you imagine living eternally the way we now live here on Earth? I can't. I wouldn't want to. Life as we know it changes every day. It is spiraling into a world of unknown tomorrows. But Jesus' world is not a mystery. It is constant. Let's make some comparisons…"

Wesley's mind was spinning. He was having a hard time understanding how so much of the world could possibly believe in something they couldn't see. And now here this man was, standing there talking about giving up all control of your life to a phantom.

"This life here on Earth is a temporary one," the Pastor shared. "The distractions that we are faced with are of this world; they are meant to disrupt our lives and disguise our real purpose for being here, which is to bring glory and honor to God. We are His creation. So if you think about it like that, it leaves you to wonder: Is making the commitment to change the beliefs of your mind and heart, and letting go of the things you let take control of your temporary life on Earth too much for Him to ask? Is walking the path that Jesus invites you to be a part of too difficult? Let's go to Jeremiah, chapter 18, verse 6b. I'm reading from the *New International Version*. It says:

"…'Like clay in the hand of the potter, so are you in my hand…' " And verse 11b-c, adds: "…'So turn from your evil ways, each one of you, and reform your ways and your actions.' "

"After all, the gift of eternal life is an invaluable one. And that gift is better than the momentary thrill of sinking deeply into those buttery, soft leather seats in your fine Cadillacs and Lincolns, or wearing those expensive, bodacious designer shoes out on the town, or even living in a fine mansion filled with all the earthly desires of your heart. Trips around the world will not compare to the beauty and the glory of Heaven!" he shouted.

Wesley stopped listening. He had heard enough. He didn't want to fill his head with all of this right now. He was going back to continue his training and possibly go off to fight a war. He couldn't cloud his mind with these thoughts now. He was intrigued, but that kind of thinking would have to wait.

Carlonian watched as Wesley tuned out the rest of the sermon and service, and then hurried his sister and the children from the church. He knew that Wesley wanted no confrontation with the Pastor or anyone else for that matter. He was overwhelmed, because his soul stirred familiarly as the perplexing thoughts bombarded his mind, causing him greater confusion. Carlonian smiled as he watched Wesley leave the little church. He was euphoric about Wesley's experience.

Wesley took Liz and the kids out to eat and splurged on a tasty meal. The next morning he caught the bus back to Georgia to begin his next phase of training.

Chapter 12

LOVE

*U*nited States Army Rangers are soldiers who have been selected, based not only on the completion of their previous training, but also on outstanding competence throughout all of their training. They are revered with higher status within the Army, and their fellow soldiers view them as elite units worthy of high esteem. Ranger School was housed at Fort Benning, Georgia, and was the next step for both Wesley and Brent. Ranger training was voluntary; however, not every soldier was accepted into the program. Both Wesley and Brent were welcomed candidates.

Ranger training was the most challenging experience Wesley had encountered. It was demanding, grueling and exhausting. One of the Ranger mottos was to never leave a fallen man behind. Therefore, a portion of the training required that each Ranger candidate be physically able to carry a man out of a battle zone; in some cases, that could mean walking for miles. In preparation for that possibility heavy weight-training was necessary, along with the other requirements.

Wesley and Brent stuck together and stuck it out. Their success as Rangers led them to the Green Berets with over two hundred other recruits. Nearly two years later, fifty-one soldiers graduated from the program and began serving as Green Berets with the 6th Special Forces Group of Fort Bragg, North Carolina.

Wesley and Brent stood tall among the group that day, and Wesley's pride in his accomplishment went deep. It had been almost three years since he enlisted with an attitude of nonchalance. He couldn't recognize that person now when he thought about who he had become. He had accomplished so much, had pushed himself farther than he thought possible, and then pushed himself more. A feeling of immense pride radiated within him. When Wesley's name was called, he turned out of formation, marched to the risers on that North Carolina field and saluted his superiors. He had never known such a feeling of indispensable dignity.

Wesley's mother had traveled from Ohio for the graduation ceremony and was smiling brightly, filled with pride. After the ceremony, she gave him the tightest hug he'd ever received from her. Then he introduced her to Brent, explaining how they had become true brothers and that he wanted them to get to know each other.

As Lorraine turned to Wesley and spoke, tears gently spilled from her eyes.

"Wesley, I don't know when I've been so proud. I knew that you were destined to be somethin, and to do somethin special with your life. I just didn't know how to show that to you. I had to come today so you would know how much I really do care about you."

"Momma, I know you care about me. You don't have to show me. I'll always love you, no matter what."

"I didn't have much to give you," she continued, "but I gave you what I had. It was hard for me to let them send you away to the detention center when you were young, but I hope you know...I had to save you from yourself and the streets, and that was the best way I knew how."

"You're right, Momma," Wesley comforted. "I didn't know it then, but I know it now, and I hope that when I have kids I'll be able to make hard decisions for them, too."

They spent the rest of the day together. Lorraine knew that Wesley had helped Liz move her family into a decent home. Tina and Andre were doing well in school, Tyrell had just entered preschool, and Liz was a teacher's assistant at their school. She was doing so well.

JoJo had gotten out of jail, but had gotten in more trouble and was waiting for his trial. They were sure that he'd be going right back to jail, and this time he might not ever get out. He was charged with armed robbery, and there were witnesses.

Chris had contacted her and was doing well in grad school. She wasn't happy with him because he had deserted the family, running off the way he had. He wasn't interested in writing anymore, but wanted to do medical research. He had won an award for some work he had been doing with a doctor, and by the looks of things, he had a chance to make some type of difference in the medical field.

Wesley was sad about his brother JoJo. He wanted him to see the man he had become. He wished there was something he could do to help his brother; JoJo had helped him so many times when he was younger. Though they wrote to each other, JoJo remained adamant about no one coming to see him in jail. He didn't want them to know what it was like there, to have a picture to hold in their minds about his day-to-day existence. So they stayed away, writing and sending money whenever they could, in hopes that it would help to make his life in jail a little easier.

Wesley and Brent were sent to Germany to the 8th Airborne Division in Wiesbaden, and then reassigned to the 10th Special Forces Group. Then they were sent on temporary duty (TDYed) to the 3rd Army European Theater Skydiving Team, where they served for one year. Germany was a great time.

While stationed in Germany, Wesley met a young lady at the PX one afternoon that was different from any other he had met. She was tall, nearly 6 feet, and looked Wesley directly in his eyes when she turned toward him to ask his advice on a gift for her father. He was captivated by her huge dimples. Her name was Claudia Montgomery. She was the daughter of one of the captains on base and the first girl he had talked to who wasn't hanging around the base trying to snag a soldier.

She bought the suggested gift and the two of them walked outside together. It was a beautiful spring afternoon, so Wesley offered to walk her home. They talked freely the entire way; Wesley knew that Claudia would be special to him.

She gave Wesley her telephone number and over the next few weeks he called her often. They got to know each other on a different level. He found himself telling her things he hadn't talked about in a long time, especially not with a female. He was amazed at how comfortable he was talking with her. Their conversations were full and engaging; they never experienced times of awkward, empty silence. But Wesley hadn't had a steady girlfriend and he wasn't sure how to proceed. So after they had gotten to know each other better, he asked Claudia to go to a movie. She told him that he would have to meet her father. The next day, he went to visit and met both of her parents.

Since her father was a captain in the Army and was used to soldiers being interested in his daughter, he looked at Wesley with suspicion, though he was friendly. Her mother seemed to like him; he could tell. Claudia and Wesley went to the movie that same night, holding hands the whole time. He could tell she really liked him. Wesley didn't know how to handle that. *Claudia was a nice girl, so what was he supposed to do next?* If she were a girl he'd met at one of the clubs, they would probably already have slept together and he wouldn't care what she thought. But he cared a lot about what Claudia thought, and he didn't want to mess it up—so he just kept everything the same: talking, movies, walks on the base, and finally, kissing…but nothing more.

Claudia was still in high school, and her father didn't like the idea of his precious little girl being with a soldier. Wesley did everything he could think of to assure Captain Montgomery that he had only honorable intentions toward his daughter. He thought he was falling in love, hell, he knew he was. She was gorgeous and she had class. And more than that, she got him. She understood him. He'd heard people talk about how it felt when you found that one person you connected with, in a way that you never connected with anyone else. He wasn't sure if this was that feeling, but he knew he liked the way he felt. One evening they were all set to go on a double date with Brent and a German girl he was trying to date. When Wesley picked Claudia up, she wanted to be alone with him.

"I know that you'll be leaving soon, so I don't want to waste the time we have sitting in a movie," she intimated. "I love you, Wesley, and I want to show you how much."

Wesley's head was spinning. *She said she loved him.* A girl had never said that to him. He pondered about his life. He knew that his family loved him, though each of them had a different view of what love was and the way they chose to show it. And up to that point, all of his romantic encounters had been just that: brief encounters.

His first crush had been on Linda Hubbard, a girl who lived in a house near the rooming house his family had lived in when he was 12 years old. He overheard her at school one day saying that her favorite color was red. He wanted to make her aware of his affection, so he picked the most fragrant red flowers he could find around the neighborhood, spent his White Castle money on a wide lace ribbon (which he carefully tied around the bouquet), and then he dressed in his most prized possession: a complete ninja shinobi, a gift sent from his Uncle Bill, who had encouraged him in a letter to learn karate to protect himself. As he looked at his image in the mirror and slipped the concealing hood over his head, he was pleased and confident that Linda would be impressed.

He ran all the way to her house and put the flowers on her porch. Then he rang the doorbell and slipped away to the safety of nearby bushes, where he could see her retrieve his precious gift. He was sure she had been watching him from the window, yet she only picked up the bouquet, smelled the flowers and went back into the house, closing the door behind her. She didn't smile or look in his direction; she simply took the flowers.

At school the next day, Wesley waited for some sign that she appreciated the flowers and was sure that she would realize how much he liked her. Nothing else mattered to him that day. He hoped above all else that she liked him, too. His anxiety grew as she stole glances of him in the hallways all morning. At lunchtime, he decided to make his move and walked toward the table where she was eating lunch with her friends.

"Can you believe he thinks I could like him?" she harshly spat as she watched him approach from the corner of her eye, making sure he'd hear her. "He had on a ninja suit and a thing over his head, slinking around the bushes like an idiot or something."

Whoa! He thought. *Did I hear her right?* All of her friends laughed. Others who had overheard her joined in the laughter. Wesley re-grouped quickly. He was determined not to let them think that anything they had to say mattered. So he held his pace, passing the table, and moved toward the exit.

Then he heard one of her friends add, "I heard he's poor. His whole family lives in one room." The laughter exploded again.

That experience had left Wesley numb. He decided that instead of being hurt or angry, he wouldn't be anything at all. Even at his tender age, Wesley was an enduring soul. He possessed eccentric nobility, coupled with an amazing resolve. He decided to leave them alone that day and every day after, pledging to stay to himself and stay close to his family.

During the years since then, Wesley's only romantic involvements had been brief bouts of companionship that were frivolous and insignificant. But he was convinced that every soul had a mate, including himself. Until meeting Claudia, he hadn't met anyone whom he considered a possibility. He had not allowed his thoughts to speculate why. Instead, he had boldly traveled his life's path, meeting every chapter head-on toward a destiny that might not include finding that special person.

Now here he was with who he thought that person may be…and she loved him. Wesley was so choked up, he couldn't speak. He had never felt this feeling before, and he wasn't sure he wanted anyone to know that—even Claudia—so he embraced her and buried his head in her hair. He felt dizzy, oddly exposed. He released her and took her by the hand, leading her to the jeep. They drove to a remote end of the base where they could park and talk. The sun was setting in the distance, a brilliant orange sky filled with lustrous clouds. Wesley turned to Claudia, who looked pleadingly toward him.

"Claudia, I have never felt about anyone the way I feel about you. I love you. I've loved you for a while now. I wasn't sure that you felt the same way."

"Well, Wesley, if you love me, why did you bring me here? I said I wanted to show you. I thought we would go to a hotel."

"Claudia, we're both still young and you're in your last year of high school. I'm 22 years old, and I've seen a lot of hardship in my time. I know what I want, and I want you to be sure that I'm what you want. I don't want to just have sex with you; I feel like you're the person meant for me. I want to know that I'm the person meant for you. I want us to wait. You're right, I will be leavin soon, and I know that nobody else is gonna matter to me. No matter how long it is, I will always, always be committed to you, no matter what happens. Can you honestly say the same thing to me and really mean it?"

"Yes, we—"

"Claudia," Wesley interrupted, "I don't want you to say *yes* now. I want you to think. I want you to know for sure or at least be as sure as you can be. I'm not tryin to put pressure on you to commit to me. You'll be graduatin from school and goin away to college. You're gonna meet all kinds of guys who are gonna be there with you, not halfway around the world somewhere."

"Listen, Wesley, I have more experience than you know. I've lived all over the place because my dad keeps getting transferred, and I have hated that. I never get a chance to make real relationships with anyone. But still, I know that I have never met anyone that I feel as strongly about as you. My grandmother has always said that I have an old soul and that I am ahead of my years. And that is sooooo true. I am not the 18-year-old that people expect me to be. I know my mind and I know myself completely. I am committed to you whether you ask for that commitment or not. You are what I want, Wesley Lewis, and I am a headstrong woman who gets what she wants."

Wesley thought for a moment and decided that he wouldn't push the issue. As difficult as it was, he didn't make love to Claudia that night. He enjoyed watching her while they bowled and went out for late night burgers and shakes, allowing himself the luxury of daydreaming of a future together.

By the time Wesley was transferred out of Germany he had decided not to propose marriage to Claudia. He was going to war. He knew himself well enough to know that if he proposed to her before he left, that he would have thoughts of a future with her on his mind. He might become careless and lose his life unnecessarily. As the time neared for him to leave they spent as much time together as they could. He bought her a gold band, which she wore on the third finger of her left hand. She gave him a thick silver locket with a picture of herself in it, for him to keep near his heart wherever he went. They vowed to write letters and stay in love, and dreamed together about one day being married to each other. As far as Wesley was concerned, that was commitment enough for him. He planned to return to Claudia and spend the rest of his life with her.

Wesley and Brent were shipped off to war, but it wasn't the war they had mentally prepared themselves for. Instead of going to Viet Nam, they were sent to the Dominican Republic-liaison with the 82nd Airborne, where they were engaged in covert military activity. It was a brief, but intense operation where the training and skills they had acquired were put to the ultimate test. When the whirlwind was over and they looked back on the exhilarating encounter, they thought of it as a prelude to the real maniacal world they were about to enter: Viet Nam was on their horizon. But first, they returned to the U.S., where they were given orders to train new troops for Long Range Reconnaissance Patrol, otherwise known as LRRP. As they were preparing for deployment to Southeast Asia, Wesley found Brent on his knees in the room they shared on base. A Bible was lying on his bed.

"What's up, B? Nervous about where we're headed?" Wesley joked.

"Not at all, man. Just not goin without prayer first."

Wesley was shocked, and he responded, "Prayin? I didn't know you did that, Brent. Never saw you on your knees before. I know you pray over food, but this is different."

"Not really, Wes. Prayer is prayer, man." He picked up the Bible, stood up and held it out to Wesley. "You should check it out," Brent offered.

"No, no, I'm good man. I'll just leave that to you and my sister, cause I gotta stay focused."

"No better way to do that than with this," Brent responded, "...but it's okay. If you change your mind let me know."

Chapter 13

SURVIVAL

*V*iet Nam was a fantastically beautiful country. Because of its loveliness, it was hard for Wesley to believe that it could be filled with danger. When darkness fell the first night they were there, Wesley admired the magnificence of the sky. It was a deep, vividly clear, black pool of endless beauty filled with dazzling, brilliant stars. It rained later that night, a fresh, soaking torrential rain. They soon learned that rain was frequent and welcomed by the American soldiers. It meant that everyone looked for cover, including the enemy. Rain meant security.

Viet Nam brought many new challenges, the first being its splendor—because at times while walking through the jungle it seemed that you weren't at war, but instead, were exploring an exotic land. The landscape was vastly different from the U.S. and other countries they had been to thus far. Known as the "bush," the jungles of Viet Nam were filled with poisonous snakes, spiders, leeches and lots of places for "Charlie" to hide.

Wesley and Brent were part of a nine-man team within their unit. They took on every assignment with a vengeance, successfully completing each mission. Though it was grueling and deadly, they thrived. Both were good at what they did, working together like a well-oiled machine.

Claudia wrote Wesley immediately after he left Germany, and he stayed in close touch as she graduated from high school and went away to college back in the States on the west coast. Their letters had been frequent, supportive and uplifting. The future seemed bright; they both had goals to accomplish and their priorities were in check. They had the rest of their lives to be together.

As time went on in the Nam, Wesley became more immersed in battle. He was sent along with the 173rd Airborne into the midst of Operation Retriever I and II in the Bien Hoa and Binh Duong Provinces, which were advanced search and destroy missions. Operations Roundhouse, Entrée and Phoenix followed. Though Wesley returned from each mission intact he was becoming aware of his need to completely separate himself from what he had left behind. He stopped answering Claudia's letters. He knew he had to, because he was too connected to her world when he needed to stay highly focused in his effort to survive. He realized that he needed to care about nothing other than his immediate task: war. He knew that if he cared, his caring would be a distraction. He had to keep Claudia out of his thoughts at all costs. If he didn't, he knew that he couldn't remain objective in his choices during combat. He had to approach each day as though he had nothing to lose.

The Battle of Dak Tó was a series of major encounters that became known as the "border battles." The fighting was intense and lasted for months during the monsoon season, which kept reinforcements of troops and supplies from getting through to either side. They ran out of food and ammunition, but the fighting continued on the ground between storms in bloody hand-to-hand combat. Many times, Wesley and Brent literally fought back-to-back. The troops that were there concerned themselves only with holding their ground until backup could get through.

When the 173rd Airborne pulled out, Wesley wrote Claudia one final letter explaining his decision to end their correspondence and to profess his love, dedication and commitment to her. Claudia wrote back immediately, but Wesley didn't read it. She continued to write letter after unanswered letter. Wesley never read them; he stopped picking them up. He didn't want mail from anyone. Her letters began to come less frequently at first, and then not at all. Wesley would never know what they said. But he still loved her, keeping her safely somewhere deep in the back of his mind. He cherished Claudia and still planned to be with her. His plan was to surprise her when he left Viet Nam. When Dak Tó erupted again and the 173rd returned with Operation McArthur, Claudia was far from Wesley's mind as he fought without fear or favor.

As the end of Wesley's tour of duty neared he tried harder not to think about Claudia. It was a soldier's belief that when your time to leave got close and you counted down the days, you became less careful and made mistakes which could cost you your life. He went along as though he had no one anywhere in the world except Brent. The remaining months flew by quickly and only a week remained before they would leave Viet Nam.

"Hey man, you think we're gonna get out of this thing alive?" Brent asked.

"No doubt."

"So then, what's next on the agenda?"

"Well, after we win this thing, I'll be ready to live a little." Wesley said.

Brent agreed. "Oh yeah, man, I'm ready to go hang out, everywhere. The money we been takin in for all this stuff we been providin everybody with will give us a nice piece a change to enjoy."

"I'm gonna get a Corvette and drive the country: New York, Miami, Chicago, Dallas, you name it. If it's in the States I wanna see it. I wanna see all I can of the land I been fightin for."

"Me, I want me a Super Sport," Brent mused, "and I'll be right there with you. Man, we're gonna have a blast, rock everybody's world. And let's end up in California, man. I always wanted to live there."

"That's cool, long as it's not L.A."

"Well, I heard the beach is realllly nice in California," Brent smiled.

"Me, too. I want one of those big, gorgeous houses right on the beach."

"Let's do it," Brent laughed. "We will be two players, livin large in a magnificent house on the beach, man. We will have it all."

"For a minute, man. But you know, I got plans."

"Yeah, man, I know; but I really think you should write that girl another letter. You don't even know what she's been sayin lately."

"B, you know that topic is off limits. I can't think about it while I'm here or I will never get out of this alive. But I will say this: I know she can feel me."

"Humph...man," Brent shook his head. "I don't think that kind of commitment exists. She ain't heard from you in over a year, man. She's a young, gorgeous woman."

"Okay B, I don't wanna hear nothin else about it. I know what we have."

. . . .

The day for Wesley and Brent to leave the war came, and they left Viet Nam. Wesley tried to call Claudia from Tokyo while laying over there for a few days. The number he had for her parents' home in Portland, Oregon had been disconnected. It had been nearly two years. Wesley flew on to Los Angeles, California and then to Portland.

Brent went to Massachusetts to see his family for a short visit. They had planned to meet up in a few weeks.

Oregon was a great place. Wesley had never been there before. He breathed in the clear, crisp November air and smiled.

"Oregon is gonna be great for me," Wesley commented to the taxi driver.

"Yes, it is very nice here, but there is a lot of rain," he replied.

"Hey, I know, before I go to the house, I'm gonna stop at the mall and buy gifts for everyone! Take me to a really good place where I can get some special things."

"What are you looking for?"

"Jewelry, flowers, things like that."

The driver took him to a jeweler where Wesley bought Claudia a flawless one-carat solitaire diamond engagement ring, a gold bracelet for her mother, and an impressive money clip for her father. Next, they stopped at a florist where he bought three dozen long-stemmed American Beauty red roses. They made several other stops, picking up Cristal champagne,

Waterford crystal glasses, imported Belgian chocolates and beautiful lace lingerie. With his many gifts and a growing excitement he had never experienced, Wesley instructed the driver to take him to the address he'd been given. As the taxi approached the house, they noticed that two black limousines were parked in front. The taxi parallel parked beside one of the limousines.

"Looks like somebody died here," the driver said. "That'll be $92.00."

Wesley looked concerned.

"You think somebody died?" he asked the driver.

The driver shrugged his shoulders.

The front door opened and Claudia's mother stepped out; she didn't notice the taxi. She was dressed in a long formal gown, and then Claudia stepped out behind her in a beautiful white wedding dress! She was stunning, more so now than ever. She was smiling, concerning herself only with keeping the train of her gown from dragging the ground. Several other young women sprang from the doorway, all dressed in long, bright green gowns. They were all joyfully, yet carefully, making their way down the steps towards the waiting limousines.

As Wesley stepped out of the taxi Claudia looked up and saw him. He almost couldn't believe how breathtaking she was—all excited and radiant...ready to marry someone else. Wesley was devastated. He couldn't have felt more foolish, standing there with a taxi filled with gifts, holding an armful of roses and an engagement ring.

"Take your time, man," the driver said, "I'll just pull over in front of this limousine and wait for a minute."

Wesley closed the door and stepped up on the curb. He stood there, unable to move, and so did Claudia. They stared at each other, not believing that this was actually happening at that exact moment in time. Claudia's mother turned, saw Wesley, and walked toward him.

"Wesley...well, I'm glad that you survived the war, um...but as you can see, today is not a good day for a visit."

She turned and motioned for all of the bridesmaids to go to the second limousine, telling the driver to drive to the next block, park and await instructions. Then she went back to her daughter, who was frozen still with a twisted look of fury on her beautiful face.

"Claudia, do I need to call your father or better yet, the police?" her mother asked, looking Wesley up and down.

"No mother," Claudia snapped. "I can handle this situation. Go wait in the car."

Wesley approached Claudia and reached out to her.

"Oh, no, Wesley...don't touch me!" She nearly screamed. "What happened to you and your undying love? You send me a letter saying you're not going to write anymore cause you need to keep you're your head straight. Well, guess what, I needed to keep my head straight, too; and that meant that I needed to tell you about my problems and what was going on in my life, and then hear what you thought about them. I needed you."

"Claudia, I thought you would understand…the only way for me to stay alive and come back to you was for me to stay focused and to—"

"Oh, NO, you are not gonna turn this around. I don't want to hear that!!! There are plenty of other soldiers who kept writing to their girl-friends, and they are still alive. I didn't believe any of that crap then and I sure don't believe it now."

"I am not them, Claudia, I am me. I know myself and what I had to do to survive that madness over there." He explained. "I never stopped lovin you for even one minute. And our plan to be together forever was always what I intended. Look…"

He reached inside his shirt and pulled a chain through the collar. The silver locket that she had given him dangled before her.

"I've kept you near, right here where you said, near my heart. I've never stopped lovin you, Claudia. And I'm here for you, see…"

He took the ring box out of his pocket and opened it, showing her the impressive ring.

She looked at the ring and then up at him, and then at her mother, who stood by the limousine shaking her head and motioning for her to come. Suddenly, Claudia began laughing.

"Oh, and that's the best that you could do?" she snapped. "Bring me a ring to make up for everything? Well, Wesley, it's not that easy. I am no fool."

She shoved her left hand out to flaunt the ring she was wearing.

"See, somebody else can do that, too; somebody who is here for me when I need him. I wrote and wrote to you, trying to tell you what I needed. So I decided that it was over. I figured you were over there with some Viet-namese chick anyway, and you'd probably be bringing her back with you, so I moved on. I can't believe that you have the nerve to come here today and ruin the most important day of my life. What did you expect?" she spat. "Did you think I would just sit here and wait for you and some 'end-less love' you claimed to have while you were over there havin fun?"

"FUN?" Wesley nearly lost it. He slammed the ring box shut, threw the roses to the ground and shrieked at Claudia. "FUN? You can't imag-ine what I've gone through. I'm ruinin your day; that's what you have to say about seein me?" Claudia cowered slightly. Wesley caught himself, regained his composure and continued in a calm, controlled tone.

"First of all, I didn't know that you were gettin married today, so no, I wasn't tryin to ruin your big day. What did I expect of you? I guess I thought that I had found my mate, a woman who had convinced me of her love and had captured my heart, and to whom I had pledged my love and devotion. So I expected that right now we'd be embracing and cele-bratin our future together. I completely misread this relationship, because instead of seein the woman that I fell in love with, I'm standin here lookin into the eyes of a spoiled, self-centered brat. So congratulations on findin your mate. I'll just keep lookin for mine."

"You do that!" She spat.

"And by the way," Wesley continued, "Thank you for showin me who you really are and sparin me the agony of what was sure to be an ugly divorce."

He turned and walked back to the taxi. Claudia stood, scowling at him as she threw up her middle finger with both hands.

Wesley returned the engagement ring, but left the other gifts in the taxi and caught the next flight to Las Vegas, where he checked into one of Caesar's Palace's most luxurious two-bedroom suites. Brent joined him the next day and for two weeks they indulged themselves with long, lavish meals, the finest cognacs and liqueurs, massages, manicures and pedicures, the best shows and lots of nightlife. When they were completely pampered beyond their wildest imaginations, they discussed the future.

"Okay, Wes. What's it gonna be? We still got plenty of cash and a whole country to explore."

"There's nothing here for me now, B. I gotta clear my head, and I do that best when I'm doin what I do best. So man, you go on and get that Super Sport and get started on that life of livin it up. I'll catch up to you later." He rubbed his head as he spoke. "I'm goin back to Nam for one more tour. I sobered up yesterday; haven't had a drink or nothin since then and did nothin but think all night. Gotta do it. Gotta go back."

"What? Nam? Are you sure? Is that the only way to clear your head?"

"Yeah, this has been big fun, but it's not enough. I have to feel useful, be useful, do what I do…and that means goin back. What am I gonna do here? I can't sit at a desk or go to college, man, that ain't me. I feel good when I'm on a mission, and then when I complete it, it's like being high, only better. I'll be fine, you know I will. And when I get back, we'll kick it like we always have."

"You're right, Wesley, we will kick it like we always have…but not til after WE get back from Nam."

"No, B, I can't let you do that. All we talked about was gettin out of there alive with all this money, and livin good and havin the time of our lives. I can't let you do this. This is somethin I gotta do."

"You are not goin back over there without me, so let's check out of this place and get back to what we do."

"B!"

"Wes!" Brent wasn't taking *no* for an answer.

"Man…what am I gonna do with you?" Wesley laughed.

"You're gonna continue fightin a war with me, that's what you're gonna do!" Brent declared.

Chapter 14

PAIN

*B*ack in Viet Nam, Wesley couldn't get back in the groove. Brent noticed it and attributed it to the fact that Wes' heart truly had been broken. Of course, he hadn't admitted it at first; he just shrugged it off.

"Man, you know, I don't know what I was thinkin," Wes began.

"About what?"

"I let her in, B. I guess I thought that Claudia and I were really linked, kind of like a resilient bond that wouldn't or couldn't be broken. I thought we could feel each other. Even when I wouldn't let myself think about her while we were fightin the war, I just kind of knew somewhere deep that we were connected, and she'd always be there like I'd be there for her."

"I know what you're sayin, Wes, but everybody doesn't have that mysteriously forever kind of loyalty that you do."

"No man, it's not loyalty...it's like, like trust, kind of, but even more than that. I've always thought I'd meet that person and have this really strong bond with her that nothin could break. I really thought she was that person. I never trusted anyone like I let myself trust her."

"Wes, man, you know you're from another time, right?"

Wesley grimaced.

"No...really," Brent continued, "You're a true gentleman of the court who distinguishes his perfect lady love, and promptly places her high upon a regal pedestal, never to be dethroned."

"Come on, B, I'm serious," Wes chuckled.

"And so am I. That's really you. You're looking for that once-in-a-lifetime love thing. I'm rootin for you, man. It's not somethin that I believe in, and I'm okay with that. My bond is with God. I've committed myself to Him, and whether He sends me someone or not, it's alright. But you, man—oh, I can see how important it is for you to have that somebody...your own somebody who you can share your inner self with and trust."

"No, B, you've got it all wrong this time. See, Claudia shocked me with what happened, but I don't need anyone. I've never had anyone, and I don't need to start now. That's why I wanted to come back to the Nam, B. This is what I know and what I can understand. They're tryin to kill me and I'm tryin to kill them. It's as simple as that, and I…can…do…this. I can't do *that*, ever again. I will not let anybody else in, ever."

Carlonian was saddened by this turn of events as he listened to Wesley's soulful thoughts. He always rooted for him and was happy for the way he had handled himself throughout his difficult teenage and early adult years. He had seen opportunities where he considered intervening more so than he did the night he whispered in Wesley's ear, trying to dissuade him from joining a gang. But even through that situation things had turned out okay. It had led him to realizations about himself through the relationships he had with his earthly sister, grandfather, and now, Brent. But Claudia had severely wounded him. So much so that he realized he would have to wait longer for Wesley. And that was okay because after all, there was much time.

Wesley and Brent grew closer and were more determined to stay together through all of the madness. They fought battles throughout Viet Nam. A year went by and they continued to fight bravely and relentlessly, though the country they fought for was a mass of confusion and contradiction. Back home there were protests about the war; there were those who supported it and those who did not. Politicians and celebrities had something to say, but despite their views the war labored on. The soldiers were caught in the web of blame, taking the brunt of misplaced responsibility. They were nameless scapegoats for those who were too cowardly to fight for themselves. Many lives were lost for a country that was too indecisive to support its own: people who were fighting an unscrupulous and self-indulgent war. The rich got richer and the poor lost everything.

When Wesley and Brent were in the Nam, SURVIVAL and nothing else was on their minds. When they went away on R & R, FUN and nothing else was on their minds. During R & R they were able to visit many interesting places. Australia, Hawaii, Japan, and Hong Kong were among them. Wesley fell in love with Hong Kong. He wanted to return there someday.

During one of their R & R visits to Australia, Wesley saw a striking woman and walked directly over to meet her. Her name was Saffi Bonn; she was Fijan and Australian, and turned out to be a fascinating woman. She didn't frequent nightclubs, but had joined friends at a club that evening. Saffi liked Wesley, so they went out the next evening. She brought a friend for Brent. Saffi was enchanting and assured Wesley that she was inexperienced when it came to men. She especially did not date soldiers who were there on R & R. For the next few days Wesley wined and dined the desirable Saffi into submission. They were inseparable for the remainder of his leave and had a lot of fun hanging out. Eventually, Saffi wildly gave herself to Wesley in a surprisingly uninhibited craze.

From that day on, Saffi dressed sexy, but carried herself regally, and Wesley didn't mind spending bundles of money on her. That leave was so sweet, before they knew it, it was time to go back to the Nam. Wesley left Saffi with a new wardrobe, jewelry, and promises that he'd be back to spend as much time with her as he could on R & R's and thereafter.

A couple days later back in Viet Nam, Wesley noticed something was terribly wrong. A quick trip to the medic brought news that the lovely, inexperienced Saffi had given him a farewell gift of the clap, an undeniable case of gonorrhea. He couldn't believe it. *How could he get it wrong again?* He had felt a connection to this woman, not like with Claudia, but something different. There had to be an explanation; he couldn't wait to see Saffi again.

He and Brent returned to Australia on their next R & R and went directly to Saffi's apartment. When she didn't answer they went to the nightclub where they had met her, and there she was in the same place—perched high on her barroom throne. Wesley watched her going through the same motions she had with him. He decided to humiliate her, right there in front of everyone. But he hesitated when he saw that the man she was performing for was a lieutenant from their unit; she was undoubtedly feeding him the same lines. Brent had been having a lot of trouble with that Lieutenant, who was unfairly riding him. That guy had done Wesley in a few times, too. So after thinking it over, he decided that leaving the Lieutenant to enjoy his leave with the beautiful Ms. Bonn would be satisfying enough. As for Saffi, he was sure that her day would come. He decided to leave her to fate.

One afternoon a few months later, Wesley and Brent were crouching in the bush on a search and destroy mission. Brent moved close to Wesley.

"Wes, man, I'm kind of glad we came back for this tour. It's been good, man," he whispered.

" Yeah, B."

"And we only have a few more weeks, then it's back to the world, baby. Our little operation over here has paid the BIG BUCKS. We got so much cash that when we get back home, the sky won't even be our limit," he chuckled a little too loudly.

"Shh, man, and don't talk about it, B. We have to stay focused. You know that!" Wesley whispered, slightly annoyed by Brent's carelessness.

Some bushes near them moved, startling them as a parrot flew out. They sighed, but were aware that a sniper was near them. The parrot probably saved their lives. Wesley was angry that Brent had momentarily distracted them both with his talk of home. He reacted quickly and began moving with Brent behind him, tracking the sniper who was masterfully camouflaged among the overgrown trees and bushes. As they pursued the sniper through the thick bush, it was apparent that he was slowly leading them farther into enemy territory. They stopped and took cover, deciding to stage an ambush instead. They concealed themselves and quietly waited for the sniper to return.

Hours passed. It was late afternoon. The sun still high, the heat, excruciating...but they waited. Nothing happened. Deciding to return to the main body, Brent motioned to Wesley and they began moving slowly, quietly, in retreat.

They crawled, rolled and waited. Nothing. They crouched and watched and moved agonizingly slowly. After an hour or so of this, they were reasonably sure that they weren't in immediate danger. They stopped to drink some water, staying well concealed and alert.

"Man, do you see, do you see what can happen when you lose focus?" Wesley posed, still whispering but agitated.

"I know, man, but I'm tired and I'm ready. It's been alright comin back and all, but I'm ready to get out of here."

"Don't start again, man. Be quiet. Listen."

They waited, hidden from view. They kept waiting and nothing happened. They decided to continue the journey back. Carefully and methodically, they made their way.

"Wesley, look man, the parrot is back. He saved our lives; I'm takin him with me."

Before Wesley could protest, Brent abruptly leaped up and across Wesley toward the parrot, just as they heard the gunshot. The sniper had returned and had aimed directly at Wesley, but Brent's movement had placed him in the line of fire. He was hit in the chest, falling limp in what seemed like slow motion. Wesley caught him as he went down, quickly laying him gently on the ground—still aiming his gun, firing relentlessly and then running a twisted path toward the sniper. By the time he reached the sniper, he was dead.

As Brent lay on the ground alone, an angel appeared above him. When Brent looked up, he smiled...he remembered the angel Joviah, his friend from the Transfer Station all those years ago. He remembered that day clearly now; it was as though he had been speaking with Joviah just moments before, asking him questions. It occurred to him how funny that was, because the entire time that he had been on Earth he had had no recollection of that experience whatsoever. And now, here was Joviah, an angel in full glory there to greet him.

Joviah was floating in the midst of a clear spotlight that led from where Brent was lying on the ground all the way up through the clouds, the sky and beyond. But it wasn't a spotlight at all; it was glistening clear air, so light, lucid and bright it nearly hurt Brent's eyes. He thought to himself that it looked like a tunnel or passageway leading to Heaven. He turned his head from Joviah and looked sideways where the bright daylight of Earth now appeared hazy and thick, a dull likeness of Heaven's atmosphere. While the beckoning heavens were joyful, jubilant and filled with promise, the earth he'd been living in was now a cloudy, baffling abyss. Brent knew that he was leaving, and he couldn't wait to be on his way.

Joviah simply said, "Hello Brent," and Brent was filled with peace. He knew then that he had made it. He had come into the world, lived the life, and upon seeing Joviah, knew that he had been triumphant there. He had fulfilled his purpose, whatever it had been, and now it didn't matter what it was. What did matter at that moment was that in God's eyes he had fulfilled his purpose and he was leaving this place. He was happy and ready to continue his journey—his life of infinity—granted only by his Heavenly Father.

As he turned to see Wesley running back toward him, his smile faded. His heart was heavy for his friend; he knew Wesley wouldn't understand and would feel heartbroken and responsible.

"I know what you're thinking," Joviah said, smiling at Brent. "You don't have to worry about Wesley, he will be okay. What has happened here today serves purposes for both of you in this life. Wesley will blame himself and he will have a long, hard battle within himself, which will lead him to many other experiences that are parts of his journey before leaving this world. Your purpose here today is two-fold. First, your death leads Wesley into the next phase of his existence, and secondly, this experience ends your time here on Earth. Your visit here was short, but your journey as a mortal being is complete."

Wesley reached Brent and checked his wound. Brent was breathing and conscious. He smiled at Wesley and tried to reassure him.

"B, man, don't worry man, I got em…c'mon man, gotta get you back, so they can fix you up."

"Wes, no…" Brent struggled to continue. "Stop man, it's okay…I'm ready, I been ready…" he breathed out with difficulty. "I'm not like you, man…I know this was for me."

"What are you talkin about, man?" Wesley cried, tears pouring down his face. "That bullet was meant for me."

"No, it was mine…and I'm glad, man. It's over. God's waitin on me… and I'm gonna be waitin on you, man. You…go on and find that soul mate, man: the one you been lookin for. She…she's out there…then…you an…her both can come…"

"No, Brent, it ain't over for you. We got a lot of livin left to do."

"No, *you* do…We're not…all…here for the same things…my time… gone, we here for…different things—"

"Brent…what? NO, man!"

"Wesley, yes, man…man, look…" He pointed upward at Joviah, and Wesley looked up to see only the sky. Brent was staring with a joyful smile of contentedness and recognition. He lifted himself slightly while stretching his arm toward the sky, his hand outstretched, as if reaching to grab onto something. Then he turned for one last look at his friend and whispered…

"Wes, I love you, man…goodbye."

As Brent reached for Joviah his soul quietly slipped from its earthly body and glided victoriously away with him. Brent's body, the shell which was his home for twenty-five earthly years, slumped back to the ground into lifelessness.

Wesley screamed in anguish and cried as he lifted Brent's motionless body over his shoulder, making his way back toward the main body.

"I got you, man, c'mon, I got you."

Carlonian looked on. His heart wept for Wesley.

Chapter 15

TRANSFORMATION

*B*rent was exhilarated as he soared weightlessly into the sky with Joviah; he had never known such joy. Shedding his earthly body felt fresh and invigorating. Joviah and Brent flew quickly through the atmosphere, arriving in Bliss, in what seemed like a matter of seconds. Thinking over the journey, Brent was fascinated at how Earth, so overwhelming to him while living there, appeared as such a small, insignificant object as they raced from it through the galaxies and beyond.

When they arrived at their destination, Brent realized that he was back at the Transfer Station. He, too, had begun his earthly journey there as Wesley and every other human being living on Earth had. He noticed that he wasn't in the same area that he had been when he came to the Transfer Station before being sent to Earth. This area, though filled with thousands of other souls, was quiet and tranquil. He reasoned that it was because they had all returned from Earth and were not nervously anticipating what was ahead. Most of the other souls were moving toward the heavens to join others who had returned from Earth and were part of the cloud of witnesses, overseeing the earth and its outcome. But Joviah took Brent to another area of the Transfer Station where only a small number of others were being led.

"Brent, your time as a mortal being on Earth is over. You were fortunate to have an early departure," Joviah explained.

"I'm happy that I'm back here in Bliss now. While on Earth, I was afraid of death. I had forgotten where I came from. Now that I'm back, I'm relieved to be away from Earth and all of the confusion there. I didn't know what I believed; I tried not to believe in too much of anything other than God," Brent admitted.

"But you did still believe in God. He knows your heart," Joviah announced.

"What's ahead for me now, Joviah? Am I going to meet my Heavenly Father?"

"Yes, Brent, you are going to meet Him. First, there is another transformation that you must undergo. Not every soul is chosen for this opportunity; the majority of those returning from Earth have gone on to oversee and wait, so I am sure that you will be happy with your outcome. Many don't return at all."

"If it's God's will, then I am happy about it, whatever it is."

Suddenly a large, magnificent shape resembling a sheet of sparkling glass appeared near Joviah. His reflection in the glass was breathtaking. Brent realized that while on Earth he hadn't seen a picture of an angel that captured their true splendor. Joviah hovered there for a moment before motioning for Brent to come near. As Brent moved, Joviah slipped away, so Brent could see his own reflection. Brent was overcome with happiness and gratitude when he saw that his own reflection was also that of an angel.

"Brent, I'll take you to Heaven now to meet with our Heavenly Father. As one of God's angels you will have the ability to travel between Heaven, Bliss and Earth, as all angels do. You'll be given a specific mission to oversee, as I have overseen your life."

"I am honored. Why was I chosen?"

"It is not for us to ask or to know. It simply is."

Joviah and Brent went to Heaven and remained there for what seemed like days or weeks or months; there was no concept of time. When they returned to Bliss, Brent's name had been changed by God. He had been instructed to return to the Transfer Station and report to the ejection ports area. He went there as multitudes of souls were arriving from their forty days in the garden for their journeys to Earth. Joviah was still with him, guiding him.

"Joviah, this place feels more familiar than it should. It is as if I were here with this same group of souls as a soul myself."

"That is because you were here with this group of souls, as a soul yourself, Carlonian. We have traveled back twenty-five earthly years in time. This is the same group of souls that were here with you when you were passing through. The soul that has been chosen for you to oversee is your earthly friend, Wesley. He will be arriving from the garden soon."

"Joviah, I don't understand. How can that be? How can Wesley be arriving here? I lived with him on Earth already. How can I oversee Wesley's life? I was part of it."

"You will see yourself at times during his life there. You will be interacting with him in mortal form, and you will be overseeing his life as his angel."

"But he is already well on his journey on Earth, how can this be?"

"Carlonian, time as you have known it, is not God's time. God's time is the past, the present and the future. God's time is timeless and unexplainable to us. And again, it is not for us to question; it simply is. Wesley was here when you were here twenty-five earthly years ago. You both went to live on Earth at about the same time. Now, you will be his guardian angel from his birth on Earth, overseeing his life while there, as I did with you. At times, you will be with him both as an angel and as his mortal friend. When your mortal form dies and leaves him, you will continue to be with him as an angel."

"The concept of is this is astounding. But I know it is the will of God." He paused. "I will be with my friend forever, and for that I am truly grateful."

"Wesley is approaching now," Joviah announced. "Go and be with him. I am always available to you, though I will have another soul to oversee."

Carlonian, formerly Brent, turned to watch as Wesley approached and was directed to his port. Filled with unexplainable emotions, he rushed to Wesley. A spiritual rapport, more zealous than their earthly bond had been, was eternally secured between them.

Chapter 16

POIGNANT

*A*rie carried many of her insecurities with her from Bliss to Earth. Her life on Earth had done little to crush those insecurities. She was born to a mother who abandoned her. She didn't bother to hold her after birth, and left her at the hospital, leaving no traces behind.

The angel Lizelle watched over little Arie as she sadly watched Arie's mother desert her.

By the time Arie was 5 years old, she had lived in a series of foster homes. Mrs. Morgan, Arie's case worker, was distressed by the lack of an adoptive situation for Arie. She became determined to find a place for her and made it a personal mission to search for a foster home with a promise of stability. When Arie was nearly 6 years old, she moved into the home of Gary and Teresa Peters, an interracial couple. Gary, a large, quiet white man with red hair and no backbone, was submissive to his wife Teresa, a plain, snobbish Hispanic woman. Arie was chosen by Mrs. Peters because of her non-ethnic appearance. She was an attractive child with the looks of a mysterious foreigner. Mrs. Peters liked that.

They lived in Kansas City, Missouri on a wide street filled with enormous trees in an older, two-story brick house with a basement. Arie's room was down there, while the Peter's own children had rooms on the second floor along with their parents' room. Arie was terrified sleeping in the basement alone and quietly cried herself to sleep every night for the first month. Later, she was happy for the solitude that the basement provided.

Her life was uneventful. She felt no love or animosity for or from the Peters family. They provided a home for her, for which they received a monthly check. That was the extent of the relationship. Arie was basically on her own. She went to school, did her chores, homework and whatever else was asked of her, knowing there was a distinct difference between the Peters' three children and herself.

Mrs. Peters adored her children, who looked much like their father. Harmony, age 5; Hillary, 4; and Wrenn, age 3, welcomed Arie into their home, but were not allowed to play with or interact with her in any way.

Arie knew that if she rocked the boat, she'd be gone to…she couldn't imagine where. So she lived those early years trying to make sure that she never upset anyone. Her mission was to stay under the radar at all costs.

One day four years later Arie came home from school and a pretty, petite little girl was sitting at the table in the kitchen, sniffling. A small suitcase was on the floor near her. Mrs. Peters loomed above her and introduced them. Her name was Beth; she was 6 years old. Mrs. Peters told Arie that this was her new little sister and that they would share the basement. When Arie took Beth down to the basement she noticed that a second twin bed had been added to the room. That was the only difference that had been made in preparation for Beth's arrival. Beth was very shy and cowered from everyone. She spent all of her time with Arie, and they quickly became close. They walked to school together, while the Peters children were driven to school. When they came home, if no one was there, they sat on the porch and waited.

"Why doesn't Mrs. Peters like us?" Beth asked one snowy afternoon while they were sitting on the front steps, waiting.

"She likes us," Arie lied, trying to calm the distress Beth was feeling as they clung to each other for warmth. "She's just busy all the time with Harmony, Hillary and Wrenn, so she forgets about us."

"But when she picks them up from school she sees us, and she leaves us there. I don't like her; she's mean to me."

"I know, but you have me and I have you, so we'll always be okay. I won't leave you, cuz you are my little sister forever." Arie bumped shoulders with her and Beth giggled.

"I love you, Arie."

"I love you too, little girlie."

Many days the Peters went out after school, for sports, shopping or to dinner, but Arie and Beth weren't included. There was always some type of food for them to warm from a can or the freezer once they were let into the house when the family came home.

The Peters provided no spiritual enrichment for Arie, Beth, or their own children. They went to the neighborhood church occasionally, usually on religious holidays to make an appearance. As Arie got older, she listened closely to the Reverend's sermons and began to attend regularly on her own, taking Beth with her. It always seemed to Arie as though the Reverend was speaking directly to her. This reassured her that she was not a mistake: that she was supposed to be living in the world and that someday she would know why. One Sunday when the Reverend gave a sermon on God's love, near its end, he looked directly at Arie. The two of them held each other's gaze as he continued:

"Never forget that Jesus loves you…open your heart to His love and

His love will dwell within you, especially in difficult times. During hardships and setbacks, God is there. Don't blame Him for the negative things that happen in your life. Those things are part of this sinful world and He will see you through them. All things that happen here are part of a plan set in motion before we came into this world. So when you become discouraged, remember that God's love will never change. It is eternal. And no matter what happens you can be sure that the power of God's love is stronger than anything present in this world."

Arie's heart skipped a beat. She had never thought much about love. Though she lived a life of quiet rejection she had never doubted its existence, especially since Beth had come into her life. She loved Beth and Beth loved her; she knew that without question. Still, she thought of her life as time passing by, never questioning the reason for her circumstances. When she left church that day she realized that a new emotion had been introduced into her life. Hope.

The angel Lizelle and Beth's angel, Margelli smiled down on the girls as they hurried home.

On Arie's sixteenth birthday, Mrs. Peters called her into the living room after she got home from school and allowed her to sit on the couch.

"In two years you'll have to move out of our house, Arie, to allow for another foster child to move into the basement in your place. You'll be 18, so you'll be out of the system," Mrs. Peters announced.

Arie was blindsided by the news.

"Where will I be living after I move out, Mrs. Peters?" Arie frantically asked.

"Well, first, calm down, but that is for you to decide. I thought best to tell you now so you have two years to make some plans," she answered, slightly annoyed at the question. "Did you think that you would live with us forever?"

"I hadn't thought about it at all, I guess." Arie's throat was tightening and she could feel the tears welling up.

Mrs. Peters chuckled, "Well, I guess it's a good thing I mentioned it today. You better get to thinking about it, then." She paused to let it sink in. "We're taking you out to dinner for your birthday. Isn't that nice? So get ready and do something with that hair. We'll be leaving in thirty minutes."

Arie called her case worker from school the next day and everything Mrs. Peters had said was confirmed.

"I'm so sorry, Arie," Mrs. Morgan said. "Some foster families grow to accept their foster children as their own and continue to be part of their lives as they move out into the world. I had hoped that it would be that way with you and the Peters."

"Oh, I know they don't care about me. They never have."

"I thought things were good for you there, Arie."

"My life has been okay there, but no one cares about me, except Beth. She's only 13 now. What will happen to her when I move out?"

"Well, Arie, she will stay there at the Peters' home until she reaches 18."

"Oh, no, Mrs. Morgan, she can't stay there without me; she's not like me. She can't handle that life by herself," Arie shrieked.

"Arie, is there something you're not telling me? Is there some type of abuse going on in the home?"

"Abuse, like somebody beating us up or something?"

"Yes, Arie!" Mrs. Morgan was nearly enraged.

"No. No one hits us, but they don't care if anything happens to us, so Beth and I take care of each other. I take care of her mostly. She gets picked on and I'm the one who's there after she gets beat up or pushed around. She's not strong like me. You can't leave her there alone with the Peters. Can't you see, Mrs. Morgan, we're sisters."

"I'm sorry, Arie, but this is how the system works. I'm sure the Peters' won't mind you keeping in touch with Beth. You'll be 21 when Beth turns 18, so if you get yourself established she can come to live with you then. This situation should motivate you to do well in school these last two years, so you can get a good job and get your life started."

Mrs. Morgan could feel Arie's sadness as she listened to her crying through the phone. She told her that she would begin looking into some options for her and quickly ended the conversation. She couldn't allow herself to become too emotionally involved. There were hundreds, thousands, just like Arie. It was overwhelming and too much for her to bear.

That night Arie told Beth that she was going to get a job so they could begin to plan for when they left the Peters' home.

"Why now?" Beth asked, alarmed at the thought of Arie not being there with her every evening.

"We have to start thinking ahead, Beth. We have to move out of here when we're 18. I want to be ready for that. It'll take money, so I have to work...for us."

"Where will we go?"

"I have to figure that out. That's why I have to start working as soon as I can; then when I'm 18, I'll find a place to live."

"What can I do to help?"

"You're not old enough to work yet, but when you're 16, you can get a job, too. Then when you're 18, you can move in with me."

"I'm going with you when you move. We'll go together, right?"

"No, Beth. I called Mrs. Morgan today and asked her about everything. She said that foster kids have to stay in the homes until they're 18."

"No, Arie, I can't do that. I can't be here without you. Please Arie, don't leave me here." She began sobbing.

"Beth, stop it, stop crying. It is two years away, and by then you'll be more independent. You'll be fine and we'll stay in close touch. On your eighteenth birthday I'll come get you."

Arie looked at Beth, who stood helplessly in the middle of the room pleading for reassurances that she couldn't give. She was a beautiful girl with striking facial features, but she didn't know her physical beauty. She was a kind person, readily making excuses for those who mistreated her. Her soul was battered and lifeless from lack of love, leaving her fragile and exposed in a cruel, intolerant world. Since the day she came to the Peters' house, Beth had looked to Arie for strength, guidance, reassurance, protection—everything. In many ways Arie was Beth's lifeline, attempting to calm Beth's fears at every turn. Memories of the past seven years rushed through her mind, and she knew that Beth's survival depended largely on her.

On the way home from school the next day Arie stopped at every fast food restaurant and applied for jobs. She was hired by a neighborhood ice cream shop and made less than minimum wage. By working there, she acquired cashier experience and established a good work ethic. She was able to get on with McDonald's after four months, making more money. She saved everything. That year rushed by, and before she knew it she was 17.

"What would you like to do for your birthday, Arie?" Mrs. Peters asked when Arie got home from work.

"This will be your last birthday celebration with us, because next year on your eighteenth birthday we'll be moving you to your new home," Mrs. Peters gushed.

"We don't have to celebrate, but thank you. I think I'll just go downstairs. I'm a little tired."

"Okay. See you in the morning," Mrs. Peters answered.

As she started down the steps she heard Mr. Peters.

"Great, this was the last birthday and we got out of it. Are you sure you want to get another foster kid next year, Teresa?"

"You know we need that money, Gary, and besides, they don't affect our life anyway."

Arie continued downstairs and closed the door. Beth was waiting and rushed to greet Arie with a cupcake and candle she had gotten from school. Arie had McDonald's burgers and fries for them both in her bookbag. The two of them secretly celebrated.

For the next year Arie worked as much as she possibly could. She was a model employee. Management could count on her to fill in, come in on short notice, or to work weekends and holidays. She saved every penny.

Mrs. Morgan had taken her to a bank and helped her open a savings account. She walked to the bank every payday and deposited her money. She overheard the Peters' talking about making her give them part of her money, but Mrs. Peters decided that if the case worker found out, they could get into trouble, so they left her money alone.

Arie and the Peters had not spoken about her moving since her last birthday. When she and Beth went upstairs for breakfast on the morning of Arie's eighteenth birthday, everything seemed normal. She thought that maybe she'd find a banner announcing her departure or some other gesture to mark the day. Instead, as Mrs. Peters placed a piping-hot bowl of oatmeal in front of her, she simply smiled. Arie was confused. *Had they changed their minds about her leaving?* She was somewhat elated about the possibility of staying, of not having to change her life. Oddly, she was also horrified at the prospect of staying and not changing her life. She and Beth exchanged glances.

"Mrs. Peters, today is my eighteenth birthday."

"Yes, I know that. And I wasn't thinking about everything clearly. Since your birthday is in February, you have a few more months before you graduate from high school, so it only makes sense that you stay with us until then. You can just pay us to live here and for your food. Is that alright with you? If not, if you've already made plans to get on with your life and you're planning to leave today, then that's alright, too."

"No. No. I'd like to stay here until I graduate." She and Beth smiled at each other. "How much will it cost me?"

"We were thinking that since you and Beth have the whole basement, that you can just give us your paycheck from now until June. I think that would be fair, but only if you tell your boss that you'll work every evening and every weekend."

She couldn't believe it. They wanted to take all of her money. She didn't bother to answer. She got up, Beth followed, and they walked out the door, leaving Mrs. Peters calling behind them.

They stopped at a grocery store on the way to school and bought a newspaper to look at the prices of apartments. Arie was surprised to see that $300.00 a month could get you a whole two-bedroom apartment in the same neighborhood. There were also rooms for rent for $60.00 and $70.00 a month. She got between $70.00 and $150.00 a month, depending on the hours she worked. What was she afraid of? The Peters did nothing for her. They pretty much never had. She was already on her own. She only stayed in their house, and felt much like an intruder. She had no contact whatsoever with their children. It was like they thought something might rub off of her or Beth onto them. Her counselors at school and Mrs. Morgan had been more like mother figures to her than Mrs. Peters had.

Later that day, Arie called Mrs. Morgan, who came and took her to look at a room in a rooming house that she had seen advertised in the paper. It wasn't far from the Peters' house, so she could be near Beth, and it was closer to her school and job.

The house was enormous and looked lovely on the outside. Inside, it was filled with Victorian furnishings. There were lace doilies, exquisite gold-patterned china and richly spun tablecloths. The owner and land-lady was a friendly older woman named Ms. Etta. She was a warm and welcoming person. She served them hot tea with cream and sugar cubes, and biscuits with real butter and honey before showing them her magnificent home. The tour ended with the second floor front bedroom that was advertised for rent. It was furnished with a four-poster bed and was royally decorated. The room came complete with fine-embroidered bedding, soft sheets and blankets and feather-stuffed pillows: a sharp contrast to the damp basement that Arie had lived in for as long as she could remember.

It was evident by the way that she talked about the other tenants that Ms. Etta was more than a landlady to them. She had carefully chosen each of the three college students who rented the other bedrooms. They were away from home and she enjoyed their company, a winning situation for all. She had a nurturing way about her that was very endearing.

The room rented for $68.00 a month. Arie moved out of the Peters' immediately. To their surprise, she did not wait for graduation. Though she knew this day was coming, Beth was devastated.

"Don't move out now, Arie; they said you could stay until June. Please!" she cried.

"Beth, try to understand that the sooner I move, the more money we'll have saved. I'm not leaving you, little girlie. I'm only going to be five blocks away. I'll come see you all the time and you can come see me, too. You'll love Ms. Etta."

Mrs. Peters overheard the girls and interrupted them abruptly. She was angry that Arie was moving and not paying her the money.

"Arie, hurry up and get your stuff upstairs so I can decide what you can and can't take with you. And by the way, you two can say your goodbyes now, cause you cannot come back to this house and Beth will not be visiting you. I am responsible for her, and I don't know what kind of place you're moving into."

"Oh, no, Mrs. Peters, you don't have to worry; it's a good place. Beth will be safe going over there."

"Did you hear me? I said that you two can say goodbye! No, she will NOT be visiting you, nor you her. And don't even think about going to her school. I am letting the school know that you are not to come in that building. I'll have you arrested if you mess with me. Now, hurry up and get your stuff so I can get rid of you once and for all," she spat. Then she turned to Beth. "You stay down here in this basement. I don't want to see your face until tomorrow morning."

Arie and Beth hugged each other and cried. Beth was inconsolable as Arie made her way up the steps, carrying her meager belongings of shabby clothing stuffed into a large garbage bag. Mrs. Peters went through it and took nearly half of the contents, out of spite.

"Mrs. Peters, please let me visit Beth here. I'm sorry if I did something to make you mad," Arie pleaded.

"Oh, so now you're sorry, huh? Well, that's just too bad!" she nearly screamed at Arie. "You should have thought about how sorry you'd be before you decided to stick it to me. You wanted to get out of this house? Well, now you're out for good. You cannot come back here, ever. Now get out!"

Arie left the Peters' house for the last time. She moved into the comfortable rooming house, and Ms. Etta could tell right away that she was troubled. Arie had a bad feeling about Beth staying behind. After she settled into her room, she knelt beside her beautiful new bed and prayed for her.

Ms. Etta prepared a huge breakfast the next morning and introduced Arie to the other young people who lived in the house. It was a wonderful beginning to her first day of independence. Everyone sat together in the dining room, laughing and talking while enjoying the delicious food. It was apparent that Ms. Etta rented her rooms out because she loved people. Arie had never begun a day in such a jovial fashion. She was so happy and wished Beth could be there with her.

Arie worked hard at her schoolwork and spent every free moment working at McDonalds. Ms. Etta saw a determination in her that was exhilarating…along with an ever-present sadness, which she instinctively knew was the motivation for her drive. Arie kept everything inside, yet she was pleasant and respectful. This made Ms. Etta want to help her all the more.

Beth was 15 years old when Arie left. The Peters decided that when Beth turned 18 and moved out, they wouldn't have any more foster children in their home. Since Beth wouldn't be 18 for three more years, they decided to capitalize on additional monthly checks by filling the empty bed in the basement with another 15-year-old.

Rhonda was a loud, boisterous girl with a bad attitude, much like Mrs. Peters. She viewed Beth as weak and stupid and treated her badly from the first day they met. As time went on their relationship worsened, and soon Rhonda was screaming at Beth, pinching her and punching her around. This went on for three months until one evening, following a bad beating from Rhonda, Beth ran out into the darkness toward McDonald's for help.

"Beth! What's wrong? You look terrible. What happened?" Arie shrieked when Beth came to her line in McDonalds.

"A…rie," Beth sobbed hysterically. "I c-can't stay there anymore." She stood shaking in front of Arie with a black eye, dried blood on her bottom lip and scratches all over her face. Her hair had been whacked off unevenly.

Arie jumped over the counter and rushed Beth to a table in the corner. Her co-workers covered her line.

"Beth, what happened to you?"

"It's th-that g-g-girl, Rhon…da. She hates me and she's-s-s…so mean to me," she cried loudly.

"Okay, don't worry. I'm calling Mrs. Morgan tomorrow. She'll get you out of there." She pulled her into an embrace and hugged her tightly. "I'm taking you home with me; it'll be okay. They can't make you stay there after this," Arie soothed.

Beth had left the house without asking. Mrs. Peters found out and sent Rhonda to find her. She had been told about Arie and went to McDonalds first. The door flew open and Rhonda stood staring at Beth, who was eating food that Arie had gotten her.

"Okay, Bethy, come on! Mrs. P says I gotta bring you home," Rhonda yelled.

"Noooooooo!" Beth cried, as she turned to see Rhonda standing there.

"No," Arie said and rushed to stand between them. "She's not going back there tonight."

"Oh, yes, she is! I'm calling Mrs. P. If she has to come over here, she'll be madder than ever. Where's a phone?"

Rhonda stomped to the counter and demanded that the manager call Mrs. Peters. He called the police instead. Suddenly, Beth stood and ran out the side door. Arie ran out behind her just as Beth ran into the busy street. At the same time, a City bus was cruising at the speed limit, because there was no bus stop on that block. The driver didn't see Beth until the bus hit her.

Arie screamed as Rhonda followed her out the door and ran the other way. Arie ran to Beth and fell to the ground beside her. She was unconscious. Arie gently placed Beth's head in her lap and held her until the ambulance, and then the medical examiner, arrived and pronounced her dead.

Beth floated above the scene briefly with her angel, Margelli. Though she was happier than she had ever felt on Earth, she wished she could've said goodbye to Arie before she was whisked away.

Chapter 17

CHALLENGE

*A*fter Brent's death Wesley completed his tour of duty, because he always finished what he started…but he was still numb. He left Viet Nam and went back to the United States. He couldn't shake his sadness. There was a hole in his heart, his life, his entire being. He didn't think that he would ever be able to smile again. Wesley believed that Brent was supposed to be alive and that *he* should be dead; he couldn't figure out that if there were a God, why He would have chosen to keep him alive and not Brent.

Carlonian read his thoughts and pushed aside the urge to enlighten his friend.

Brent was a good person, better than me, Wesley thought, taking stock of all of his shortcomings, but only Brent's strengths. Brent won out every time, at least in his mind. *So why was he still here? Why had he survived Viet Nam? So many died there; why couldn't he have died, instead of Brent?* He went to sleep thinking about it every night, that is, when he could sleep. And when he woke up, there it was again, waiting for him to think about it some more.

What kind of life had he had before the military? Sure, he had his sister, and now her children, who adored him; and his mother had come back into his life. She had her own apartment in Cleveland, and though she still worked for the Kingstons, had assured him that she would love for him to come visit her and stay as long as he wanted.

Wesley had not found the love that he had been searching for and now he didn't care, because he didn't want to be close to anyone. He wasn't going to open his heart to a woman anytime soon, if ever. Every time he had done that, it ended in catastrophe and humiliation for him. And the ending with Claudia led to him losing his closest friend, the only friend he'd ever had, who knew him completely and loved him for himself without reservation.

Wesley blamed Claudia for Brent's death. If she had loved him, he and Brent wouldn't have gone back to Viet Nam, and he'd still be alive. The three of them would be living in the breathtaking coastal town of Carmel, California in a majestic beach house overlooking the ocean. With all the money he and B had made in the Nam, life would have been spectacular. *How could he have thought that Claudia was his mate, worthy of his devotion?* That day in Portland, she had been someone he didn't recognize: cold, non-caring, cruel. She wasn't the person he fell in love with. The only true friend he had ever had was gone, and she was the reason why.

Wesley had the money, but it didn't matter or lessen the pain. Life was pain. He would go out and drink to feel better, but he didn't. He'd have something to eat, drink some more, get high, meet someone and they'd party together; then he'd move on. And still more pain. Everything he did reminded him of B. On some level deeply burrowed within himself, covered by layer and layer of pain, life was there—but he didn't want that. He didn't deserve that. He should be dead.

It was all running together, colors were flashing by, one long day followed by a long night: day after day after day. Sleep was too hard; it brought B back and then he awoke…and being awake was too hard. So he turned to drugs more and more. First marijuana, until that wasn't enough; then pills and cocaine, and when that wasn't enough he would add alcohol to the mix. When he got high it felt good for awhile, and then it didn't, so he would sober up and start the cycle again. He wandered through months of numbness, searing pain and distorted, drug-filled days and nights.

One day Wesley woke up at 5:00 in the evening and didn't know where he was. He looked around the small room searching for a clue. It appeared to be a motel room, a cheap one, sparsely furnished with a well-worn chair, lumpy bed and lopsided table. The evening sun peeked crookedly through a tear in the ragged, faded purple flowered curtains. He could hear life in full motion outside the little room.

He forced himself to sit up. His first thought was that he was serving no purpose on Earth anymore. His life had become miserable. He wished he had died with Brent. Maybe he should end it all, so he could stop his mind from cracking up. But he couldn't take his own life; to him, that would mean defeat. As all of the heartbreaking thoughts began to resurface in his mind, he threw up his hands and shouted:

"Why am I still here?" He felt as though he was standing in the midst of an intersection with numerous paths—all leading to an outcome of pain.

Carlonian watched Wesley and decided that he must intervene. He knew that Wesley hadn't completed his purpose on Earth and that he must move forward or the darker forces would prevail. He gently nudged Wesley by speaking to his subconscious.

"You have a specific purpose in this life, and you must move forward to complete that purpose. Get back to life. Your destiny will prevail."

All of the negative thoughts stopped abruptly and Wesley's mind was suddenly and completely blank. Though he didn't have peace, his mind was silent, and a comforting stillness slowly overcame him.

He began to remember good things and positive relationships that he had managed to carve from his life of turmoil. He remembered that being in Viet Nam was the last place he had felt useful and whole.

He pulled himself together and re-enlisted for another tour of duty, returning to Viet Nam for the third time. When he got there, he wore Brent's absence like a medal. There was no conversation with anyone he met that did not include Brent. Brent was with Wesley wherever he went. He wore Brent's dog tags. No other soldier could measure up. Wesley did everything alone.

Well known throughout his company for his accomplishments and valor, Wesley was revered and treated like a celebrity. Many wanted to be his partner in combat, but he refused them all, opting to fly solo within the squad. During recon patrol in the bush, he was the leader, though without Brent there beside him Wesley felt strangely exposed. In the past, the thick, lush jungle of the Nam had given him a calming sense of security and an invincible sense of excitement. There was no excitement now.

A particular mission took the squad deeper into the jungle than Wesley had been since he had returned. The group moved cautiously through the tropical forest late one afternoon. When the bushes about 100 feet to Wesley's right began to flutter, he signaled the other soldiers to stay put while he inched his way through the bushes into a rice paddy to investigate. The mission was eerily reminiscent of the final episode of Brent's life. However, Wesley felt that there was no threat and turned to look back. He realized that he was standing in a small minefield.

Carlonian drifted above the minefield. He had chosen Wesley's steps as he had explored ahead of the group, safely leading him through the minefield to his present position.

Before Wesley could warn the other soldiers who had began walking toward him, one of them stepped on a mine, which exploded on contact. Shrapnel flew in all directions. Everyone was wounded, including Wesley, but the soldier who stepped on the mine was severely injured and incapacitated. Before they had time to react to the explosion, they were suddenly under attack. They had been led into an ambush. Gunshots were exploding all around them. They immediately began firing back while seeking cover. Two of their men dropped and Wesley was hit, but managed to scuttle into the bushes. The battle went on for what seemed an eternity until finally, there was complete silence. No one moved. Wesley took stock of his squad. Three soldiers lay still in the open, including the one who had stepped on the mine. Wesley and three others were hidden, watching, listening and waiting. Both sides of the conflict sat quietly, contemplating their next move.

Darkness came and brought the blessing of a ravaging monsoon. The rain and wind were staggering, and they had never been more thankful. As the Vietnamese soldiers retreated, searching for cover, Wesley and the other three soldiers were able to drag the badly wounded into the bushes, as they, too, took cover from the storm. All of the squad members were alive; they administered first aid to themselves and to each other as best they could while they waited for the turbulent storm to pass.

Just before dawn the rain stopped and the sopping wet and torn jungle once again became the deadly war's backdrop. The squad assessed their conditions. The radio had been destroyed, so there was no way to call for evacuation. All of the men were injured with shrapnel, bullets or both, but were able to travel, except the soldier who had stepped on the mine. Though Wesley had been shot, he hoisted the soldier over his shoulder and began the long, arduous retreat back to the main body, just as he had done with Brent. Due to his own injuries, he struggled tremendously. As he carried the wounded soldier and encouraged the badly injured squad to press on, his own injuries were worsening.

The group moved slowly for two days. Wesley was overcome with fever, and his pain was nearly unbearable. He trudged forward, pushing, pulling, dragging and sometimes rolling the others. He was bleeding and out of water from sharing it. Overcome with exhaustion and dehydration, he was determined to get them out of the jungle. He knew that he could be dying, and all he thought of was the other men. The rugged, jungle terrain, the threat of animals, the heat and their physical conditions assured Wesley that they were not going to make it. But he was too stubborn and driven to give up.

On the morning of the fourth day when he stopped, laid the soldier down and fell to the ground to rest again, he knew he wouldn't get back up. All of the men were in the same, or worse, condition. His last thought before he fell unconscious was that he didn't feel at peace about dying as Brent had, and he wondered why that was.

Carlonian looked down upon the group of wounded soldiers. He also saw a unit of their fellow soldiers searching for them far away, heading in the wrong direction. So he interceded because he knew it was not Wesley's time. The other angels present awaited Carlonian's intervention. Suddenly, a flare went up from the unconscious group of soldiers, capturing the attention of the search unit. When they found them all unconscious, they wondered who had fired the flare, and moved quickly and cautiously, commandeering the rescue.

· · · · · · · · · · · · · · ·

Wesley woke up and knew he was in a hospital somewhere, *but where? Was he a prisoner, or was he back home in the States? No, he couldn't be. This hospital was makeshift: put together quickly to be taken down just as quickly.*

"Hey, somebody, where am I?" he blurted out.

A nurse carefully approached.

"You're awake, huh?" she said gently, smiling a foolish smile.

"Of course, I am. Where am I...how bad is it?" he struggled to speak.

"Just a minute, I'll get the—"

"No, can't you answer a simple question?" he pressed.

The doctor marched up and snatched the clipboard the nurse was holding.

"I got this. I told you to get me when he woke up," he snapped. "Just go, please!" He waved her away.

"How long was I out? Is it bad, huh, Doc?" Wesley asked. "Okay, look, just be straight with me."

"Is that how you want it?" the doctor asked.

"That's the only way I'll take it, and I mean be straight. Don't hold back, man."

"All right, you were hit pretty bad...heard you carried a man for four days to get him out. That is commendable. I—"

"Doc, straight, remember?"

"Yes, well uh, you were hit pretty bad. Your wounds went untreated for so long, it's a wonder you're alive. We were able to treat you pretty successfully, but it has been touch and go for weeks due to infection. You had two bullets lodged inside your body. We removed one and the other would be best left alone. It could and probably will shift at some point in your life. It's close to your spine, and could paralyze you, but it could also never bother you. Time will tell what will happen with that one. There may come a time that surgery may be necessary, but it would be risky; it's hard to say. It's too unpredictable to take it out now."

"You were also cut up pretty badly from shrapnel, especially your left hand. We've got it wrapped up pretty good now so it can heal. We had to take three of your fingers and some of the palm of your hand. Gangrene had set in and there was no other choice. Your other injuries are not life threatening and..."

Wesley listened, showing no sign of emotion. The doctor droned on about the complications that they were able to overcome and how proud he should be, and that no doubt he would receive a Purple Heart, etc., etc.; but Wesley had stopped listening after he heard that part of his hand was gone.

"Where am I and when can I get out of here?" Wesley asked. He was ready to end the conversation, his life in the military, and just give up.

"I thought that I mentioned you're in Qin Yong, out of the line of fire. Physically, you're not stable enough to move. You'll remain here for at least a few weeks, and then we'll send you on to Japan. From there, you'll head back to the U.S., where you'll receive rehabilitation and all of the medical attention that you'll need to adjust to your new life style. You will have to make some adjustments; take it easy. Rigorous activities could cause the bullet to shift, and we don't want that to happen."

Wesley thought again, *Why didn't I die that day in the bush? What am I suppose to do now?*

Chapter 18

HOODWINKED

*F*ive weeks later, Wesley was released from the U.S. Army Hospital at Camp Zama, Japan, transferred to the airfield and sent home to the United States. The plane was filled with injured soldiers and military personnel to care for their needs during the flight to Travis Air Force Base in Redwood, California. Wesley used the long flight home to reflect on his life. He was returning a hero, not a coward as many were, so he began to get excited about being welcomed back home. He had willingly fought for his country for nearly five long years. The judge that was responsible for sending him into the Army didn't think that he'd amount to anything. For all he cared, Wesley Lewis could have been killed in combat and he wouldn't have lost a minute's sleep over it. He probably wouldn't have known about it.

Wesley would be the recipient of a Purple Heart and a Silver Star. He was a real-life hero. That didn't mean much to him though, because he was just being himself. Deal with it: that was his motto. Whatever it was, confront it. Do what needs to be done to resolve it and end it, whatever *it* may be. That's what he had done. Viet Nam had been a chapter in his life that was now closed. He had known war and the bond between those who fought together. Without living it, one couldn't truly understand the meaning of that bond. Many soldiers would never go back to the homes they once knew. They couldn't live as they had before after experiencing the madness in the Nam. Some were blown apart and held in the arms of fellow soldiers as they whispered last words for loved ones, cried, or simply died. A soldier lost pieces of himself with every loss. But most importantly for Wesley, he had lost the closest person he had ever known and cared for.

He analyzed Brent's last moments again. He had expected Brent to be angry and afraid when he came back to help him on that awful day. But now he marveled at how Brent had been peaceful and at ease; and at the very last moment before he died, he smiled, as though completely abandoning this world. It was like he saw something beautiful and was happily moving on toward it. Wesley wanted to know what Brent found on that day. He decided that he would seek God out and see where that route would lead.

The plane lurched slightly and Wesley was nudged back from his private thoughts as the plane prepared to land. He had seen on television and heard from other veterans about how troops of past wars had been welcomed back after defending their country. This war wasn't over yet, but soldiers were going home every day, and surely the crowds would be there, cheering them. He could feel the enthusiasm and could easily get caught up in the happiness of the moment.

The plane landed, and since Wesley was on a stretcher, he waited to be carried out of the airplane. When the door opened he could hear the crowd of fellow Americans waiting, as they shouted and chanted. He could barely contain his excitement. Two soldiers lifted his stretcher and moved to the door. One of them suggested that Wesley cover his head with the blanket, but he dare not miss any of the triumphant moment. As they moved out of the plane into the sunlight, Wesley lifted his upper body and turned toward the sky to soak in the American sun, now that he was back home for good. He looked at the crowd, smiled broadly, and began waving as the soldiers carried him down the plane's steps.

Then he noticed that the crowd didn't look friendly. Many of their faces were distorted in anger, and they were shouting profanities. Wesley was confused and raised himself higher on the stretcher, struggling to understand what was going on, when an overly-ripened tomato came hurling into his face. He wiped his eyes and realized that the soldiers carrying him had reached the bottom of the stairs and were now running to avoid the bottles, cans and rotted fruit that was being thrown at all of them. He looked closely at the crowd and read the signs they were thrusting in the air, protesting the Viet Nam War. Everything began unfolding in slow motion. The crowd was pushing, screaming, fighting, climbing the fence, and shoving the guards who attempted to hold their ground. *Surely, this wasn't happening. Surely, he had fallen asleep on the plane and was dreaming this nightmare.*

"WHEN WILL I WAKE UP?" he shouted over and over, as the soldiers fought their way through the debris and into the building.

Chapter 19

STRENGTH

*W*esley was sent for recuperation to the VA Hospital in West Haven, Connecticut, so he would be near his family. Liz came to visit him a week later. Though he was happy to see her, she could see that he was troubled and was concerned about his state of mind. She went to the library to find some books, in hopes that reading would help him take his mind off of himself.

Joyce Ann Morrison, known as Joy, was a biologist at the hospital. She was an unusually outgoing woman in her mid-thirties who enjoyed people. She particularly liked the soldiers and reading to them. The soldiers loved looking at her voluptuous physique as she sauntered throughout the hospital, and were captivated when she read to them.

Liz met Joy in the library and liked her right away. She explained the troubles that her brother was having re-adjusting to his life. Joy volunteered to help. Together they selected a few books that Liz thought may interest Wesley. They took the books to him and Liz introduced Joy.

"Wesley, I want you to meet someone," said Liz, "This is Joy; she works in the hospital."

"Hey. Got some great books here, and I'm heading out to the hospital gardens for some fresh air…care to join me?" she brightly offered.

"Thanks, but I don't feel like going outside." He didn't bother to sit up or to move. "And I don't read much."

"I read a lot and can read to you if you like," she offered. "The air is fresher and cleaner out there." She pointed out the window.

"No, thanks."

Liz was more concerned; Wesley was not one to turn down a good-looking woman. She was worried about her little brother. With the exception of her children, he was all that she had. She and Cimarron were divorced now. He was out of her life and the lives of the children, who were now 12, 11 and 8 years old. JoJo was in the sixth year of a fifteen-year sentence. Chris was still off living his version of life. Their mother checked in by phone, and Grandpap was aging and ill. She couldn't lose Wesley to suicide or insanity. She had to do something to help him pull it together.

"Joy, thank you for taking the time to come and meet my brother. I'd like to spend a little more time with him, and then I'll stop by your office before I leave."

"No problem, Liz," Joy nodded, realizing that Liz wanted to be alone with Wesley. "I'll see you in a bit. Wesley, the offer stands anytime. My office is on the third floor; just ask for Joy. Everyone knows me down there." She shrugged and slowly walked away.

Wesley didn't answer. He stared out the window.

"Wes! Wes!" Liz reached over and shook him.

"I'm listenin, Liz."

"Wesley Lewis, you have got to snap out of this. I won't let you check out of here. You and me, that's how it's always been. We have to be here for each other."

"I'm here for you, Liz."

"Then snap out of this funk. I can't take this. I can't leave you here and drive back to New York, wonderin if you're gonna be okay or if I'm gonna get a phone call about you."

"You won't. I'm fine."

"How long you gonna lay in this bed feelin sorry for yourself?"

"I don't feel sorry for myself, Liz." He struggled to sit up, gasping slightly for breath as he felt a tingling pain in his back. He glanced at his bandaged hand as if checking to make sure that he really had lost part of it.

"I'm just a realist. I'm weighing my options, tryin to figure out my next move," he said unconvincingly.

"Don't try to fool me with that talk. I know you. You are hurt and upset, and that's okay. But you know we can't be those people...the ones who fall apart. We have to be who we are...we are the ones who say, "It is what it is," and we go from there. We deal with it. We always have. We always will. I can't stand lookin at you pining away like this. If you don't get up from there and get it together, this is gonna be your life."

"Liz, you don't understand what I've been through."

Liz lost her patience and lit into Wesley. "No, I don't and I never will; but Baby Brother, you don't understand what I been through either, and you never will!" Liz shrieked. Wesley winced.

Liz regrouped and softened her tone. "Don't you see, Wesley? We all have a path filled with stuff we got to get through. Some people's paths are harder than others, but the Lord don't give you no more than you can handle. You are a strong, beautiful man, and your path is waitin outside this hospital for you to get back on it." She paused.

"I'm leavin now," she said. "I'm drivin home to New York, and I will be back here on Saturday morning with your niece and nephews to see you. So you think about what you want them to see when they get here: an ole, broken down piece of a soul they can't wait to get away from, or the wonderfully supportive, enjoyable uncle who they have always adored."

Liz stood up, leaned over and hugged Wesley tightly; then she kissed him on the cheek and turned from him quickly. As she slowly walked from the room toward the elevator, she felt the anguish that would be with her until she returned. *Had she done the right thing? Said the right thing?* She silently prayed that she hadn't pushed him too far as tears fell from eyes that rarely cried. She knew within that he was near the edge, but knew no other way to help him.

Wesley sat sideways on the bed watching his sister walk away. He knew that she was tormented about him, but couldn't bring himself to quiet her fears. He was drained, empty of emotion. When he looked ahead in his life, he saw empty space. With no idea of what he could do with only one good hand and the possibility of paralysis looming over him, he felt an unshakeable lifelessness within his usual positive nature.

On Saturday morning when Liz stepped off the elevator, her three children ran ahead to Wesley's ward, excited to see him. When she turned into the room and saw Wesley's empty bed, her heart nearly stopped. The bed was neatly made as if waiting for a new occupant. Liz began fanning herself while struggling to reach a nearby chair. Her daughter Tina ran for a nurse, who rushed to a nearly hysterical Liz.

"My brother, my brother, Wes!" she sobbed. "Where?"

"Oh, no, don't worry, your brother is fine. You must be Liz," she said, smiling. "Just relax, sit back and breathe. I'll get you some water."

"No, no, I don't need water. You said he's okay?"

"Yes, he's better than okay. He's doing great…really! He's a different person this week."

Liz's heart lifted. "But where is he? His bed is all made…did you move him?"

"No, actually, that is still his bed. He made it himself this morning when he got up. He's been doing that every morning since Monday. He does it much better than we do," she chuckled.

"Uh, oh…that was really a scare. I have been so worried about him since I left on Sunday."

"Well, he has pulled himself up out of that deep, dark hole, and he spends a lot of time outside on the terrace now. In fact, that's probably where he is right now."

Liz smiled. *Outside. Of course.* Wesley was sitting on the terrace listening to Joy read. The children ran to him, showering him with hugs, kisses and lots of questions. Wesley loved it. He pulled them into a group hug, and for an hour or so, he gave them his undivided attention. The five of them left the hospital and went to a nearby park. Liz and Wesley sat watching the children enjoy themselves.

"Liz, I really like Joy. She's so different, a free spirit. I've never met anyone like her. I've had a good time being with her. We hang out and don't talk about anything serious."

"That's great. I am soooooo happy to hear that. You had me really worried."

"I know, sis." He sat, staring at the children. "Thank you."

"Okay, so I know you need to thank me for a whole lot of stuff, but what are you thankin me for right now?" she playfully teased.

"For kickin me in the rear. For makin me get it together…for being there," he calmly stated. "You were right. We are survivors, so there's no other choice. I have to survive this, and I have to survive it in our usual way…which means, full force ahead."

Realizing the enormity of the moment, Liz stiffened, placed her hand over his, and simply answered: "You're welcome, Baby Brother."

They sat in silence, equally thankful for each other.

Chapter 20

JOY

"I do," Wesley simply stated, as he looked into the eyes of the woman who would be his wife in a matter of moments.

Inside, he was alarmed. *Are you sure about this?* he thought.

Carlonian watched with understanding. He was well aware of the void that Wesley was searching to fill.

On the one hand, this marriage seemed to be a drastic move; while on the other hand, it felt entirely right. Wesley decided that he wanted a shot at a normal life: the life that the commercials on television hinted at, like the wife doing laundry or the husband coming home with flowers to a well-cooked meal. And kids, there were always kids…happy kids who were active in school and sports. If only life were that simple.

Joy was the most unusual person Wesley had ever met. Her physical appearance was the first of many contradictions about her. She had a fantastic body and short, sandy brown hair, which sharply contrasted her large hazel eyes. Her facial features were rounded and her movements were quick and smooth. She was lighthearted, upbeat, and had a brilliant mind. She seemed to know something about nearly everything. Delightful in her own right with an endearing, erratic personality, Joy seemingly skipped through each day without a thought of what may happen tomorrow. She was refreshing for Wesley. He was happy not thinking about tomorrow, and he certainly didn't want to dwell on his yesterdays. He looked forward to spending as much of his life as he possibly could with Joy.

It started with readings in the library, and then walks around the hospital grounds. Soon, they were leaving to have lunch and eventually shared evenings out on the town. When it was time for Wesley to be released from the hospital, Joy invited him to stay with her. He wasn't sure what he felt for her, but he did know that he had never felt that way about any other woman; so he decided to take a chance and go home with her, temporarily.

Wesley expected Joy to live in an apartment. He was surprised to find out that she owned her own home. It was an old, large two-story brick house with a big concrete porch, filled with a variety of blooming potted plants and two wicker rocking chairs. Multi-colored wildflowers adorned the front yard. Joy loved the outdoors.

Surprisingly, the inside of the house was traditional in decor. There were brown leather couches and chairs, large wooden and bronze antique pieces and dark colored, thick woven rugs throughout. Joy's unconventional nature was becoming more apparent.

"There are four bedrooms, Wesley. Take whichever one you want. You can choose mine and sleep with me, or you can have your own," Joy offered.

Wesley wasn't sure what she was offering.

"I don't know, hmmmm, where would *you* like for me to sleep?" he asked tentatively.

"Well, since we haven't had sex, maybe we should, so we can get that uncomfortable feeling out of the way," she stated in a logical tone.

"O…kay. Maybe we should."

And they did. Right then. Wesley was dumbfounded.

He was attracted to Joy, but he wasn't sure if he loved her. Everything they did was done in such an unexpected way that he was continually thrown off balance. He began to think that since he had never known anyone like her, or that he had never felt the way he did (even though he was confused about what he felt), that maybe this was how it was supposed to feel when you were in love. It didn't feel wonderful like it did with Claudia. And it didn't feel awful like when he was a teenager. And it wasn't a fly-by-night affair, like his encounters while in the military. It was comfortable and enjoyable.

Wesley proposed; Joy was ecstatic. Opting for simplicity, she set the date for two weeks later. Wesley was stunned. His head was spinning, but maybe that was okay. He felt this was right. It was different; she was different; even he was different, so it had to be right.

The wedding took place on a hot August evening at dusk behind Joy's house. The yard was lit with luminaries covering the walkways and large white Japanese paper lanterns hanging from the trees. White wooden folding chairs with yellow, orange and purple colored twine tied around each, were evenly placed in rows facing the huge, old oak tree that shaded most of the yard. An arch wrapped with the same twine and filled with matching colored wildflowers stood waiting beneath the tree for their nuptials. Wesley wore white linen slacks and a matching white shirt, while Joy dressed in a simple white linen dress, pearl necklace and earrings, with one orange flower in her hair.

Joy's two sisters and both of her parents were there. Liz, Tina, Andre and Tyrell drove up for the day, along with Rick, a man Liz had met while Wesley was in Viet Nam. They had been dating since and were moving toward marriage themselves. He was good to Liz and the children.

The ceremony was simple as planned, followed by a no-frills reception of finger sandwiches, raw vegetables, wedding cake, punch and sangria. A three-piece band of a guitar, bass and banjo played jazzy country music that was both upbeat and whimsical. They moved the chairs, and most of the guests happily danced the evening away. It was unconventional, prompting Wesley to embrace it all the more. Later that night after consummating the marriage, Wesley lay in bed thinking about how happy he was to finally get a chance to be normal. *Was he dreaming?* He checked his finger to be sure, and there it was: his intricately-carved wooden wedding band that matched Joy's. She had chosen them for their simplicity.

Living with Joy was nice. They didn't argue. They didn't make plans. They didn't have deep conversations, because Joy didn't like to get too involved in any one thing. She felt that life should be harmonious. Her philosophy was that if you got into deep discussions, only negativity would surface.

Life was good. Wesley felt content. All of their needs seemed to be met, yet Wesley wasn't ready to completely trust Joy. He hadn't told her about the small fortune that he had hidden away. He had divided the money that he and Brent had made equally and sent Brent's half to his parents. His half was safely nestled in a safe deposit box, of which only he and Liz held keys. He was taking things slow and easy with Joy and he wanted to trust her with everything, but for some reason he wasn't ready to trust her with that. He gave his full monthly disability check to the marriage. He had been classified 100% disabled and was receiving a hefty sum.

Wesley's rehabilitation was going great. He had been fitted with a prosthetic for his hand that was much like a hyped-up glove with built in fingers for the ones Wesley had lost. The coloring matched his skin tone. He went to therapy daily and performed his exercise regimen several times throughout the day, every day. His determination was admirable.

One afternoon eight months later, Wesley was sitting on the front steps in the sun enjoying the onset of spring, when Joy pulled her car into the driveway. She had a carload of men with her. They all got out of the car as two more carfuls of people, men and women, parked in front of the house. Joy bounced happily across the lawn toward Wesley; the small crowd followed. Everyone laughed and sang. They were ready for a good time.

"Hi, honey pie. These are some of my new friends," Joy laughed, pointing to the guys who had ridden with her. "Some of them have been at the hospital for months, so I called a few of my old friends and my sisters to come over so we could all party."

"Okay," he said. "Let's all go inside. You want me to fire up the grill?"

"Oh, no, honey. It's not gonna be that kind of party," she laughed.

They went in the house and everyone seemed to take over. Wesley watched as someone turned on funky music to full throttle. Some danced provocatively. They took over the kitchen, rambling through the refrigerator and cabinets. Everything happened so fast that Wesley was speechless. He saw Joy across the room pressed against one of the men; they were entwined, moving to the music and kissing sensually.

"Joy!" he shouted, but his voice was lost in the deafening noise.

He fought his way through the wild room and pulled Joy away from the man, through the house to their bedroom.

"What's wrong with you? Why did you do that?" she questioned, still a little off-balance.

"Joy, what's wrong with you? What are you doin?"

"What do you mean? I just think it's time to liven things up a bit around here."

"What are you talkin about?"

"Wesley, don't act like that. You know I'm a free spirit in every way. Now that we've been together awhile, I'm ready to explore some new things with the man I love. I want us to be able to do whatever we want and to include each other in our fantasies. This is one of mine; we're having an orgy."

Wesley was shocked. "Joy, I am not gonna watch you have sex with anyone else. You're *my* wife. What about the vows we said about marriage? Were those just words to you?"

"Now it's my turn to ask, what are *you* talking about?" she crossed her arms. "I love you and I married you to be with you, but everyone knows the only marriages that are successful are those that are open…to everything."

"I married you because you are who I want to be with. If I wanted to keep havin sex with other women, I wouldn't have gotten married. And I'm certainly not havin sex with my wife and another man!" Wesley was shouting now.

"Don't scream at me."

Joy pushed past Wesley and walked into the living room. The orgy was in full motion. No one had noticed their dispute. Joy was annoyed because the man she had been kissing had moved on to someone else. She went back to the bedroom and glared at Wesley.

"You chased him off!" she shouted.

Wesley couldn't believe what he was hearing.

"I thought you understood who I am, Wesley. I love life and plants and animals and people; I love everything. I can't be limited for the rest of my life. I have to be free to be with whoever I want, like my mother and father. They have never limited each other. I wanted to be honest and do it *with* you, instead of having some secret affair. You have to allow me that or this marriage will never work. If you are truly my mate, you'll understand."

Wesley stared at Joy. He was speechless. He kept thinking that she would start laughing: that the whole thing was a sick joke. His mind was racing. He was confused and felt betrayed.

"Joy, honey, I do love you and I wanted to spend the rest of my life with you. But I know without a shadow of a doubt that we are not meant to be together."

Chapter 21

EXPLORATIONS

*W*esley and Joy ended their marriage as simply as they began it. It was over and that was that. Joy didn't hold a grudge, and to Wesley's surprise, he felt no bitterness. In retrospect, he viewed their marriage as a bridge that had led him from a painful chapter in his life to the new life that was waiting ahead. His relationship and marriage to Joy had been a needed transition.

Wesley said his goodbyes to Liz, Tina, Andre and Tyrell as he passed through New York from Connecticut. He decided that it was time to take that long-awaited road trip across country that he and Brent had planned. What a better way to clear his head and get started on a new life. He still believed that there was someone special out there for him. He also believed that he would eventually discover his life's purpose.

He paid cash for a brand-new Nevada Silver Corvette convertible with some of the money he had stashed with Liz. He split the remaining money with her, leaving her with a substantial emergency fund in case things didn't work out with her and Rick. He had enough left to get a good start somewhere.

When Wesley pulled onto the interstate and New York City was behind him, he felt a rush of excitement like he hadn't known since the Nam. He felt free, weightless, happy. He drove fast with the top down and the music blaring loudly as he raced to Philadelphia, stopping there as a tourist for several days.

His next order of business was to see his Grandpap, who had had a stroke and was in a nursing home. Wesley drove south to the North Carolina farm, and was overcome with sorrow when he saw that it had been sold. He went on to the nursing home in Belhaven. His grandfather was sitting outside on the patio behind the main building enjoying the spring Carolina sunshine. Wesley watched him for awhile and was saddened to see that his grandfather had lost most of his movement on one side. He was sitting in a wheelchair wearing freshly starched cotton pajamas and a light robe.

"Grandpap, it's me, Wesley."

"Wes...ley, my boy...look...at...you." His eyes watered as he struggled to speak.

"Hey, Grandpap, look what I brought you: a great big ole watermelon, just like we used to sit and eat on the porch."

"Go head...Wesley,...throw it...down and...break...it open."

"I will, Grandpap, just like we used to, so we can scoop it up with our hands and eat the heart right out of it."

He threw it on the concrete and the melon broke open. Grandpap laughed wildly. Wesley joined in, and then dug his hand into the melon, scooping out the heart for his grandfather, who ate it hungrily. They talked until dinnertime, catching up. Wesley pushed his grandfather into the cafeteria and promised him that he would be back in the morning.

He checked into a nearby motel and visited his grandfather every day for a week. It did them both good. Wesley had questions and his Grandpap had the answers.

"Grandpap, I've always wanted to know about my father. Momma doesn't talk about him and won't answer my questions."

"It's haaaard...for her...son."

"Do you know him?"

"Knew...him. I'm...sor-sor-ry to tell...you, but...Wes...ley, he...is dead."

Wesley's heart sank. Though he never knew him, he thought that one day he would meet his father. He was filled with contempt for him and wanted to tell him so. Now he would never have that opportunity.

"You...met...you...fatha...once. He was...your Aunt...Clara's husband...Frank...Bosworth. Let's...call Jean, she...will tell...you a...bout him."

Aunt Clara's husband was his father! Wesley was stunned. He dialed his Aunt Jean's telephone number and listened as his grandfather told her to answer Wesley's questions.

"Hello, Aunt Jean, how are you?" Wesley asked into the receiver.

"I'm fine, Wesley. I knew this day was comin. Now, I'm gonna tell you all about what happened, then I don't never want to talk about this again. And don't you bring this mess back up to ya momma; she moved on from this. You hear me, Wesley?"

"Yes, ma'am. You have my word."

"Okay. Well, your momma met your daddy, Franklin Bosworth, before he went into the Army. He was one good lookin man, and honey, you are his spittin image. The two of them was inseparable. Your momma loved that man right away, and he loved her."

"But your nasty Aunt Clara had a thing for Franklin. She had tried and tried to catch his eye when she was around him, but he only had eyes for ya momma back then. He was sent off to the war and while he was there, he wrote love letters to Lorraine, and she wrote him back."

"What none of us knew was that ole Clara had started writin to

Franklin, telling him lies about your momma, sayin that she was runnin all around with a whole lot a men. Franklin started questionin her, and all they did was fight on the phone when he paid all that money for a long distance call from Germany just to talk to her."

"She didn't know she was pregnant with you til she was nearly six months along, and so when she told Franklin she was pregnant with you, he believed what Clara had been sayin, what with her havin had three other kids before and all. So when he came back, him and Clara got married. Broke your momma's heart for good. You know they lived five minutes from the farm, and Clara just couldn't stand you being so close because you looked so much like your daddy. Franklin only saw you one time, and he knew right then that he had made a big mistake. By then, him and Clara had been married for bout five years. And you ain't missed a thing not knowin your daddy; he was a coward. They couldn't never have no children of they own, either."

"But I do give him a little credit," she continued. "After he saw you, he start sendin money to Lorraine for you til the day he died of a heart attack."

Wesley didn't say anything. He handed the telephone receiver back to his grandfather and went outside to walk the grounds and gather his thoughts. When he returned, his grandfather was waiting.

"You al...right now...s-s-son?"

"Yes, sir. I'm fine now. Thank you."

In spite of the shocking revelation, it was an enjoyable week for them both.

"I have a question to ask you, Grandpap."

"Wh-what is i-it, son?"

"When you came to my boot camp, you said somethin that I didn't understand. You said for me to give you flowers while you were livin, or somethin like that. What did you mean by that? I've never heard that before."

His grandfather chuckled. "I-it meant d-d-do some...thin good for m-me while I-I-I'm here to enj-j-joy it, not after I'm g-g-gone when I w-won't know about it. I wanted m-my grandson to sh-show them wh-what you were m-m-made of. A-And you did. For me, th-that was a huge b-bouquet of fl-flowers." They laughed and Wesley began telling his grandfather stories about many of his military escapades.

At the end of the week when Wesley left, he drove northwest to Cleveland, Ohio, where he visited with his mother, staying in her apartment with her for a month. Realizing the heartache that she had endured throughout her life, he indulged her with his time and money. She couldn't have wished for a more enjoyable visit with her son.

Moving on to Chicago, Wesley looked up a couple of buddies from the war and partied with them for a few weeks before driving to St. Louis, then to Dallas and Houston; back north to Lubbock, Texas to visit a friend, and then on to the majestic city of Denver, Colorado. It was an amazing city with a beautiful backdrop of snowcapped mountains, even in early summer. He stayed in Denver for awhile, and then was off to Albuquerque, New Mexico, Phoenix, Arizona, and eventually San Diego.

He loved California and San Diego. It was the right mix: a small-town feel with a spectacular coastline and remarkable scenery. He stayed there; it was an alluring place. The climate, the pace, the dazzling ocean…it was fresh and felt new. He found an apartment near the ocean in the northern suburb of La Jolla, so he could easily enjoy it. He loved the ocean for as long as he could remember, but not like he loved it there. The warm Pacific water lazily lapping the coastline of the sleepy shore of La Jolla was mesmerizing.

Wesley fit in with the natives of the San Diego area. He dressed comfortably, adopting a less formal approach to life, and appreciated his newfound home. There was an abundance of quaint shops and restaurants in La Jolla, many with views of the ocean. Wesley never tired of his daily explorations. In late fall, the weather shifted, and light rain was the norm. Still, San Diego was amazing.

A man approached Wesley's table while he was seated at a favorite café one evening, enjoying jazz and an overcast view of the ocean while sipping a cognac. Wesley was aware of his presence, but didn't let on. He sat at the same table daily. Though his back was to the door, he positioned himself in such a way that he could monitor activity in the café through the reflection in the window's glass to his left and a mirror to his right. It was a drizzly afternoon, but the reflection remained clear.

"Sergeant Wesley Lewis?" the man asked. "Is that you?"

Wesley turned and was surprised to see his superior from Viet Nam. He jumped up, and out of respect, nearly saluted, but caught himself and awkwardly moved to shake the Major's hand.

"It is you!" Major Wright bellowed in a loud voice, slapping Wesley on the back and pulling him into a manly hug.

"Major Wright! It's been what? It's been two years?" Wesley said, still astonished.

"And then some, my boy." He laughed loudly, happy to see Wesley.

Major Joseph Wright was Wesley's Battalion Commander in Viet Nam. He had gotten to know Wesley because of his excellence as a soldier. They enjoyed catching up, ordering drinks, then dinner, and then after dinner, liqueurs. They were loud and boisterous, telling stories, laughing at jokes, and wildly dancing with women they didn't know. It was getting late; the café had nearly cleared out. Suddenly, Major Wright's mood altered as he moved closer, lowering his voice to speak softly.

"Wesley, you were always good at what you did." He was serious now. "Are you interested in work?"

Taken off guard by his one-time superior, he quickly gathered his composure.

"Do you have work for me?" Wesley always answered a question with a question, gaining time to think.

"That depends on you, your situation, and your willingness to be discreet."

"Major, if those are the requirements needed, I'm definitely interested in work."

"I thought as much." The Major smiled briefly. "I'll be in touch."

Wesley turned to take a pen from his jacket so he could write down his telephone number. But when he turned back, the Major was gone. Wesley knew then that he had been sought out, and now that contact had been made, the games were about to begin. He couldn't have been more elated.

He went on with his life as though nothing had happened. Nearly a month went by when one day, while stopping at the post office to pick up his mail, Major Wright appeared from around a corner. He made eye contact with him and slipped a piece of paper into the mail that Wesley was holding as he walked past him. It said, "Come only if you are ready to 239 Spring Street La Mesa—15:00."

The hair on the back of Wesley's neck stood up. He had been waiting for this moment for the last month. Now that the Major had contacted him with instructions, he wasn't sure that he wanted to pursue this.

Though he was excited, and was searching for his life's next chapter, he had also become comfortable enjoying the safe, quiet life he was leading. He had heard stories from other soldiers about the covert operations they had engaged in since their time in Viet Nam. Some of the stories were equally as intense as the war itself, though undercover, without the scrutiny of the general public—which could be a good or a bad thing.

He decided that though life was good, he knew that it would not go on like this forever, and that a next step was inevitable. He was intrigued, and it felt good to be respected to the point that he had been recruited based on his abilities. Wesley knew that he would go, and he knew that he would enjoy whatever he would be asked to do.

The address on the paper led him to a small two-story building on a narrow street in the small suburb of La Mesa. He arrived early, well before 3:00 p.m. The door was unlocked, so Wesley cautiously opened it, checking his surroundings both outside and in as he slowly moved into the building, quietly closing the door behind him. He was in a hallway with three doors and a stairway leading to the second floor. The door to his right opened and a woman of Asian descent stepped into the hallway.

"Wesley Lewis?" she asked.

"Yes."

The woman thrust her hand forward to shake his.

"My name is Kailise Chang."

They shook hands. Her grip was more firm than he had expected. She was vaguely familiar.

"If you will, please follow me!" she commanded.

She led Wesley to the top of the stairs and into a small, sparse office.

"Have a seat, Mr. Lewis. The Major will be with you. Would you care to have a cognac?" she offered.

"No, thanks." He had to keep his mind clear.

She said nothing else, closing the door as she left the room.

Wesley sat waiting for 2 ½ hours. He was sure that he was under surveillance and used the time to think. So he waited, expressionless, showing no sign of irritation, contempt or anxiety. Viet Nam had taught him patience.

When the door opened, Major Wright was standing there, shaking his head.

"Just as I thought, a true professional."

"Yes, sir."

"Well, Wesley, I'll get right to it. Our little organization here is a small glimpse of the company. It's worldwide. We operate under the name of Global Inc. We need highly-trained people like you to carry important, highly-classified items around the world. You will be an International Courier. You will be expected to protect the packages—no matter what happens. I will not go in to detail about what you will be carrying or who you will be carrying them for; that does not and will not ever concern you. Do you understand?"

"Yes, sir."

"Knowing you as I do, I know that you being here is a commitment."

"Yes sir, you know me well."

"You'll be based in Hong Kong and receive your instructions for each of your assignments from the office there. How soon can you leave?"

"As soon as you have things in order for me."

"Good, I thought as much. There will be a first-class ticket for you on TWA on the 8:00 evening flight to Tokyo this Friday. You'll travel on to Hong Kong, where you will receive further instructions. I assume your passport is in order."

"It is."

"The next time we meet, it will be in Hong Kong."

The meeting was over.

Wesley left the little building and hurried to his favorite café for a stiff drink and a good meal. He had three days to put his business affairs in order. He decided to keep his apartment in San Diego for downtime, and so he would have a U.S. address.

He called Liz, his mother and his grandfather, explaining that he had a wonderful career opportunity and would be traveling most of the time. He assured them that he would keep in touch by calling periodically. There was no one else that mattered, except for JoJo. It was time for him to see his big brother.

Chapter 22

REUNION

*O*n Tuesday night Wesley took the red eye to New York City, arriving there early on Wednesday morning. He had a small carry-on, and hurried from the plane through the terminal to the taxi line. When he arrived at Attica Prison he was conflicted. He hadn't seen his brother in nearly thirteen years and didn't know what to expect. JoJo had been clear about no one seeing him behind bars, but thirteen years was a long time, and he hoped that his brother would be happy to see him.

Visiting hours didn't start until 10:00 that morning, so Wesley sat in a waiting area thinking over the early years when they had all lived together in the rooming house. He looked up to JoJo, convinced that there was no one greater in the world. He was angered about his brother's incarceration, remembering JoJo as a natural leader who could have done great things. He had been a warrior on the streets, revered by his boys and feared by those who weren't. *Who is it that decides the destinies of people? If I had been the older brother,* he thought, *would I have made choices that may have led me to confinement? Why is it that I'm a free man with a future, sitting on the outside, while my resourceful brother sits conforming to the powers that be, on the inside?*

Then, once again, he thought about God. *If God is in Heaven watching all of this, then what was God's purpose for sending JoJo here to sit in prison for most of his life? It's a waste of a life.* Yes, that would be the question he would ask God if he was ever given the opportunity.

Carlonian was relieved to hear that Wesley was once again questioning God's motives, because it meant that he still considered the possibility that God existed. He could see that Wesley was getting closer to believing that God has purposes for each of us, just as He had in sending Carlonian to live on Earth as Brent. He felt that part of his purpose for living had been to take the bullet meant for Wesley, thus prolonging Wesley's time on Earth.

The waiting room door opened and a guard announced that visiting hours were beginning. Everyone stood and lined up to go through the process of registering and being searched before being allowed into the

107

facility. The whole thing took nearly an hour before Wesley found himself seated in a guarded, internal visiting room, waiting for his brother to be brought in.

When JoJo entered the visiting room his ankles were chained, causing him to shuffle slowly toward Wesley. Wesley watched his brother, who looked very much the same, only better. Prison life had not aged him as negatively as Wesley had expected. His body was thicker, but muscular from weightlifting, his skin smooth and his hair full and wavy. His eyes met Wesley's...it was as if they were back on the block, like time had not moved. They were brothers, and at that moment nothing else mattered. JoJo reached Wesley and wrapped his brother's entire body within his arms. They stood, clutching each other in an intense embrace until a guard ordered them to sit down.

"My little brother, look at you, man. You look like it's all been good. You survived the war and you a hero, man."

"JoJo, it shoulda been you. You were the one out there takin all the chances for us."

"Don't go there, Wes. This is what it is. I'm not complainin. Man, you don't know how much easier you have made my life by sendin me money every month."

"You took care of all of us, Jo. It's the least I can do for you. I wish I could do more."

"How is Liz, Wes, I mean, really?"

"She's doin good."

"I love that girl. She comes up here now. I finally started lettin her come see me, but not the kids. At first, I was just so mad at the world for me being so stupid. I didn't want nobody to come up here feelin sorry for me. And I didn't want ya'll to feel bad seein me in here. But now, it's just good when I see her and hear about the kids."

"Yeah, those kids are somethin else. Liz is a good mother: a real good mother," Wesley added.

"Momma writes; she always has. I didn't answer her at first, but I do now. She's glad to know about what's goin on with me in here, and I know it gives her as much peace of mind as she can get, concernin me. But seein you is, wow...I can't even explain that. I didn't think I'd ever see you again, man."

"I thought that too...especially when I was in the Nam. Some nights, when it was quiet and I was sittin in the darkness of the jungle, I would think about you, Liz and Chris, wonderin what ya'll were doing at that moment."

"Whew! Chris...now there's a mystery. How in the world did all of us come out of the same place and he end up to be such a selfish fool? When the last time you saw him, Wes?"

"The day his father came and got him."

"What? You haven't seen him since then?" He pulled back with a look of shock. "Wes, he came here to see me."

"He did? When?" Wesley was stunned.

"About two years ago. He came up here with some mess, wantin to know if I wanted to be in some study where they shoot you up with some drugs. Of course, they only want to use convicts."

"I didn't think *anyone* had seen him, not even Momma."

"Yeah, he is one selfish dude. He won't call her. He lives in Boston, works at one of them fancy universities. Believe me, you don't want to see him. I never thought I'd say it, but I don't even think of him as my people, let alone my brother."

"Well, I guess he really is dead to us, huh? Liz always said that."

The two brothers sat talking, re-acquainting, and rebuilding their brotherly bond until the visitation was nearly over.

"Look, JoJo," Wesley quickly added before leaving. "I wanted to see you because I'm about to leave the country again. I got a job that's gonna pay me well. I set up money for you; it will come straight here every month. I can't write or call, but you'll get the money. I'll come back and visit when I can, but I don't know when that will be."

"You go out and conquer the world, my brother. I will be right here when you come back."

Wesley walked out of the building and took a taxi to JFK, where he caught a flight back to California. The next two days were a whirlwind of activity as he prepared to leave San Diego. The unknown loomed before him again; however, this time he was prepared and welcomed it with anticipation.

Chapter 23

EXHILARATION

That Friday, Wesley left the United States on Trans World Airlines (aka: TWA) Flight 261 to Tokyo, Japan, where he connected on to Hong Kong. As the flight began its descent into Hong Kong's Kai Tak Airport, also known as Hong Kong International, Wesley was once again fascinated with the amazing view of Victoria Harbour. It reminded him of how much he enjoyed this breathtaking city the last time he was there with Brent on R & R.

After clearing customs, he was met inside the airport by a uniformed driver holding a sign with his name imprinted on it. He was treated like royalty. The driver quickly commandeered the collection of his luggage and escorted him to a green Rolls Royce that was awaiting his arrival curbside. Inside the luxurious vehicle, a second uniformed driver welcomed him, offered him a cocktail list, and used a car phone to call the hotel's lobby bar and place his order. When the car arrived at The Peninsula, the most lavish hotel Wesley had ever seen, his drink was served to him on a tray as he stepped into the magnificent lobby. It was sizzling with activity. Although it had been a long, exhaustive week and flight, Wesley was instantly rejuvenated. He was excited to experience Hong Kong again, this time on a more affluent level.

After checking into his room he showered, changed and went downstairs for a meal of local cuisine at one of the hotel's extravagant restaurants. When he climbed into bed that evening he slept for nearly fourteen hours. The next day was spent relaxing and waiting to be contacted. He took a long walk, passing the Hong Kong Museum, absorbing the atmosphere, preparing himself to be a part of all that he saw. That night, he went out into the city's nightlife, soaking it in. He was a man alone in a foreign place on the brink of a fascinating ride; he was anxious. He thought of all that had happened during the last week and was amazed, yet he remained unruffled and primed.

The following afternoon he received a telephone call from Kailise

Chang, the woman from the La Mesa office. She gave him an address and instructed him to meet her there in ninety minutes. He dressed business casual—grey Yves St. Laurent slacks and sweater, Florsheim suede shoes, and a London Fog jacket—and took a taxi to the address.

Unlike the small townhouse-like structure in California, Global Inc's Hong Kong headquarters was impressive. The building was no less than fifty floors, contemporary in design, while displaying a distinct British architectural flavor. There were enormous windows throughout. A glass elevator whisked Wesley to the penthouse offices, where Kailise Chang was waiting in the elevator corridor.

"I trust you're well rested, Mr. Lewis," she said efficiently as she again thrust her hand forward.

"Yes, the hotel was very relaxing."

He shook her hand, noticing how different her appearance was this time. At their first meeting she was plain, no make-up, hair pulled back and carelessly dressed. With her hair down and wearing a rose-colored St. John's knit suit with stylish heels, she was actually very attractive. As they walked toward one of the main office suites, Wesley couldn't shake the feeling that he knew her from another time.

He was introduced to the director of the Hong Kong headquarters, Chester Bluffington. He was a small man sitting behind an enormous desk. When he stood and came around to meet Wesley, he was no taller than 5 feet, 5 inches, but when he spoke his heavy baritone voice filled the room with confidence, leaving no room to doubt who was in charge. Wesley was given a quick summary of what they did, which was no more than what Major Wright had already told him. Though Wesley would report directly to Major Wright, from time to time he would also work with Bluffington. Kailise Chang was identified as Wesley's assistant, the person who would handle the details pertaining to his assignments. She would fill him in on everything else that he needed to know.

They left Bluffington's office and proceeded to Kailise's, a smaller one in a different suite of offices on another floor. She handed him an agenda for the following month of training that he was scheduled to undergo with four other recruits. There were procedures that must be followed, licenses to be attained, and a variety of assessments that must be conducted before their first missions. He would be carrying firearms in and out of the countries in which he would be working. And there were the covert strategies that he must learn and never deviate from, especially when something did not go according to plan. All information and any elements needed to complete every mission would be provided for him, without question.

"Mr. Lewis, I have arranged appointments to view three apartments where you may be interested in residing. They are scheduled for this afternoon. I have a car waiting, shall we go?"

"Yes, yes, of course. But first I'd like to get on a first-name basis, if that's alright with you, Ms. Chang."

"Of course, Wesley, that will not pose a problem at all."

Wesley liked Kailise's Asian accent and her formal use of English.

"After you, Kailise…"

Comfortably seated in the rear of the hired Mercedes, Wesley and Kailise conversed.

"How long have you been workin with Global?" Wesley asked.

"I have been employed with the company for four years now."

"Is this home for you?"

"Yes, it is now, though I am originally from Taiwan. I lived most of my life in Taipei. My father is unhappy with my choice to leave our country and pursue a different career than what he had planned for me." She smiled. "I am considered a rebel within my family."

"You know, I can't shake the feelin that I met you somewhere before."

"We met years ago, Wesley. It was while I was visiting a friend in Honolulu. You and your friend Brent were visiting there on R & R."

"Kay!" Wesley turned to stare into her face. "You're not Kay, are you? You can't be."

"Yes, Wesley; Kay is short for Kailise. I think about that visit often, about how much I enjoyed spending time with Brent. He was such a special person. We met one other time in Japan."

"I didn't know about that, Kay," Wesley said. He was surprised by this.

"Kailise, *please*…Kay was a different person that I no longer recognize," she intimated.

"Kailise it is."

They rode in silence for a few moments as Wesley processed what Kailise had just told him.

"Through Brent, I met Major Wright in Japan," she continued. "He became aware of my exceptional organizational abilities and recruited me into the Global network. I am part of his internal core, as you are now."

The car came to a stop on a hill in a residential area overlooking much of Hong Kong.

"This area is known as V. I. P. Hill, Wesley," Kailise said, changing the subject. "Many Americans, as well as local and foreign politicians, dignitaries and celebrities reside here."

They went into the first building; the apartment was on the second floor. Wesley didn't look at it, opting to have an apartment on a higher floor. They continued to the next building, the Magazine Gap Empire, a luxurious, modern building, elegantly decorated with a stoic doorman stationed inside the sophisticated foyer. They toured the tenth floor apartment, which was complete with upscale furnishings. Wesley knew that he was home. He signed a one-year lease, paid the deposit and first month's rent, and moved in the next day.

Life in Hong Kong was exciting. His apartment was the most incredible place he had ever lived. The view from his balcony didn't seem real. It was like looking at a picture of a stunning view that existed in the mind of an artist. Sometimes Wesley would sit on the plant-filled balcony for hours, absorbing the peace and tranquility of his surroundings.

He thought about his conversation with Kailise. *She knew Brent; how could he not have remembered her?* Brent liked her a lot. *It's a small world,* he thought. Oddly, he was reassured knowing that Kailise was someone from his past. No matter how small a part she had played, they had history. She held a vital role in his present situation and for that he was glad.

Wesley began his training. It was long and tedious, but the extravagant evening dinners and nightlife diversions with his colleagues and superiors were rewarding. He couldn't believe his good fortune.

Some evenings after training he met with Kailise in her office to continue briefings and further familiarize himself with protocol. Though Kailise was a beautiful woman who was both smart and easy to talk with, they kept the relationship purely professional, partly because of Brent, but also because they didn't believe in confusing the work environment with what could potentially be an emotional situation. Occasionally after working with Kailise, they would have dinner together. They came to learn and respect each other's expertise and established a good working rapport.

One evening Wesley and Kailise were working into the night when they realized it was nearly 11:00.

"I didn't realize it was so late. I think I'll stay here at the office in one of the overnight suites since class begins at 6:00 tomorrow mornin. You should think about stayin, too; we've had a grueling day."

"No, but thank you for your concern. I must be at home when my son awakens in the morning. I have never been away from him overnight."

"Son? You have a son? I didn't know that."

"How would you know?" she chuckled. "We have not had the occasion to speak of our personal matters."

"Hmm, I guess you're right. I don't know if you're married or not."

"I am not." She lowered her head slightly. "I brought disgrace to my family by having my son. My parents demanded that I terminate the pregnancy, or they would no longer recognize me as their daughter."

"I'm sorry to hear that."

"I have no regrets concerning my decision. My son brings me such happiness."

"Is his father in his life?"

"No, Wesley. His father is Brent."

Wesley couldn't believe what he had just heard. He just stared at Kailise. He was dumbfounded.

"Did Brent know about him?"

"No, I lost contact with Brent. We were not in love, though we cared for each other. I planned to tell him, but by the time I was able to locate him, he had already departed this life. My son was born shortly after."

"How old is your boy?"

"He is 4 years old. He is my life."

"I'd like to meet him. I hope that you'll allow me that."

"I've thought about this moment since the day that I saw you in San Diego. I've known about your life. Major Wright searched for you; he instructed me to research you since you left Viet Nam. I was torn, but in the end decided that seeing you and the possibility of you being a part of my son's life was something that I could not deny. It appears to be part of all of our destinies."

Kailise went home, leaving Wesley with his thoughts.

When his training was over Wesley was informed that his theater of operations would be within Asia for the most part, but occasional trips to other continents might be necessary. He was given his first assignment, which was a routine pick-up from the U.S. Embassy in Singapore. Everything went like clockwork and continued to flow seamlessly for the next three months. Wesley Lewis was on top of the world.

A few weeks later, when he returned home from an assignment that had taken him to the Philippines, he had a message to call Kailise.

"Hi, I just got home. What's up?"

"I know that you have been patiently waiting to meet my son, and I would like for you to know that I have appreciated your patience," she calmly began.

"I knew that you'd let me know when you were ready."

"That time has come. Tomorrow is his fifth birthday. I am having a celebration for him and I thought that it would be a good time for you and him to meet."

"I'll be there. What time?"

The next day Wesley stopped at a toy store and with the help of an employee, purchased an abundance of toys that a 5-year-old would enjoy. All of the gifts were wrapped and loaded into the rickshaw. When Wesley arrived at Kailise's home, he was surprised that there were no other children there. She and an older woman, whom Kailise introduced as Miss Li, her son's caregiver, were busy placing food on the table around a small cake.

"Am I early?"

"No, you are right on time. We are all here now, so the celebration can begin."

Wesley had a flashback to his own childhood birthday party and felt a sudden pang of sadness within. A small boy walked into the room. He looked at Wesley with enormous black eyes. Wesley could see his friend's physical presence in this handsome little character.

"Hello, sir, are you my Uncle Wesley?" he asked while running to greet Wesley with a BIG hug.

Wesley could barely contain himself as he picked the little fellow up, holding him tightly with a vengeance.

"Yes, Julian, this is your Uncle Wesley whom I told you about. He will be able to tell you many things about your father." Kailise smiled, happy that Wesley wanted to be there.

"Julian?" Wesley said aloud.

"Yes, sir," Julian said. "Julian Watkins Chang; that's me," he giggled, showing two missing front teeth.

The three adults sat with Julian for the birthday lunch as he slurped the long, flat noodles filling his mouth to capacity, as was tradition when celebrating a birthday in Hong Kong. The noodles symbolized a long life for Julian, so the more he was able to fill his mouth with them, the better. He was delighted that a new guest was there to celebrate with him and take part in the special meal that followed. Stir-fried crab with ginger, green onion, and egg, along with clear soup and steamed rice was one of his favorite meals. After they had eaten and the longevity peach birthday buns were served, Julian opened his presents...but he quickly pushed them all aside and climbed onto Wesley's lap. He was ready to hear stories about his incredible father, whom his mother had praised through the years.

For nearly an hour Julian sat listening, laughing, and asking question after question about his father, Brent. Both he and Wesley couldn't have been happier.

Carlonian was also very happy, as he watched and listened to his earthly son and his closest friend.

Chapter 24

FRENZY

*T*wo years went by without friction in Wesley's life. He enjoyed his job, loved the travel, and had a couple of women that he regularly dated, whom he liked a lot, for different reasons. Everyone back home was well. Liz had married Rick and they bought a house in Long Island. Liz was ecstatic. She called Wesley and left a message on his San Diego answering machine that said:

"Imagine me living on 'hoity-toity' Long Island..."

Wesley laughed to himself as he sat aboard a Malaysia Airlines flight en route to Kuala Lumpur. Remembering the sound of Liz's voice mimicking the Queen of England was hilarious.

A bell sounded and the flight attendant's voice came over the speaker in Malaysian, announcing that they were preparing to land in Kuala Lumpur. It was 7:00 in the morning.

After landing, Wesley picked up his rented jeep, which had no windows or windshield. He was told that only certain vehicles were allowed on the country roads due to the rugged terrain. With no other option, he headed into the hills of Malaysia, following the highlighted route on the map that Kailise had prepared and included in the mission packet.

The road was narrow as he left the airport and narrowed still more, eventually changing from rugged pavement to hard-packed dirt. It would be a dusty ride. He stopped and tied a rag around his head, covering his nose and mouth. As Wesley maneuvered the jeep through Malaysia's wilderness he compared it to Viet Nam. The thick, lush canopies and trees of the jungle clung closely to both sides of the road. Periodically large, colorful birds flew across his path. He encountered one truck head-on about an hour into his journey. Both vehicles came to a complete stop. Because his jeep was the smaller of the two vehicles, Wesley had to inch the jeep into the trees, enabling the truck to slowly press through.

There was virtually no one else on the road. It dipped and curved and every so often, the jungle faded away revealing a small village or secluded wooden house. The drive to the appointed meeting place was long, tedious and exhausting. He reached his destination nearly four hours after his flight had landed.

Wesley was met by a Malaysian man who spoke flawless English, as he steered the jeep off the road and parked it near the large green barn with an enormous frog painted on its side, as indicated on the map.

"Good day," the man called out while approaching the jeep. "Do you need assistance?"

"I do. Car trouble," Wesley answered loudly.

"Come inside. I can help you."

Inside the dilapidated barn-like building, there was a comfortable living room, dining room, kitchen and bedroom. Wesley was led to the rear of the building, and through a hidden panel that led to a back stairway. Upstairs, there were state-of-the-art offices with the advanced technology that Global routinely used. There were ten others in the offices, busily going about their various tasks.

"Welcome, you made it and in good time. I am Said Zubir."

"Yes, I recognize you from your photo. As I'm sure you recognize me, if that's possible through all of your country's dust." He gestured over his dirty face and clothing. "I am Wesley Lewis."

Zubir chuckled. "Here is a phone for you to use after you check-in and freshen up. Then we will dine."

Wesley was shown to a small room on that floor, furnished with a comfortable recliner and an adjoined bathroom stocked with toiletries and a shower. A change of clothing in his sizes hung on the door. After showering and eating a delicious Malaysian meal served in the dining room on the first floor, Said Zubir gave Wesley the sealed package that he had come to collect. The time was logged as 1:00 in the afternoon. With no questions or further conversation, Wesley was in the jeep on his way back to Kuala Lumpur.

The drive began as it had earlier that day. Wesley was more confident because he was familiar with the road. He hoped that he would not encounter a vehicle traveling in the opposite direction, as he had earlier. An hour and a half passed, smooth sailing.

As he drove, he allowed himself the luxury of daydreaming. He thought about the good life he had, and the relationship he had developed with Julian, who had become like his own son. He spent most of his free time with Julian. And he was leaving on vacation next week: a full month off to travel within the U.S. He had plans to visit his mother, sister and grandfather. His grandfather had made enormous progress since Wesley last saw him. He had regained some of the use of his paralyzed side and his speech had improved. Kailise was allowing Julian to go with him. He couldn't wait for all of his family to meet Julian.

As Wesley continued driving he noticed a jeep in the distance coming toward him. His first thought was that he would stay on the road this time, forcing the other vehicle to squeeze into the trees. As the jeep got closer, Wesley noticed that there were two people inside. His defense mechanisms kicked in. He un-snapped the strap of his 9 millimeter Smith and Wesson, took it from the holster and removed the safety, holding it out of sight in his lap.

When the two vehicles met and stopped nose-to-nose, the other jeep's passenger leaped from the jeep and approached in an offensive manner, speaking loudly in Malay, a broken dialect. Wesley was alert and sat quietly, observing every detail within a wide radius. When the driver slid out of his seat, Wesley's finger was on the trigger of the automatic weapon. Both men stopped short of Wesley's jeep and stood watching him.

It was at that moment that Wesley wondered what was inside the package safely nestled on the floor beside his seat. He rarely thought about what may be inside the mysterious portfolios and boxes. But now, as he faced a potentially-tragic outcome, he realized that not knowing the contents of the package put him at a grave disadvantage. If he knew what was inside, he may be able to determine the lengths that one may go to get it. But none of that mattered now.

"American?" the driver smiled.

"Yes...American," he laughed.

"Give me your money, fool."

Money? Wesley couldn't believe what he was hearing. They were trying to rob him. It would have been easy for him to shoot them both and drive away...but at what price to himself? He had hoped that his killing days were over. *It was one thing to kill in the name of war, but here today, would killing be necessary? Could he avoid this?*

"My money?"

"Yes, fool, get out of the jeep and give us your money. All of it. And your package, too."

Ah, so it wasn't a random robbery; they were just making it seem so.

In one swift movement, Wesley lunged from the jeep, landing in a protected squat with his weapon perfectly positioned at them and his package tightly in hand. The men were stunned. As they began to draw their guns, Wesley fired, spraying both of the driver's legs. The passenger ran into the jungle, firing back, as Wesley drop-rolled into the forest. He was at home in the jungle, so he quickly moved outward away from the road, in an effort to avoid the passenger. He estimated that he was a little over two hours' drive from Kuala Lumpur. He would just have to make it on foot.

The passenger pursued Wesley as he made a wide circle back toward the road. They exchanged gunfire twice, then nothing. He didn't know whether he had hit the man, or if he had stopped the pursuit and returned to his partner. The men were no longer a concern, as long as they posed no immediate threat.

Wesley worked his way through the jungle; his objective was to reach

Kuala Lumpur and follow the deviation strategy. He would be missed soon when he didn't check in at the appointed time.

At 6:00 that evening Wesley's check-in call did not come, and at one minute after the hour, Kailise called Bluffington on the red telephone. All alerts were placed, and by 6:05, special agents were dispatched in Kuala Lumpur. They followed the little road that Wesley had taken toward the meeting point. They found his abandoned jeep and determined there had been a conflict. Assuming he was on foot, en route to Kuala Lumpur, they turned around and began the search, taking his jeep with them.

Now that Wesley knew the men who had confronted him were not merely robbers, he took every precaution as he traveled slowly on foot through the thick jungle. Keeping the road to his right, but staying far enough from it to remain undetected slowed the journey even more. It was totally dark now: the clear nighttime Malaysian sky only partially visible due to the dense foliage. He came into a small clearing that backed up to a hill with a recessed cove beneath it, resembling an overhang. Wesley checked the area for snakes and other threatening animals. He huddled into the cove, placing his back against the rear wall so he was facing the clearing with an unobstructed view. He decided to stay put until daylight.

Carlonian stayed put with him.

Meanwhile, back in Hong Kong, Kailise was frantic. This was uncharacteristic of her. She had worked with other couriers before Wesley. One had disappeared while on a mission and was never found. She knew the dangers involved with the work they did, and had been prepared for any outcome. However, this time was different. Wesley had come into her and Julian's lives, and had made an incredible difference in both their worlds. The thought of never seeing him again was devastating.

It was midnight when Major Wright came into her office as she sat waiting for news.

"Nothing yet," he calmly stated. "Go home."

"I can't do that just yet, sir, I—"

"Kailise, I know. Wesley and I have talked. I know that you have allowed him into Julian's life. Believe me when I tell you that it is a very good thing. Worst case scenario…Wesley doesn't make it, well then, your son has had an enriching two-year experience with a male figure in his life that cared about him. He will be sad if Wesley doesn't make it back, but he will still be the better for that two years of male companionship and guidance. Now…on the other hand, I know Wesley Lewis. Seen him in action. He will be back."

"It's been six hours, and nothing…"

"And there will be nothing tonight. Wesley has found shelter in the jungle for the night. He's a resourceful soldier with determination and a reason to want to get back here: that son of yours. Now go home. I will be here all night in one of the overnight suites."

Chapter 25

INDIGNATION

*J*ust before sunrise the next morning, Wesley heard a twig snap, but didn't move. He was and had been on alert throughout the night. He focused his attention toward the clearing. He could vaguely see a shadow moving slowly in the slivers of moonlight that were filtering through the cloudy sky. He pressed his back further into the soil of the hill within the cove, and watched, gun positioned and ready. The shadow was inching around the fringes of the clearing toward him. He held his breath. As the shadow moved closer Wesley could see the outline of a man holding a gun.

Suddenly three other figures appeared near the clearing. The four men moved slowly, methodically around the edge of the clearing, partially concealed by the trees around it, toward Wesley. He reasoned that he could take two of them out, before possibly being shot himself.

Just as he aimed for the nearest man, he heard a series of gunshots. In the commotion that followed, Wesley grabbed his package and crawled quickly out of the cove and into the bushes, concealing himself as the men either fell or ducked for cover. The next few moments were filled with the exchange of gunfire until everyone's ammunition ran out. Two of the attackers lay lifeless on the ground. The other two attackers were jumped by two men who suddenly appeared. The two surviving attackers were experts in martial arts and were effectively battling. Though Wesley still had his loaded gun, he didn't know who was who, so he waited in the bushes. As the sky was slowly shifting from black to gray, the clearing was filled with brutal violence as the four men fought a ruthless battle, knowing that they may never see the sun rise that day in the jungle. The fight labored on until two of the four men lay motionless on the ground. Wesley was quiet and still as he watched and waited for the code.

One of the two men loudly whispered, "Painted Pelican."

For every mission a code word was assigned and included in the mission packet, in case something went wrong. Wesley's mind made a mental scan of the packet Kailise had prepared for this mission. He could see the words *Painted Pelican* typed on the covert page that he was instructed to read and then destroy.

"Wesley Lewis: ten, seven, five," he replied and moved into the clearing while holding tightly onto the package and the gun.

No one said anything else. The three men moved in unison as though none of it had been out of the ordinary. It was what it was. They quickly gathered anything that would tie them to the site, including their opponent's weapons. The three of them, bloody and exhausted, hurried back through the jungle and climbed into the two waiting jeeps, rushing away from the tragic scene to a safe haven in Kuala Lumpur. A cryptic message was sent directly to the office of Major Wright, informing him of the outcome.

Wesley stayed undercover for a week as ordered, allowing things to blow over, especially in the media. Four bodies had been found in the countryside and one man was crippled from gunshot wounds to his legs; it was all being swept under the rug. When Wesley was driven to the airport and boarded the aircraft as a dignitary with a new name, passport and documents, he realized the magnitude of Global's influence and power. The power to extract him from a foreign country following his involvement in the deaths of four people was inconceivable. He wondered more than ever what the packages that he had protected with his life contained. This situation had domination written all over it and felt wrong in every way. The contents of these packages had to be world-altering. Wesley felt used and abused. He had been kept in the dark too much. He was angry with his superiors, and he was angrier with himself for allowing it.

When the plane landed, he went directly to the Global Building and walked into Major Wright's office before the secretary could announce him.

"I was expecting you," Major Wright calmly stated as he stood looking out the window at an incredible view of Hong Kong.

"Major, what is it that we do here? I never cared before now," Wesley demanded.

The Major turned to look Wesley directly in the eye.

"Have a seat, son," he offered.

Wesley stood defiantly. He felt like a schoolboy being told to go sit in the corner. Major Wright moved around the desk and sat on one of the richly-upholstered, cream colored couches to observe Wesley more closely.

"I know how you feel, son. You put your life on the line every time you go out there on assignment, and this time you came close to losing it."

"And for what?" Wesley turned, glaring at the Major.

"I don't understand, Wesley. I watched you put your life on the line everyday in Viet Nam; no, not just on the line, but sometimes on the edge. You never flinched, you never faltered, you never questioned. How is this any different?"

"I knew then what I was fightin for. It was for my country."

"Who repaid you with what, Wesley? Contempt!" he shouted.

"When I was fightin in that war, I didn't know that I was hated by my own country. I was doin what I thought I needed to do for freedom and justice. Last week, I fought and nearly lost my life, and I don't know what it was for. I don't know if I'm one of the good guys or the bad ones. Can't you understand that I need to at least know that?" he pleaded.

They both said nothing. There was silence as Wesley stood staring at the Major, and he sat staring back.

"We're not boy scouts, Wesley. But we're not criminals, either. What we do here insures the life of freedom and justice that you, your family, and the families of all the American people enjoy. We're doing a better job of protecting those rights than the Viet Nam war ever could have."

"What am I carryin in those packages, Major?"

"It varies. Some of them are documents needed for negotiations; others are orders."

"Orders for what?"

"This is where I stop this conversation, Wesley. I will not answer that question."

"I can about answer it for myself, Major. Have my actions directly resulted in the loss of an innocent life?"

Major Wright sat staring into Wesley's eyes before abruptly turning his head away. Wesley had his answer. Though he had not pulled a deadly trigger outside of war, he suddenly felt like a senseless murderer. He walked out of the room without another word and took the steps down to Kailise's office. When he opened the door, she was sitting at her desk, and though she wanted to jump up and hug him, she refrained, because she could see the distress on Wesley's face.

"I am very happy to see that you survived that mission," Kailise began tentatively. "What is it, Wesley? Has something else happened?"

"Yes and no. I need to think. The trip home will give me my answers. Is Julian ready?"

"After the ordeal that you have just been through, I wasn't sure th—"

"I'm leavin as soon as possible," Wesley butted in. "I'm on the way home to pick up my things, and then to pick up Julian."

"O…kay, but Wesley, are you sure you are up for the trip right now?"

"Kailise, don't worry. This trip is the *only thing* that I'm up for. This time with Julian is the one thing that I know is real. It is more important to me than you can know."

Chapter 26

HOME

*B*eth's death devastated Arie. She blamed herself for not fighting harder to get Beth out of the Peters' home or taking Beth and running away. Though it had been nearly two years, it felt like yesterday. She cut herself off from the students who lived in the house, refusing to enjoy life on any level. They accepted her dismissal and went about their way. Ms. Etta was determined to keep Arie from slipping away and forced herself into Arie's life, if only for a stolen moment here or there.

"Arie," Ms. Etta would call as she pushed her way into her room. "Here's a nice, hot cup of tea and some fresh muffins. Get up now and eat. Got to keep up your strength for work."

"No, thank you. Ohhhh, please don't open the drapes."

"But just look outside…" She pulled them fully open. "It's a glorious day. I know you're off today, and I need your help. I'm taking donations to the church and I can't carry everything myself. Please come and help me."

"Ms. Etta, please ask someone else."

"Everyone is gone. They had commitments. So up and into the shower you go. I'll be waiting downstairs."

Ms. Etta used every opportunity to pull Arie back during those two years. It was a long battle. Eventually, she got Arie to visit her church, where the Pastor was able to begin counseling her. He was patient and understanding, and allowed her to explain her feelings while helping her to come to terms with the tragedy.

Arie began soaking in the kindness that Ms. Etta so readily offered. They established a wonderful rapport. Ms. Etta didn't have any children, and her only surviving sibling was an older brother who lived far away. Arie and Ms. Etta sat in the parlor or in the warm, inviting kitchen (or, weather permitting, on the huge front porch) and talked about nearly everything.

"Ms. Etta, do you think Beth is okay?" Arie asked one afternoon early in May while they sat on the glider, watching the neighborhood bloom.

123

"Pastor Jenkins says that she is in the arms of our Heavenly Father, and that's where she's supposed to be."

"I believe that, Arie. Beth was a gentle soul, and I think this world was too hard for her."

"She had such a sad life. It seemed like a cloud cast a shadow over her wherever she went. But even so, she sure made me feel loved for the first time in my life." Arie began sniffling.

"I know, honey," Ms. Etta said reassuringly, "I'm sure that she knew you loved her too. And I'm sure that she's happy now. Once she left this place, she left that shadow behind her. Isn't that a beautiful thought?" She smiled.

"When you put it that way, I guess so. Maybe she is happy, blissfully so, I hope," Arie mumbled.

"Yes, I like that: blissfully happy in Heaven. And here we remain, waiting to leave this place; we're walking in the shadows of bliss," Ms. Etta eloquently stated.

Lizelle smiled as she enjoyed listening to the relationship that had developed between Arie and Ms. Etta.

Under Ms. Etta's close guidance Arie learned how to cook, properly clean, sew, budget her money, as well as many of the social graces. She was a patient woman who valued the opportunity that she had been given. Arie was like her very own daughter, and Ms. Etta filled a void in Arie's life. They were a blessing to each other.

Ms. Etta introduced Arie to Mr. Tilton, the vice president at the Citizens Bank on Vine Street, where she had banked for the last forty years. Mr. Tilton agreed that Arie had potential and hired her as a teller-in-training for the next class. Arie learned quickly, completed the teller training classes and began a career in the banking industry.

When she left the house for work each morning, Arie carried a strong sense of security within…and Beth in her heart. Her life had turned a corner, yet something was still missing. She couldn't shake that feeling.

At 20 years old, Arie had never been involved in a romantic relationship. She'd never held hands, kissed, or even hugged a boy. There had always been other issues that were paramount in her life. Now that she had Ms. Etta's motherly love, a comfortable home, and a good job, she began to think more and more about the possibility of meeting her mate.

"Do you think there's a mate for everyone in this world, Ms. Etta?" Arie asked.

"Oh, yes, Arie. I think there is a mate for every soul," she tenderly stated. "But some never find that mate while here in this life. I think those souls find their mates in the next world. And some make mistakes thinking they've met their mate. They end up divorced or unhappy. But I met my someone and we were together for forty-three years before he left this place."

"How did you know he was the right one?"

"Oh, I don't know how I knew…I just knew."

"I think there's someone for me here, too; I just know it. I sometimes wonder where he is and what he's doing at that moment. Do you think that's crazy?"

"I think that's wonderful, Arie. Your life hasn't been filled with promise. It would be easy for you to expect the worse or become bitter. You're blessed, Arie. Your spirit is a blessing to you and it will help you in life. Right now, it's a blessing to me." She smiled warmly.

Intuition told Arie that her soul mate was out there, somewhere. She began to search, paying close attention to every male that happened to come into her world. On the day that Charles Knight walked into the bank and paid extra attention to the lovely Arie, she was primed, accepting his attention.

"Well, hello there, Miss, uh…" he dramatically swayed to read her name on the nameplate positioned in front of her teller window. "Arie… what a beautiful name for a beautiful lady."

Arie smiled and began to blush.

"You must be new here. I know all the tellers."

"Yes sir, I am. May I help you today?"

"Oh, yes, Miss Arie Jones. You can help me every day."

Charles handed Arie the paperwork for his transaction and slyly looked her up-and-down while she was busy.

"There you are, Mr. Knight." She handed him the deposit receipt.

"Oh, no, no…Charles, please."

"Charles…" she shyly mumbled.

He smiled, turned and walked briskly out of the bank lobby.

"Watch out for that guy," Crystal, the teller beside Arie, warned. "He is trouble: a womanizer."

"Don't worry about me," Arie assured. "I'm not looking for that kind of man."

"*That one* will sneak right up on you before you know what hit you."

Arie laughed…but she was intrigued by Charles Knight. He was not a particularly handsome man; in fact, he was kind of plain. But he had a sensational presence. He dressed impeccably. His clothes were crisp and tailored, and he showed his straight white teeth with an infectious smile. She noticed how he interacted with others in the lobby before he came to her window. He carried himself with such flare, it was captivating. It was not something she had ever noticed and she liked it, a lot.

The next day, Charles Knight came into the lobby and walked directly to Arie's window, as if on a mission.

"Miss Jones, have dinner with me this evening," he stated. It was not a question.

Taken off guard, Arie hesitated and stammered an unintelligible response.

"Good, I'll pick you up when you get off at 6:00. If you need to check me out, ask any of your managers about me."

After he left, Crystal looked at Arie and shook her head.

"You better think about that long and hard, little girl. That man will eat you alive."

Arie had never been pursued. It was exciting. She had never been out to dinner with a man. It was an invigorating thought. *She couldn't go. How would that look? But how exciting; she could just go this one time, so she could tell him that she was not interested in his type. Yes, that's what she would do: Go to dinner, let him pay for it, yeah, and she would order a steak. That would teach him to take her so lightly, he could just ask her out and she'd come running.* No, he wasn't her mate, she was sure of that, but going on a date with him would be good practice for the real thing.

At 6:00 sharp, Arie walked out of the bank. Charles was there waiting, with one red rose that he held toward her.

"Oh, uh, thank you," she stammered.

"Shall we?" He lifted his arm formally for her to hold on to, just as she had seen in the movies. *Maybe he's a gentleman,* she thought.

"I made a reservation at The Angus House, one of my favorite restaurants. Have you been there?"

"No, I..." She had heard of it and never thought she would ever go there. It was a landmark restaurant in a prestigious part of town. It was elegant and very expensive.

They sat quietly in the comfortable Lincoln Continental as Charles drove. When they arrived at the restaurant he used the valet parking service and dramatically whisked Arie from the car into the lavish restaurant. A captivating golden sun slowly slipping from the sky cast a mesmerizing glow throughout the elegant room. The maitre d' escorted them to a formally-set table at the window's edge as a dynamic jazz trio filled the room with vibrant music. A bottle of wine was ordered; Arie's glass was filled and Charles moved close, gazing into her eyes as he took her hand in his, declaring his desire to please her. She was filled with dizzy delight and felt like the luckiest girl in the world.

Charles was charming and gave her his undivided attention. He was not cocky, as he had appeared at the bank. She was enthralled by him and forgot about her plan to put Mr. Knight in his place. The evening was enchanting.

Ms. Etta disliked Charles Knight immediately when she met him on the front porch that night. She didn't invite him inside, and watched warily as he lightly kissed Arie on her cheek.

Arie fell in love with Charles, and despite Ms. Etta and Crystal's warnings, freely gave herself to him: mind, body and soul. The relationship quickly changed and Arie was soon subjected to a myriad of emotions. Charles took her to insurmountable peaks of ecstasy, as well as scathing lows so tangled with lies that Ms. Etta worried if her darling Arie would survive with her wits intact. Ms. Etta grew to hate Charles over the next three years.

Arie openly gave Charles dedication, which served to feed his robust ego. When the novelty of Arie, the virgin, wore off, Charles became less and less interested, using her when other options weren't available. At first, he wouldn't call when he said he would. He began standing her up, but always with an excuse later. He stopped picking her up for dates, instead telling her where to meet him. Many of those nights ended with her sitting in a nightclub while he slipped away with another woman. She always forgave him. When she heard stories about Charles and other women, she didn't believe them and fiercely defended him.

One Friday Charles came into the bank and went to one of the new teller's windows to conduct his business. They laughed and talked, and then he left without speaking to Arie or even looking her way. She was devastated. When she got off work she called his office, pager and his apartment: all to no avail. She took taxis to four of the nightclubs they frequented, but never found him. She was frenzied from the search and emotionally distraught from her speculations, and eventually went home. Ms. Etta was watching an old movie on the couch. Arie told her what happened.

"Listen honey, that is NOT how a man treats a woman that he cares about…" Ms. Etta gently started. "Charles is a fool not to see what he has in you, and you have to stop accepting this from him."

"But Ms. Etta, I love him. Love is so special. I never loved anyone in the world except for Beth, you, and now him. He said he loves me too."

"Arie, a man will say whatever he has to say to get you to do what he wants you to do. If he really means it when he says he loves you, then he is not going to hurt you over and over the way that Charles does."

"But he doesn't mean to hurt my feelings. Things just come up, and he doesn't have time to stop and call me."

"Okay, Arie, if that is true, fine, but what was his reason for not even acknowledging you today at the bank?"

"I'm sure he'll explain that. I haven't been able to reach him yet."

"Have you been calling him, Arie? Please tell me you haven't. Never mind, don't answer that; I'm getting sick just thinking about it. Don't call him anymore. Stop chasing behind that man. Let him call you."

"But he might not. If he thinks I'm mad at him, he might turn to some other girl."

"You should be mad at him. And it would be a blessing for you if he turned to some other girl."

"I can't be mad…I am upset because I don't understand what he's doing or why. I've been hearing things about him, that he's going out with other women…but I just keep thinking that if he's doing that, it's because he wants to be sure that I'm the right one for him."

"Oh, Lawd, please help me. Arie…honey, do you believe that?"

Ms. Etta couldn't believe what she was hearing.

"You need to be asking yourself if he's the right one for you, baby," Ms. Etta pleaded.

The doorbell rang. Ms. Etta looked at the clock.

"Who would be ringing my bell at 1:00 in the morning?" she said.

Arie jumped up and ran to open the door. Charles stood there holding a red rose.

"Hey baby, come on with me."

"Charles, you came! What happened today at the bank? Why did you go to another teller?"

"Oh, that. I did that for you, baby. I didn't want them to think you're doing any favors for me, just because I'm your man. C'mon, let's go baby."

Ms. Etta came around the corner.

"And why are you coming over here in the middle of the night to pick her up? She isn't good enough to be seen with you during decent, respectable hours?" Ms. Etta scolded.

"Ms. Etta, it's okay," Arie explained. "Don't worry. I'll see you later, okay?"

Arie left with Charles and came home on Sunday afternoon in a taxi. She was wearing the same dress she had on Friday night, though it was torn and dirty. Her eyes were swollen from crying and dried makeup was smeared on her face. Her purse and one of her shoes were missing, so she didn't have money for the taxi or her key. When Ms. Etta opened the door and saw Arie's condition, she was enraged.

"Oh, no! Baby, come on in the house."

"Can you pay the taxi driver please?" Arie sadly asked.

Ms. Etta took care of the taxi driver, wrapped a blanket around Arie, and walked her upstairs to her bedroom.

"Arie, I'm gonna call the police; but first, tell me what happened."

"No, don't call the police, Ms. Etta. This is my fault."

"Arie, no its not! This is that no good monster's—"

"Ms. Etta, you have been right about Charles," Arie gently started as she looked past her through the window. "I have learned my lesson."

"What happened to you, honey?"

"I'll tell you, Ms. Etta, and then I want it to be over. Really over. I don't want to call the police. I don't want to do anything but get over this."

"Alright, whatever you want."

"When we left here on Friday night Charles drove to Topeka. A friend of his was having a party. We went in and sat down on a couch; then his pager went off. He said he had to take care of some business and he'd be right back. He went toward the back of the house. I sat there, waiting."

Arie took a few breaths and continued, "I started getting nervous because I wasn't sure where we were, and I thought he might have left me, so I went to look for him at the back of the house. I opened the back door and stepped outside. I could see Charles' car parked down the block. He was standing near it talking to someone. As I started walking toward them, they moved together and started kissing. I was so angry. My first thought was that all of the rumors about him cheating on me were true.

I decided to confront him. I walked really fast toward them, and as I got closer I realized that Charles was kissing a man. A man! Can you believe that?" she cried.

"I stopped walking. I thought my eyes were playing tricks on me. So I ducked into the bushes and tried to make sense of what was happening. They hadn't seen me and kept kissing and fondling each other. Finally, the other guy pulled away and walked off to his car, all the time waving and blowing kisses to Charles, who laughed. After the guy drove away, Charles went back inside the house. I climbed through bushes so no one would see me, and when I made it to a busy street I started running. That's how I lost my shoe, and I must have dropped my purse somewhere."

"Oh, honey, how awful. I knew he was a dog, but even I didn't think he'd do something like that. Where were you all day Saturday?"

"I was trying to get home. I hid for a long time because I didn't want Charles to see me. Then I tried hitchhiking. I walked a lot. When I finally got back to Kansas City today, I told a cab driver you'd pay for me if he would just bring me here."

"You did the right thing, honey. You should have just gotten a taxi in Topeka. I'd have paid for that, too. Don't ever think you have to be out there in the street like that. You hear me, Arie?"

"Yes, ma'am." She hung her head. "Here I was worrying about rumors of him being with other women. A man! I am some lover, huh? I can't even make a man happy. My man leaves me for a man."

"Oh, no, you don't blame yourself for this one, missy. If that man likes men, he's been liking them for a long time, since way before he met you."

"You don't know that for sure, Ms. Etta. Who am I? I am nobody."

"Arie, it breaks my heart that you can't see your worth. You are a blessing to everyone who is blessed to meet you. Your caring spirit shines brightly from within. Everyone can see it, except for you. It's unfortunate that a worthless leech latched onto your kind heart. That relationship was not good for you. A good, solid relationship that is filled with real love will not feel confusing and painful. It will feel wonderful to be in love."

Arie quietly thanked God for bringing the past three years to an end. She took off from work the next day and rested. When she awoke and went downstairs, Ms. Etta was distraught.

"What is it, Ms. Etta?" Arie asked.

"It's my brother. He's dead. Oh, Lawd, and it was a horrible thing that happened to my Thomas."

She explained that he had been killed in a fire. Ms. Etta was grief-stricken. Though she and her brother spoke only once a week on Saturday mornings, they were close. He was her only surviving sibling.

Ms. Etta had to go home to Belhaven, North Carolina for her brother's funeral. She started packing as she sang childhood songs aloud, and told Arie stories of her and Thomas' lives growing up in the South.

Arie offered to go with her to North Carolina for the funeral. Ms. Etta was touched, and gladly accepted. She was relieved to have Arie in her life, and realized just how much she loved her that day.

Arie was glad that she could offer Ms. Etta emotional support. Ms Etta had done so much for her and had made an invaluable difference in her life. It was also a good time for her to get away from everything that had been going on, especially lately. A change of scenery would be like a breath of fresh air. After all, she had never been to North Carolina, or anywhere else for that matter.

Chapter 27

SORROW

*T*he trip to the United States turned out to be just what the doctor ordered for Wesley. The moment that he and Julian boarded the flight headed to Los Angeles, Wesley pushed Global, Inc., and all of his theories about the company, to the back of his mind: at least for the time being. Wesley and Julian had a great time. It was turning out to be a fantastic trip.

They flew to San Diego, where they spent a week at Wesley's La Jolla apartment. After taking care of business matters that required Wesley's attention and he had made all of the necessary phone calls to family, Wesley began the business of showing Julian the time of his life. They went to the famous San Diego Zoo and to Sea World, places that Wesley had never had a desire to see, but enjoyed just as much, if not more, than Julian. Julian discovered tacos and burritos and a favorite restaurant in Old Town.

It seemed fitting to enjoy a cross-country road trip with Brent's son, so the following week they began. The first stop was the Los Angeles area, with a two day visit to Disneyland in Anaheim. Then on to San Francisco where Julian was amazed by Ghirardelli Square and Fisherman's Wharf. They drove through Nevada, Idaho, Wyoming, Nebraska and Iowa, stopping in small towns, taking it in and marveling at the diversity of the United States.

"I can't believe there is nobody around anywhere," Julian bellowed.

"It is amazing, isn't it? But just wait until you see New York City, and then the Carolina countryside. You're going to love it all," Wesley said.

"This is the best time I ever had, Uncle Wesley."

"You know what, Jules, me too."

They laughed and turned up the music, bouncing in their seats and singing the lyrics at the top of their lungs.

When they finally reached Ohio to visit with Wesley's mother, three weeks had passed since they'd come to the United States. Wesley began to contemplate his future and what he would do about Global. The time he had spent with Julian had been uplifting. He realized that he wanted no part of anything that would rattle the sense of inner peace he had gained during their mindless times the past three weeks. He looked at Julian sleeping in the passenger seat...*so young and innocent.* He wondered what it would be like to actually have a child of his own. When he was married to Joy, he thought they would have children one day.

But if they had, he would not have met or known that his best friend had a son. He allowed his mind to wander to a place it hadn't visited for many years: the existence of God, and that his meeting Julian had been orchestrated by God so that he would be a part of Julian's life. *Was this his reason for being on Earth? Did it all come down to something as simple as being a father figure to Julian? Or was this part of a plan for him that may still include his soul mate, his other half, and other reasons for him to still be here?* He was determined to play this game out to its end and see.

When Wesley's mother opened her door, he could tell that something was wrong. Lorraine hugged Wesley a little tighter and longer than he expected. She listened quietly as Julian described their journey, and then took him to her bedroom to watch television with cookies and milk. When she returned to the living room, she told Wesley that his grandfather had died in a fire. Wesley went numb, his ears rang, and he didn't hear another word that his mother said.

He didn't care about the details at that moment. Instead, he cursed a God who would not allow him to see his grandfather again. *He was nearly there; he would have been there in four days. What purpose did this serve?* Wesley was angry with himself for not going there first: for not putting his grandfather first. *Why had he planned the trip this way, making his grandfather his last stop? What did that say about the place his grandfather held in his life? He should have gone immediately to him. He had bragged about his grandfather to others and talked about how important he was in his life.* At that moment he hated his own hypocrisy. He hated himself. He hated God. And now, here his mother sat, attempting to be a real mother, breaking the bad news to him.

Lorraine attempted to rattle on about the details of her father's death, but Wesley silenced her.

"Don't tell me what happened to him. I won't hear it from someone who cared nothin about him."

"Wesley, don't talk to me like that. My relationship with my father was complicated, and you don't understand it."

"I understand it enough to know that Liz had to sneak around behind your back to call or write him, and even though he never got to see us, he still cared enough about us to send us money and help us."

She was stunned.

"What are you talkin about, Wesley?"

"That's right, Mother, your father took care of us from afar when you couldn't."

"Why would Liz keep somethin like that from me?"

"Because you wouldn't hear it then, Mother. You tried for awhile, and then you gave up on us. You took the easy road and made off for yourself. Claimed a better life for yourself, complete with new children. We were still there, sitting there in the life you laid out for us. How do you think we could've made it without some help? Help you weren't givin."

Lorraine was sobbing loudly, and Julian ran into the room to see what was wrong. Wesley took Julian by the hand and walked out of the apartment, leaving the door wide open. He didn't speak as they got back into the car, and Julian instinctively knew not to, either. They drove to a hotel and checked in to a two-bedroom suite. Wesley knew that he needed some time and privacy. After settling Julian in one of the bedrooms he called Liz from the other. Together, they cried into the phone as Liz recounted the horrible story of their grandfather's death.

They made plans to meet in Belhaven, North Carolina. Wesley took some time to reflect on what had happened. He could feel himself sinking into a deep hole. The only thing that held him together was Julian. He called Kailise in Hong Kong and told her what had happened. She was saddened for Wesley and made plans to meet them there.

Wesley was livid. He wanted retribution. He needed retribution. *This was somebody's fault, and he would find out whose, and that person or people would pay. It was his mission now, and he would not rest until it was done.* He was not there for his Grandpap when his Grandpap needed him; this tormented him. *He had failed him in life, but he would vindicate him in death. God had done nothing. He had stood by and let this happen. He didn't need God now; He could handle this on his own. He would show God—he would show them all. Wesley Lewis would make them all pay.*

Carlonian knew that this day of spiritual reckoning would come for Wesley, but he had been unsure of its magnitude. He knew that for all souls who visit Earth, this day comes. For some, the day is an earthly lifetime of turmoil, and for others the day is brief. This is the day that determines the direction, and in some cases, the continuation of the journey. Carlonian was prepared to be with Wesley throughout his turbulent walk.

Chapter 28

VICTORY

One Day Earlier...

The Falstaff Nursing Home where Thomas John Lewis lived was anguished by his death. He had been getting better since the stroke, though he still couldn't manage on his own. The paralysis kept him in the wheelchair. He looked forward to three things since being confined to the nursing home: He liked sitting in the sun, talking with his sister Etta every Saturday, and attending church on Sunday mornings.

On the fateful Sunday morning of his death, Thomas went through the slow, methodical process of readying himself for church. Dressing was difficult for him, but going to church was special, and he took greater care preparing for it. With the help of a favorite nurse, his shoes were shined and he was flawlessly dressed in a gray pinstriped suit, freshly pressed shirt, matching green paisley tie and hanky, and a gray brimmed Stetson. He sat ready and waiting in his wheelchair on the main building's massive veranda, for his daughter Clara to pick him up for church.

Clara was the only child of his that lived near him, and the one with which he had the most friction. She had not stopped blaming her father for her own unhappiness due to Wesley's presence in their lives during the early years of her marriage. She harbored hatred toward her father, seeing him only on Sunday mornings when she picked him up for church. Clara didn't attend church with him or spend any time visiting; she merely provided him a ride to and from church once a week.

Thomas was wheeled into church by Deacon Harold Brown, who unloaded his wheelchair, and patiently helped him into it every Sunday when Clara pulled her car to the front of the church. The deacon rolled him up the side aisle as he did every week, carefully parked the chair beside the third row pew, and locked the brakes before joining his family in the rear.

The service was particularly enjoyable for Thomas that day. His

134

favorite choir sang, and a soloist with an angelic voice crooned one of his favorite songs, "Total Praise."

When the service had nearly ended, an electrical fire started in the lighting system encased within the ceiling of the church. At first, there was a faint electrical burning smell. As the altar call was given and the congregation crowded closely to the pulpit, the smell became a little stronger and many people began to notice it, looking around for its cause. Reverend Carter made a mental note to call an electrician.

Smoke lightly oozed from the ceiling tiles without anyone noticing. Marjorie Daye, an 8-year-old with a vivid imagination, was the first to notice the smoke. Instead of closing her eyes for prayer as Reverend Carter instructed, she sat gazing dreamily toward the ceiling, imagining herself grabbing onto the puffs of smoke, guiding them out the windows and up to the magnificent sky. She smiled as she thought about how fun it would be to ride on one of the smoky puffs to the clouds, where no one could ever yell at her ever again.

The congregation was in deep prayer, most with heads bowed and eyes closed. As the smoke began to thicken on the ceiling, Marjorie decided that something wasn't right and started patting her mother's arm while pointing upward. Her mother was annoyed and began to scold her daughter; then she looked up. Flames sprang from the ceiling and the lights. Mrs. Daye screamed, "Fire!" and pandemonium followed.

Everyone began running, screaming and scrambling for the exits. Mothers grabbed children, husbands pulled wives…many were trampled, but managed to scramble to the doorways. The flames became ferocious and quickly took over the wooden building, as many of the fiery ceiling beams began crashing to the floor.

Thomas Lewis knew that he would not survive the fire that day. In the urgency of the moment, no one remembered the nice old man who was parked near the front of the sanctuary in his wheelchair, and that he was unable to move it himself. Thomas felt no malice toward Deacon Harold Brown; after all, he had a young family to worry over.

In the last moments before the beam above Thomas fell to crush the life from his body, he knew that there was no other place on Earth that he would have chosen to die. He was victorious. He hadn't known the Lord his whole life, as many had. He had come to the church after Lorraine had come and taken his Wesley away. He and his wife Lois had been afraid for their little grandson to live in New York City. Together, they joined the church and became faithful followers. Only the power of the Holy Spirit had been able to calm their fears and give them a sense of peace.

As Thomas looked up, he saw that the blazing beam was about to give way…but more importantly, he saw an angel bathed in a searing bright light, with wings spread wide. He recognized the angel, who reached for him as Thomas stretched his anguished body from his wheelchair as he hadn't been able to do in years. When their hands touched, he was filled with a peaceful relief as he was lifted from the wheelchair, looking back briefly to see his earthly body crushed beneath the beam. As he and the angel Narwith sailed gloriously into the atmosphere, he thought only of Wesley.

The day that Thomas Lewis died had been an awful day for the town of Belhaven, North Carolina. A church had burned to the ground, and a well-respected elder of their community had burned with the building. The congregation was ashamed that no one had thought to help Brother Lewis. And Reverend Carter took all responsibility upon himself. He agonized over it, vigorously praying openly in public, and privately as he fell on his knees within his home.

He went to Clara to express his condolences and to pray with her. The congregation rallied around her, the grieving daughter. Reverend Carter organized a revival the next day in an effort to begin healing the grief-stricken community. The revival was held in another church and was packed with the congregation and town folks of every ethnicity. An offering was taken for the family; everyone dug deep, paying their guilt away. Clara accepted all of the money, thoroughly basking in the town's remorseful attention.

Chapter 29

RAGE

Wesley slept for six hours and gently placed the sleeping Julian into the passenger seat of the Corvette around 1:00 in the morning. He drove straight through to North Carolina, stopping only for food, gas and bathroom breaks. They arrived in Belhaven at 2:00 that Tuesday afternoon.

Wesley checked into the River Forest Manor, an upscale boutique hotel housed in a beautiful Victorian mansion on the Pungo River. Liz and her family flew into the airport at Raleigh/Durham and rented a van. She, Rick and the three children drove to Belhaven, where they, too, checked into the lovely, antique-filled hotel.

Wesley was so enraged that Liz didn't recognize her brother for the first time in their lives. He ranted on and on about how the minister would pay. She decided that they should rest that night and face the sorrowful ordeal that was ahead on Wednesday. The funeral was planned for Saturday, four days away. Rick took the kids, including Julian, out for burgers to give Liz some time with Wesley.

"Wesley, you have got to calm down. We're not even sure of all of the details," Liz said.

"Did you see the newspaper, Liz? Did you?" he shrieked, on the verge of tears again.

"Yes, I did," she calmly responded.

"Well then, you should know. It was practically murder...MURDER!" he screamed. "And that minister, who is he a minister for: SATAN?"

"Wesley, I feel just like you do. I'm angry. I'm hurting. I loved that old man, too. But we have to lay him to rest in a peaceful manner. That is what he would've wanted. You've got to know that."

The room was quiet. No one spoke for a few moments.

"Wesley...let's just wait til tomorrow when we speak with the minister... okay?"

"Liz," Wesley's voice was suddenly so low and controlled that it gave her chills. "That man will pay."

The next day Rick stayed at the hotel pool with the kids while Wesley and Liz drove to the nursing home. The staff was happy to see them, greeting them warmly. It was evident in the way they were treated that their grandfather had been well thought of.

They were taken to his room. All of his belongings were still there, undisturbed. No one had come to check on or get his things, which heightened the pain both Wesley and Liz were feeling. The administrator came in to express her sympathy and told them that she had made several calls to his daughters and left messages about his belongings, but no one had returned the calls.

She arranged for boxes to be brought in for them to pack. They carefully went through his earthly belongings. Wesley stared at a bulletin board filled with the post cards that he had sent his grandfather from everywhere he had been. And Liz reminisced while fingering a cuddly throw she had sent him for chilly evenings. They packed his clothing for donation, and selected certain keepsakes for themselves, the children and JoJo.

Their next stop was the funeral home. A small wooden house with a sign in front identified it as The Briargrass Funeral Home. When they went inside, they were met by a woman who said that they were right on time because some other relatives were there to make the arrangements. They were led through the hallway, and when the woman knocked lightly and opened the door, they saw their mother, Aunt Jean, Aunt Clara and an older woman who was silently crying, seated at a table, waiting.

A young woman stood behind her looking out the window. She turned toward the door and her eyes met Wesley's. They both felt a sudden rush of emotion. Neither could pull their eyes away from the other.

Lorraine quickly crossed the room to Liz, hugging her. Jean watched and waited for a reaction, while Clara turned her head away.

"I'm so glad that you're here, Liz," Lorraine said.

"Why, Momma?" Liz asked.

"Well, because, this is a difficult time for all of us and—"

"So difficult that you couldn't go out to where he lived and get his stuff?" Liz sarcastically spat.

"Liz! Wesley! I don't know what is wrong with you two. You are so hostile toward me. I thought we had gotten past this."

"Let's go, Wesley," Liz said, as she noticed that Wesley wasn't responding to the situation at all. He was staring at the woman neither of them knew. She gently took his arm.

Wesley was frozen and looked as though he'd seen a ghost. He couldn't tear his eyes away from the young woman. Liz pulled him down the hallway.

"We have somethin more important to take care of now, Wesley. What's wrong with you?"

"Who was that girl in there?" Wesley asked.

"What? Here we are, trying to get to the bottom of things, and you're checkin somebody out?"

"No, it isn't like that. That was strange. It was like I knew her from somewhere."

They drove to Reverend Jonas Carter's house in silence. When Mrs. Carter opened the door, they introduced themselves. She expressed her sympathy and began talking about what a wonderful man their grandfather was. Wesley turned and walked to the van without a word. Liz found out that the Reverend was at the church site going through the rubble. When they arrived, he was there. Wesley leapt from the car and marched directly to him before Liz could say anything.

"Are you Reverend Carter?" Wesley demanded as he was approaching.

The Reverend turned and saw Wesley rushing toward him. He stumbled backward with his hands raised, as if to shield himself.

"Are you Carter?" Wesley shouted.

Liz was running toward them.

"Wesley, Wesley!"

"Well...y-yes...I am Reverend Carter."

Wesley confronted the minister: nostrils flaring, eyes wide and accusing. As he reached to grab the minister, Liz pushed her way between them, holding onto Wesley.

"I...AM...Wesley Lewis, Thomas Lewis' grandson, and I blame YOU completely...for the death of my grandfather!" He screamed. "Why did you let him burn to death and save yourself? You call yourself a man of God, and yet you're here and he's not." He paused to gather his breath. "He sat there, believin in you and WHAT you were sellin, and then WHAT? Suddenly, he needed you and you were gone...you and the rest of your people. Nobody gave a damn about that man. He just sat there and burned—TO DEATH. Where were you, huh? Where were you? Outside sayin, "Whew, that was a close one—"

"Wesley, stop it!" Liz pleaded. "Stop it."

The minister bowed his head. All of the money he had raised for the family and the relentless prayers for forgiveness suddenly seemed insignificant. Everything that this man had just said was exactly how he felt.

"Mr. Lewis, I know that this will mean nothing, but I am so sorry and—"

"You're right about that! It means nothin. And there is nothin that I can say to explain the actions I am about to take. I will destroy you."

Wesley walked away to the van. Liz looked at the minister, who appeared to be broken by what had happened. She could see beyond her grief to his pain. She turned and followed her brother to the van.

Neither of them spoke during the drive back to the hotel. When they got there, Kailise had arrived from Hong Kong. Wesley was happy to see her, hugging her tightly.

Later, they all went to eat dinner in Greenville about an hour away. While the four kids rummaged the buffet and enjoyed sitting together at their own table, the four adults talked about the day and got better acquainted.

"Who do you think the older woman was at the funeral home, Liz?" Wesley asked.

"Well, when we got back to the hotel, I called Aunt Clara's house to talk with Aunt Jean. She said that the woman is Grandpap's sister. Her name is Etta. She lives in Missouri."

"I didn't know he had a sister."

"Me, either. Aunt Jean said she's a nice woman, and that when she found out what happened to her brother she was heartbroken."

"I want to meet her," Wesley announced. "Where is she stayin?"

"At a friend of hers somewhere in Belhaven. She grew up here on the farm and knows people here."

"Let's go see her tomorrow. Was the younger girl with her? Is that her daughter?" Wesley asked.

"I didn't ask about her. We can find out tomorrow. She's probably our cousin."

"Did you find out where our mother is stayin?"

"Yes, and you won't believe it. She and Aunt Jean are both stayin at Aunt Clara's house. They apparently have mended their relationship. Aunt Jean said they all sat up the first night they got to Belhaven and had a tearful reunion."

"Humph," Wesley snorted.

"Okay, time to change the subject before you get worked up again. So now on to other matters of importance," Liz kidded. "What exactly is the nature of this relationship?" she said while waving her finger at Wesley and Kailise.

"Friends," Wesley stated, and then looked at Kailise. "Good friends."

"I would do anything for Wesley, Elizabeth. He has been very good to me and to my son. We both love him."

"Call me Liz, please Kailise." Liz smiled. "Well, is there anything in the future for this friendship?"

"Yes, Ms. Nosy, more friendship," Wesley said. Kailise barely smiled.

Later that night when everyone had turned in, Wesley was sitting on the couch in the living room of the two-bedroom suite he shared with Kailise and Julian, waiting for the day to begin in Hong Kong. Kailise came into the room dressed provocatively in a red gown of silk and lace. Her jet black hair cascaded onto her shoulders. She was stunning. Their relationship had never gone there. They had kept it professional at work and platonic in their personal lives. He resisted the urge to comment; instead, he shared his intentions with her.

"I've decided to call Global."

"You've decided to return to Hong Kong?" She was hopeful, as she perched on a chair across from Wesley. She crossed her legs allowing the split in her gown to open, revealing her legs to her upper thigh.

"Probably. It depends on the next few days," he said. "I'll know shortly after I make a few phone calls."

"I hope you know that I am completely dedicated to you, Wesley. I will do whatever you ask of me," she offered.

"And I know that, Kailise. It was great that you came, but I didn't expect that. I called you because I thought you may have wanted me to send Julian home before I came here. This may turn out to be an unpleasant situation."

"It doesn't matter. I am here for you. You are our family, Wesley." She stood and walked to the couch, standing directly in front of him, and took his hand. "What do you want me to do for you?"

He could smell her perfume. It was intoxicating. He didn't want this now, not now when he was in the midst of righting a wrong.

"Right now...I think you should go to bed and get some rest. I'm going to make these calls and turn in myself. We need to be clear-headed tomorrow."

Kailise reluctantly went to her room and eavesdropped beside the cracked door as Wesley picked up the phone and dialed Major Wright's private number.

"Yeah, Major here."

"Major, it's Wesley."

"Wes...heard about your grandfather. Sorry to hear it."

"That's why I'm callin. I'm callin in a favor. I don't know if I have a favor to call in, but it's important to me, very important, so I'm askin."

"Okay, I take it that if you're calling in a favor, you have decided to table the questions and move on with Global, business as usual? Is that what you're saying, Wesley?"

"Yes. I am. I want to expose someone. The preacher at my grandfather's church. I know he's a sham, a hypocrite, and I want to show that to his church: all those people who look at him like he's some kind of saint. I want the whole town to know what he is. I want it to be a scandal that shakes the whole Baptist community."

"Do you know what you're saying, Wesley? Is this just grief talking?"

"I want to remove all of his credibility. I want to destroy his reputation, his marriage, his credit, his life. And when that is done, I want to destroy him. He is the reason that my grandfather is gone. He has to pay for it."

"I understand that, Wesley. But before you decide to do this, make sure that this is what you want."

"It is."

"Give me his name, and the name of his church."

"Reverend Jonas Carter of the Greatest Power Baptist Church in Belhaven, North Carolina."

"I'll do some research and be back in touch."

Wesley placed the phone in its cradle and sat down on the couch. He thought about his last conversation with his grandfather.

"Can't wait…to see you and meet th-th-that little fella who s-s-stole your heart…Wesley," Grandpap had said.

"Yessir, Grandpap, you're gonna love him. Him and me are like you and me were. We're on the way to Momma's now, so we'll see you in a few days. I'm bringin you more flowers for you to enjoy while you're livin," he kidded. They both laughed.

"O…kay. I'll g..get my v-v-vase ready. A-And don't forget t-t-th-the watermelon," his Grandpap laughed.

Now he sat thinking, *If only I had gone there first, Grandpap would be alive. I would have been there with him at church. I would have saved him myself.* Wesley blamed himself. He was in agony; he held his head in his hands. He closed his eyes, and a picture of his Grandpap sitting in the church clapping his hands and listening to that preacher came to his mind.

He was startled when he felt hands slide slowly down both of his arms. He looked up to see Kailise. She wrapped her arms around his neck, holding him tightly and stroking his hair while moving into his lap. They embraced. Her touch was soft and silky, her scent invigorating. She pulled him to her, showering his ears, cheeks and lips with light kisses. He didn't want this, but she was relentlessly brushing her body against his, kissing him, pawing him and pulling at his clothes. He gave in. He needed to fill his mind with something else. He needed to; he had to, and so he did. He let himself fall fully into the moment, abruptly scooping Kailise into his arms and carrying her to his room, where their friendship was forever changed.

As the sun began to rise Wesley watched Kailise sleeping in his bed. He was ashamed of what he had let happen and agonized over it. He didn't love Kailise romantically, and he knew that she cared for him in that way. She turned over and saw him watching her from the chair.

"Kailise, I'm sorry," he said. "This shouldn't have happened."

"Wesley, I wanted this. I love you. We are good together."

"No, Kailise. You don't understand. This shouldn't have happened. This changes our relationship. We work together, and there's Julian."

"Yes, I know, Wesley, and this will make it better now. We will be closer, we will be a family."

"No, Kailise, we won't."

"Why not, Wesley?" she pleaded. "I have watched you with the women you go out with in Hong Kong. You do not care about them. You treat me like someone special, not them. You treat them as though they do not matter in your life at all."

"Yes, that's all true. You are someone who's special in my life, and they're not, Kailise. I love you like I love my family, not like I would love a wife. I'm sorry, but I just don't love you that way."

"Wesley, I do not care. You will grow to love me that way. It will happen."

"Kailise, it won't happen that way. Please...let go of it. We will not be together that way. I am truly sorry. Please forgive me."

Kailise stared at Wesley for several minutes. He waited for her to continue the dispute. She didn't. She snatched the sheet from the bed, wrapping it around her as she left the room, and walked through the suite to her room, slamming the door tightly.

Chapter 30

GRIEF

*I*t was Thursday, two days until the funeral. Later that morning, Wesley and Liz took their little group with them. Everyone was enchanted by the lovely little town as they drove through it. Kailise looked out the window of the van and daydreamed about a life with Wesley and Julian in a sweet little town like Belhaven. She believed that once she, Julian and Wesley got back to Hong Kong that Wesley would realize they should be together. She attributed his reluctance toward her to the grief of losing his grandfather. She was sure that it would all work out in her favor.

The first stop was the funeral home, to check on the service details. Reverend Carter was there finalizing things. When Wesley saw him in the office, he turned and walked back outside to wait in the front yard. Reverend Carter followed.

"Mr. Lewis, I'd like to talk with you."

"You're talking," Wesley stated.

"Mr. Lewis, I know there's no way that I can express my distress over what happened or explain how your grandfather was left in the building."

"No, there is not," he curtly agreed.

"I just want you to know that the moment I realized your grandfather was still in that building, I tried to re-enter to help him. I'm not making any excuses."

"That's what it sounds like," Wesley accused, his annoyance rising.

"No, Mr. Lewis, I blame myself completely. I'll take this to my grave."

"That may be sooner than you think," he said in a menacing tone.

"If that's what happens to me, then it would be the will of God," he conceded, looking into Wesley's eyes.

Wesley was taken aback, but only for a moment.

"So that's your game, huh? Con us into thinkin that you're so sorry and that whatever happens to you is God's will. You acceptin the blame isn't gonna bring my grandfather back."

"Mr. Lewis, I can't change your mind about me."

"That's right. So get out of my face."

Wesley walked away to the van. When Liz, Rick, Kailise and the kids came back outside, it had begun to rain lightly. The rain was refreshing. It's scent, the mixture of rich, moist earth and salt water from the nearby ocean, was soothing. They piled into the van and drove to Clara's house on the outskirts of town. She had a lovely home surrounded by trees and vacant land. The older lady from the funeral home, their grandfather's sister, was sitting in a rocking chair on the front porch. It was raining harder now, and as they ran toward the house, she called out to them.

"Morning! Don't you just love a good, rainy day?" she smiled.

"Yes, when you don't have to be out in it," Rick shouted back through the rain, while herding everyone onto the porch.

As they shook the cool water from them, laughing and enjoying the moment, Lorraine came outside, cautiously watching Wesley and Liz, not sure how they would receive her that day.

"Good mornin, Mother," Liz said, flatly.

"Good mornin, everyone," Lorraine replied dramatically and rushed to hug her grandchildren, who warmly embraced her.

Etta noticed the cool reception that Lorraine received from her children. Lorraine turned to her Aunt Etta and introduced everyone.

"Auntie Etta," Lorraine started, "is your grandfather's only livin sibling."

"Hello, Aunt Etta." Liz went to her and hugged her tightly. Tina, Andre and Tyrell followed, hugging her and kissing her on both cheeks.

Etta was overcome with emotion. She had never met them and had no other family that she interacted with left in the world. She was touched by their warm acceptance of her and embraced them all lovingly, squeezing the children to her.

"Oh, my," she said. "You all are sure making me feel wonderful."

"Where is your daughter, Aunt Etta? Is she inside?" Liz asked.

"Oh, no, honey, I wasn't blessed with any children of my own," she answered.

"Oh?...I thought the young lady who was with you at the funeral home was our cousin."

"No, no...though Arie is like a daughter to me. She lives with me. I have a big house that my husband left to me and I fill it with young people. They rent my extra bedrooms, and Arie is one of them. But she is more than just a renter; she is my family, baby. You'll meet her and love her just as much as I do."

Liz chuckled. "If you love her so much, I'm sure we will, too."

Lorraine looked at Wesley, who stood staring at her coldly. She turned to the children.

"Yes, well...uh...Go on inside, children, and dry off. Your Aunt Jean has hot chocolate waitin on the stove for you."

"Oh, yay! I love hot chocolate," Andre bellowed.

"Me, too," Tyrell echoed.

Andre, Tyrell and Tina rushed into the house. Julian hung back near his mother, remembering the scene in Ohio when he and his Uncle Wesley had abruptly left Lorraine's apartment. Lorraine looked at him, and then at Kailise.

Wesley noticed and said, "Mother, this is Julian's mother, Kailise. She's a good friend of mine. I didn't have a chance to tell you about her when Julian and I were in Cleveland, since our visit to Ohio was cut short."

"Hello," Lorraine said warily. She wasn't sure how she felt about him being there with a woman of a different ethnicity.

Kailise felt her disapproval and nodded her head slightly. Liz noticed the exchange. She and Rick went into the house, pulling Kailise along; Julian followed. Lorraine stared at Wesley for a few moments, then slowly turned and followed them into the house.

Wesley walked toward Ms. Etta and sat in one of the other rocking chairs. They stayed on the porch together enjoying the rain. From what Ms. Etta had been told by her brother and the scene she had just witnessed, she knew that Wesley needed time. So she waited.

The rain subsided and eventually stopped. The sun glided from behind the clouds as the temperature began to soar, replacing the cool, fresh morning mist with Carolina's usual hot humidity.

"Aunt Etta," Wesley said, breaking the silence after nearly an hour. "I didn't know that Grandpap had a sister. It makes me realize how selfish I was. All I ever talked about was what was goin on with me," Wesley sadly began.

"Well, that's alright, Wesley. Your grandfather could have talked about other things to you if he had wanted to, so don't go blaming yourself for that." She paused. "He was a private man."

"Are there other brothers or sisters?" he asked.

"There were, but we were the last ones still living. Now it's just me. There were ten of us in all: six girls and four boys. I'm the youngest, and there were three between me and Thomas. He was my big brother." She smiled.

Wesley was quiet, not knowing what to say or do.

"Your grandfather thought the world of you, Wesley. He talked about you every Saturday when we spoke on the telephone. I've heard so much about your life that I feel like I've known you the whole time."

"It's good to know that he had you in his life. After the farm was sold and he was put in that nursin home, I felt so bad for him. I thought that he didn't have any life or anybody."

"Oh, he was still full of life, and he was making his way back. That was a strong man. That stroke wasn't gonna keep him down," she chuckled.

"I know you're sad that Grandpap died and that you'll never see him again. I want to help you get through this, Aunt Etta. You should know that I'm doin somethin about his death."

"Yes, Wesley, I am sad because I won't see or talk to Thomas again, here on Earth; but I'm not saddened by his death."

"What?" Wesley was shocked. "They're the same thing. He died and he's gone, forever."

"Oh, no, baby, they are *not* the same thing. I'm sad because I can no longer call my brother on Saturday mornings and have our talks and laugh about this life. But mostly, I am happy for Thomas. He is in a wonderful, holy place. I'll see him there one day, I pray. We're the ones who have it hard; we have to struggle on in this world until it's our time to get out of here," she said.

Wesley was stunned by this. *How could she so easily accept death?*

"But Aunt Etta, look at how he died. You can't be happy about that. He was alone. They left him there alone to burn to death."

Etta winced at the mention of the horrible fire that took Thomas away.

"Yes, Wesley." Her eyes moistened as she pulled a hanky from her tote bag on the floor. "That is a terrible thought, and whenever I think about it, I am horrified for my Thomas." She openly cried.

"That's what I'm talkin about, Aunt Etta. That preacher, he's to blame. It's his fault Grandpap burned…he should have made sure that somebody helped him." Tears rolled from his eyes.

Etta reached out to him, and Wesley dropped to his knees, burying his head in her lap. Together, they cried tears of agony for Thomas.

"God has His reasons for allowing Thomas to die that way, Wesley," she gently continued. "That isn't for us to question. There's something to be learned somewhere in this, by someone, for some unknown reason. I have faith that one day I will know why, or that one day it won't matter to me; and I know within that Thomas was not alone in that church when he died. The Holy Spirit was there with him. I simply have faith in my Lord, Jesus."

Wesley pulled back and stared at her in disbelief. He wiped his face and moved back to the chair.

"It's not that easy for me to accept, Aunt Etta. You're right about one thing. Someone must learn from this, and it's that preacher. He's gonna learn a lesson that he will take to his grave."

Wesley stood and took his aunt's hand and kissed it.

"Wesley, don't do anything foolish. Your grandfather would NOT want that."

"What I'm about to do is NOT foolish, Aunt Etta. It's what I feel I MUST do for the memory of my grandfather."

"Wesley, stop. Stop it. There's something that I need to show you. Let's go for a ride, just the two of us, if that's okay with you."

"O…kay, Aunt Etta. How long will this take?" he asked, impatiently.

"Not long. Please. Come with me, Wesley. It's important."

"Alright…Okay. Well, I'll let them know that we're goin out."

Wesley drove Aunt Etta's rented sedan, following her directions. After backtracking into Belhaven, they went through the town's center and turned onto a two-lane highway that took them into the countryside from the opposite end of town. Wesley was mesmerized by the beauty of North Carolina. Because it was summertime, everything flourished. The leaves and branches of the fully-bloomed trees spilled into the path, shading the small road. The fragrances of gardenias, rosemary and the like were abundant. Though the thick, sticky heat of the Carolinas was hindering, its splendor was charming, causing Wesley to remember the joys of his childhood in the southern countryside.

They rode for nearly thirty minutes on the little highway before coming to a fork in the road. Wesley followed to the left, as instructed, and then turned onto a wide dirt road, which led through the trees into a clearing. There was a wide expanse of land, bordered on two sides by the thick trees of the forest and brilliant wildflowers. A well manicured, one-story yellow and white cottage with a wrap-around porch stood in the center of the lot. Behind the cottage, the waters of the Pamlico Sound stretched beyond the picturesque marshlands. The cottage was adorned with an array of flowers bordered by blossoming herbs and unusual shrubbery. Strategically-placed trees provided much needed shade, and a wheelchair ramp led from the circular driveway up the left side of the wide porch.

Wesley parked the car in front of the cottage. He inhaled deeply when he smelled the pungent salt water in the air as he got out of the car. Aunt Etta came around to stand beside Wesley. She wore a wide smile as she stretched her arms toward the cottage.

"Is this what you wanted to show me, Aunt Etta?" he asked.

"Yes, Wesley, this is OUR family's home, yours and mine; it's what's left of the Lewis family land. A homestead, if you will."

"But I thought you lived in Missouri…"

"That's right, I do," she said. "Come on inside and I'll fill you in on a little secret that Thomas and I have had for years."

All of the furnishings in the cottage were bright and airy. It gave a sense of bliss. There were pictures of nature throughout. The furniture had a Caribbean flair and the rugs were made of natural fibers in bright, welcoming colors. All of the windows were covered with beautifully handmade cotton curtains, with tie backs to give full views of the surrounding wooded area and the water's edge. Vases filled with fresh flowers and potted herbs bloomed in every room.

As they entered the house, the young woman Wesley had seen at the funeral home stood watching from the counter that separated the kitchen from the combined dining and living room area.

"Arie," Etta called out. "Come and meet my nephew."

Arie's feet would not move. As she looked at Wesley he returned her steady gaze. Again, their eyes were riveted to each other, as they had been at the funeral home. Arie picked up a tray with three glasses of the iced tea that she had poured when she saw the car pull into the front of the cottage.

"Okay, Ms. Etta." She forced her eyes from Wesley's and took the tray into the living room.

"I thought you may be thirsty after the drive from town."

"Oh, yes, I know I am. Thank you, honey." She raised one of the glasses to her lips, taking a long, slow drink…as Wesley and Arie warily observed each other, both bewildered by the magnetic pull they were experiencing.

"Oh, my, that was delicious. You've gotten the hang of making real southern iced tea now, Miss Arie," Etta chuckled. "Wesley, this is my Arie. She is the closest thing I have to a child of my own, so that's what I call her: my daughter." She smiled.

"Nice to meet you, Arie." he said.

"You, too," she shyly responded.

"Well, come on, sit down Wesley, and let me tell you about this little place I call my haven."

The three of them sat on the two couches that faced each other in front of the big bay window.

"You see, Wesley, when my Thomas started getting sick, I told him that we had to make some decisions while he still could; so if something happened, he wouldn't be taken advantage of. The farm wasn't sold after he moved into the nursing home, like everyone thinks. We sold that farm way before, and then rented it back from the owner so Thomas could still live there."

Wesley caught his breath.

"But, we didn't sell all the land. We kept this part where this little cottage is. It's 5 acres on the edge of the 93 acres our family owned, the most beautiful section of the land."

"Ninety-three acres?" Wesley whimpered.

"I know. I know what you're thinking. We did give up a lot of prime real estate, but we were getting older and Thomas didn't trust his children. He knew that none of his last three wanted to live on the land. Your momma and Jean been in Ohio for years, and Clara is such a spiteful person, he didn't trust her even in his sight. So he decided to sell it and keep a little piece of his happiness, and this is it.

"I came down here and together we had this place built. We didn't tell nobody. We even used contractors from Rocky Mount and Raleigh. And when this place was finished and he saw it, he was elated. He sat out on that back porch for hours and hours, just enjoying the view. He loved watching the tall grasses and reeds of the marshlands swaying lazily in the soft, humid breeze. And every now and then, a boat silently glided by in the distance, and he would smile and wave. All of the natural beauty surrounding this little piece of Heaven on Earth was nothing short of a true blessing for us both."

"Wow, that's somethin. He had this wonderful place, and then he got sick and never got to see it again," Wesley sadly realized.

"Well now, that is not entirely true, baby. After he went into the nursing home, once a year I came down to visit your grandfather for a month, in the early fall. I hired a nurse from the East Carolina University Hospital, and we would pick him up and bring him here for the whole month. It was wonderful for us both. We talked and reminisced and played music, and I cooked any and everything he wanted to eat. And..."

Wesley was silent as his aunt continued to talk, telling him the details of her visits with his Grandpap. As the story sunk in, he began to feel better. He imagined his grandfather sitting on the back porch of the house, and it soothed his soul for the first time since he'd learned of his death. When his aunt stopped talking, Wesley got up and went out to sit on the back steps and stare out into the waters, as his grandfather had.

Chapter 31

DISCOVERY

*A*rie went out to check on Wesley after a while.

"You doing okay? Like some more tea?" she asked.

Wesley looked up and again was amazed at the sensations he felt when he looked at her.

"Have we ever met anywhere?" he asked in an urgent tone.

"I've actually been thinking about that, too," she said. "We must have. Have you ever been to Kansas City?"

"No."

"Oh, okay. Well, hmm. I don't know, then; been there all my life."

"No, I think you just remind me of someone," he reasoned.

"I'm sure that's what it is. What are you thinking about out here?" she asked.

"Just thinkin about my grandfather."

"He sounds like he was an incredible man. Ms. Etta sure loved him." She sat down on the step beside him.

"I've always wondered what it would be like to have a brother or sister or a parent," she continued.

"I'm gatherin that you don't?" Wesley asked.

"Nope, just me," Arie answered. Thoughts of Beth drifted through her mind.

"Come on, there must be someone?" He turned and stared into her eyes again.

"There was; she was like a sister. Her name was Beth. Now, there's only Ms. Etta," she quietly answered, returning his gaze with one of her own.

"I've mostly been alone in this life. It's my walk, my journey, and I accept it."

Wesley was startled by her intensity. They continued to look at each other. He was drawn to Arie; he couldn't understand it. It was an unfamiliar feeling for him, as though there was a new dimension within his being. Arie was also bewildered: not only by how she felt at that moment, but by her desire to be near this man.

151

They moved from the steps to the candle lit back porch and talked about their lives well into the night. They shared things they hadn't told anyone else, beneath a cloudless, starlit sky. They listened intensely as they hadn't listened to anyone, and they talked openly, honestly: sharing things that stunned them both. Wesley talked about Kailise and the complication their friendship had just encountered. Arie told Wesley about Charles. They shared their losses of Brent and Beth, and the scorching pangs of loss were subdued in them both. They wildly laughed, whispered, and even subtlety cried together.

"Have you ever thought that you had a soul mate?" Wesley asked.

"Yes, I know I do. For years, I've wondered where he was and what he was doing at that very moment," she said, staring directly into his eyes.

"I've always known I had a soul mate somewhere. I've been waitin for that person. I was fooled a few times thinkin that it was some people I met before now."

Wesley slid closer to Arie until his leg was against hers. He covered her hand with his. An immediate rush of joy washed over them both as they interlaced their fingers of both their hands.

"I know you're gonna think I'm crazy, but I KNOW that we're gonna be together, that we're suppose to be together," Wesley declared as he marveled over her with amazement.

"No, I don't think you're crazy," she whispered as they moved even closer.

Wesley leaned in, brushing his cheek to hers while whispering in her ear.

"I know that you're my soul mate. You're gonna be my wife."

Arie was giddy with excitement. She couldn't admit it, but she felt the same way. There was something about him. Something strange was happening. She had never felt such intense emotion for anyone, ever; it was magical. She had just met this man, and yet she felt she could trust him with her life.

Wesley got on his knees on the step in front of her. He gently took her face in his hands and pulled her so close, their noses nearly touched. They stared into each other's eyes, seeking an explanation for the overpowering emotions. Wesley slowly pressed his lips onto Arie's. They pulled each other into a tight embrace, their bodies igniting with crackling explosions of glee. Their souls reunited. A feeling of intense elation overcame them both. The two became complete, yet they didn't know that. They only knew that their souls had soared.

Carlonian and Lizelle drifted above them. They rejoiced this long-awaited moment in time as two halves joined. Their souls reunited to continue their journey together.

Wesley led Arie to a hammock that hung between two pillars on the porch. They climbed into the hammock, where they slept in each other's arms and awakened to a breathtaking sunrise over the dark waters of the Sound. It was a brief, but blissful, rest...the calm before the storm.

Chapter 32

REVELATIONS

*W*esley had called Liz the night before from Etta's cottage, telling her that he and Aunt Etta had gotten tied up and would not be coming back to the house. He said he would meet them back at the hotel.

Kailise was devastated that he had not asked to speak to her, and had left no message for her with Liz or at the hotel when they returned there. She was beside herself with anger at first, and later with worry, because at 11:00 that night Wesley still wasn't there and hadn't called her.

She didn't sleep, pacing the floor in the living room of their hotel suite until the sun rose and beyond. Because of the nature of their work, anything could have happened to Wesley. It was late Friday morning when she decided to call Major Wright. When she picked up the receiver to make the call, she heard a key in the door.

Wesley came into the living room of the suite and was surprised to see Kailise waiting there.

"You are okay. I am so happy to see you," she gushed and ran to hug him.

"Wha-what's wrong?" he answered.

"I was worried. You did not call. You should have called to let me know you were not coming back last night."

"Kailise, our relationship hasn't changed. I don't report to anyone," he blankly stated.

"I know that, but I am here to support you. I am out of my comfort zone. You could have called me. You called your sister."

"Kailise, I'm sorry I didn't call, but don't expect that from me. You and I have never had that kind of relationship." He was annoyed. "I told you that I'm sorry about what happened between us. I wish I could take it back."

"I do not, Wesley. I will cherish our time together. It was wonderful. You will see it too, one day." She continued, "Your sister called this morning and I did not know what to say to her. I told her that you were sleeping."

"What? Why did you lie to her?"

"Because Wesley, she thinks that you and I are good together; that we're a couple. We spent a lot of time together talking yesterday. She worries about you and she thinks that I would make a difference in your life, if I were your wife. So I did not want her to think badly of you, if she knew that you stayed away all night."

"Kailise, I'm glad that you and Liz got to know each other better because both of you are very important to me. But I told you that the love I have for you is like the love I have for a sister, like Liz. I thought that our relationship was clear to both of us."

"It has been until recently: especially since I came here. You seemed so happy to see me, and then I was accepted by your sister and her family. I realized that other than Julian, you are the most important person in my life. I also realized that I love you in more than a platonic way. And the fact that you have love for me, any kind of love, is enough. Marriages have been based on less than that, Wesley."

"Marriage!" Wesley exclaimed. He was confused about how the conversation had turned so quickly to this place, and couldn't imagine where it would go if he didn't stop it.

"Kailise. You and I will never be married."

Kailise froze. The room went silent. Kailise looked at Wesley with a sadness he couldn't understand.

"I'll be back in a few minutes," he said. "I'm goin to see what Liz wanted."

Liz, Rick and the children were in the restaurant having breakfast. Tina, Andre and Tyrell were having the time of their lives. They swam everyday and were given permission to attack the buffets at mealtimes with no restrictions. They were away from the table when Wesley found Liz and Rick.

"Good mornin," he said a little more joyfully than even he expected.

"Well, good mornin there, Baby Brother," Liz said, eyeing him suspiciously.

"I see you haven't had a chance to change your clothes, man," Rick observed. "Late night?"

"Long story." He turned his attention to Liz. "Kailise said you called."

"Uh-huh, and I see you weren't sleepin. No matter. What does matter is that a lawyer called here this mornin. Grandpap had a will and his lawyer wants to get everybody together to hear Grandpap's wishes before we leave."

"Oh, really."

"Yes, he said we could hear it today, or if we would rather wait until after the funeral, it would have to be on Monday."

"What does everyone else want to do?" he asked.

"I don't know. He's contactin them. I told him that we would do whatever they want to do. He's suppose to call me back as soon as he talks with them. So, I would suggest that you go get yourself together in case we have to go today."

Wesley went back to the suite to find that Kailise had closed and locked her portion of the suite off from the living room. He knocked on her door to check on her, but she didn't answer. He showered, changed and ordered room service while waiting for Liz's call about the will.

His mind drifted to the early morning when he was in the hammock with Arie. He had been relieved to find her wrapped within his arms, sleeping peacefully. Before opening his eyes, he thought that maybe it had been a lovely dream. But it wasn't. He laid with her in the hammock fully clothed, not wanting to move, not wanting to disturb that surreal moment. His heart was so full, it nearly ached. He looked at Arie and wanted to have her near him, with him, always. He felt an overwhelming need to care for and protect her from anything. He had never felt happier.

The door to Kailise's room opened and Julian ran in to see Wesley.

"Where were you, Uncle Wesley?"

"What? No *good mornin?* No *how are you?*" he laughed as he grabbed Julian, tickling and kidding with him. Julian laughed, and then attacked the food Wesley offered. He had ordered for all of them since they hadn't left the suite. Julian dug into a cheeseburger.

"My Mommy's crying. She said you want her to go home."

"Well, I don't want her to go home. She's my friend."

"Does she know that?" Julian asked.

"Yes, she does, Julian. I'm gonna talk to your Mommy now. You stay here and eat your lunch."

When Wesley went into Kailise and Julian's room, their suitcases were packed and stood waiting. Kailise was dressed and sat staring out the window.

"I've always been honest with you, Kailise. You are an important part of my life, and I don't want that to change. I leaned on you, which resulted in me treatin you differently than I normally do, because this is a situation I have never found myself in. What happened the other night shouldn't have, and I feel terrible about it. I blame myself. I misled you with my actions, and I'm sorry. It's just that because we are such close friends, I was completely at ease and shared my grief with you. You misread that for somethin that it isn't. We've never played this relationship-game stuff. Please don't let it end our friendship."

Kailise looked at Wesley and nodded.

"If you are going out, please take Julian with you. I need some time to myself," she said.

"I will. Take all the time you need."

Wesley went back to the living room as the telephone rang. It was Liz. Their mother and her sisters wanted the reading of the will that day. Aunt Etta was mortified, but would go along with the majority. They were to meet at the lawyer's office in Belhaven at 3:00 that afternoon. It was already

1:00. Rick took the four children on an outing to Greenville to find a bowling alley while Liz and Wesley headed to the lawyer's office.

Steven J. Barringer, Esq. was the only lawyer that lived in the town of Belhaven. He was a personal friend of Thomas Lewis. They had grown up together. Steven and Thomas were the best of friends, never understanding or accepting the restraints that the South forced on them because of their economic backgrounds. They had chosen to ignore the town's protocol, and their friendship had survived for nearly seven decades.

It was unheard of for a man of an affluent family to be with a poor woman, but Steven and Etta secretly loved each other just the same. For the sake of his family name, Steven had let the love of his life leave Belhaven without him. He regretted his cowardice and watched her life from afar, vicariously enjoying her escapades through Thomas' stories. They had not spoken since she moved away and eventually married some fifty years ago. Steven had never been happy. He hadn't married. He longed to go back in time. He would have given up his career, his respectable life in Belhaven, to have been with Etta.

Etta was the first to arrive at Steven's office that afternoon, with Arie by her side. She purposely got there early because she was unsure of how he would receive her. The office was a large room on the first floor of Steven's home, an old, massive house near Main Street. She and Arie were greeted by the staff, and Arie was led to a study where she was served tea. Steven met Etta in the opulent foyer before taking her arm and escorting her into his private office. Filled with dark wooden office furniture and a brown paisley couch, the room was an ominous backdrop for the reading of the will. They sat together on the couch as Steven clasped both of her hands in his.

"For years I have imagined this moment," he said.

"Why, Steven?" Etta asked, genuinely confused.

"Because Etta, I was a fool. I saw that too late. I loved you. I love you still. No matter what does or doesn't happen, I had to tell you that today. I loved your brother, too. And when this happened, I realized that I placed importance on the wrong things back then. I have wasted so many years of my life. I have a brilliant career and nothing else."

Etta reached out and gently rubbed Steven's cheek. They still enjoyed each other's company.

"If nothing else, have dinner with me tonight, Etta," Steven said.

"I would love to have dinner with you, Steven."

There was a knock on the door. The others were beginning to arrive. Wesley and Liz were the last to get there. When they entered the lawyer's office, their mother, Aunt Jean, Aunt Clara, Aunt Etta, and a woman and man they didn't know were already seated and waiting. A maid offered water, coffee or tea to everyone, and just before the meeting began the door opened and Chris, their long lost brother, walked into the office and sat down at the rear of the room.

Wesley and Liz looked at each other. No one spoke a word.

The will was short and to the point. The woman there was a nurse who worked at the nursing home where Thomas lived his last days. She had been kind to him, helping him to dress and with other tasks. He left her $5,000.00 and a tiepin for her husband, one that she had repeatedly admired.

The man in the room was Deacon Harold Brown, the man who helped him into church each week. He left him $5,000.00 and a savings bond for each of his young children.

Thomas had an insurance policy for $30,000.00, which listed his three daughters as equal beneficiaries. He also left each of them a small wooden box, which he had carved in his rehabilitation class. The carving strengthened his tired hands. Inside each box was a personal memento for them to remember their father. In Clara's box was the cross he wore around his neck with a note encouraging her to seek the Lord to soften her cold heart. In Jean's, the gold watch he loved more than any other personal possession with a note thanking her for her love, though it was from afar. And in Lorraine's box were her mother's wedding rings—with a note proclaiming his and her mother's love for her, something she doubted throughout her life.

Through the advice of his attorney, Thomas had purchased stock in Coca Cola and IBM and sold it at the right time, making him very rich. That money, along with the proceeds from the sale of the farm, had been used to pay Thomas' bills while he was living. The remainder, which was in excess of $2 million, was left to Liz, Wesley and JoJo equally. The money had been liquidated, as instructed. Steven handed Wesley and Liz certified checks and informed them that JoJo's portion had been placed in a trust fund for him.

The sisters were stunned. They couldn't decide if they were more upset about what their father had left them, or the fact that he was a millionaire.

It was revealed that 5 acres of the farm's land were still owned by him, and that a house stood on that land. The land and the house were left for Etta, Wesley and Liz to oversee, but its main purpose was to give JoJo a home to come to when he was released from prison.

A trust fund had been set up for Liz's children, so they could each attend college and get a good start in life.

Steven went to a box and removed a felt bag, before turning toward Chris, who sat quietly observing. When Steven pulled a large, unusual pipe from the bag he explained that Grandpap had left Chris his antique peace pipe with a message to reconcile his relationships with family. Chris stood and left the room without a word, leaving the pipe behind.

After the reading was over, Chris was waiting outside. He walked up to Wesley and embraced him. Wesley had stopped caring about Chris a long time ago. He stood motionless until Chris released him and stepped back.

"Wes, what is it, man? I thought you'd be happy to see me. I've missed you," Chris said.

"No, man, you haven't," Wesley answered. "I waited to hear from you for years, man, and guess what? I didn't. Why are you even here?"

"That lawyer called me, said the old man left me something in his will."

"Don't you call him that!" Wes shouted, and then paused. "And we all see that it means nothin to you." He quietly continued holding up the felt bag. "No problem man, I'm glad you didn't want it, cause I sure do; so thanks."

Liz walked up and glared threateningly at Chris. "How dare you show up here for a payday. You have no shame whatsoever, do you? But then again, you never did. Once you found out there was no money in it for you, you were through, huh?" She threw her hand up at Chris. "Go on, MAN, get out of here. You being here is an insult to the memory of our grandfather."

Lorraine rushed over and hugged Chris.

"I'm so happy to see you, Chris. I'm glad you came for your grandfather's funeral. He would be happy about that, too. Come on, let's go somewhere and talk."

"Uh, sorry Mother, I don't have time for that. When I heard the will was being read today I changed my return flight, so I'm heading to the airport in a few minutes, I'm just waiting on the taxi."

"Chris! You mean to say you're not gonna attend the service tomorrow?" she asked in disbelief.

"No, I'm not. I don't like funerals, never have."

"You haven't changed one bit," Liz spat. "You are still as self-centered as you ever were." She walked away, pulling Wesley with her.

Ms. Etta found Arie in the study and told her the details of the reading of the will. She also told her about the conversation with Steven and that they were going out to dinner. Arie had never seen Ms. Etta so excited. She was happy for her.

"Arie…" Wesley called out as he entered the study.

She turned to see him approaching. He reached for her hand. She reached for him, and he pulled her into a protective embrace. She felt light-headed and magical. Their connection was mystifying.

"Wasn't my Grandpap somethin else?" he bragged light-heartedly.

"He was, indeed," she chuckled.

"I'm going to head back to the hotel with Liz. I have to make sure that all the loose ends are tied up on a work thing. And I need to talk with Kailise again; I have to make sure she understands. I'm tryin to salvage the friendship after what happened between us."

"I hope she can understand. I know it's important to you. I hope it works out okay for you both. I'm a little tired anyway. I'm going back to the cottage and turn in. Are you sure you're alright?"

"I couldn't be better."

Chapter 33

BATTLE

When Wesley got back to the hotel, Kailise wouldn't open her door to talk. So he called Major Wright.

"Okay, Wes, you're not going to like this," the Major began.

"Well, go ahead tell me. It is what it is."

"The preacher appears to be the real thing, Wesley. He's squeaky clean, solid marriage, no playing around, no legal problems—ever; volunteers at a soup kitchen, the homeless shelter, AIDs clinic, hospital, works tirelessly with the youth…the man is trying to make a difference. He's nearly a saint. I found out that your grandfather had only had three visitors since he went to the nursing home: you, your grandfather's sister, and the Reverend."

"And since he's so wonderful, it's okay that he let my grandfather die?" Wesley shrieked into the phone.

"No, Wes, I'm not saying that. I'm just saying be sure that this is what you want to do. Be sure that this is something you can live with."

"I am sure, Major. Do it."

"Okay, Wesley. I'll get things started. When will you be back in Hong Kong?"

"As soon as the funeral is over, and I look into the eyes of that scum and watch his life drain away to nothin."

· · · · · · · · · · · · · ·

Carlonian was angry. He had watched Wesley all his life and waited for him to see the light. Now he was convinced that Wesley's heart was turning. He was becoming something that Carlonian could no longer recognize as good. He was losing him.

Wesley poured a glass of cognac and sat staring from the balcony of his hotel room. North Carolina was truly beautiful. He looked out at the tall pine trees, billowing gently in the night's breeze above the charming wild-flowers. He took a deep breath, filling his nostrils with the moist, thick air of Carolina heat and remembered the joys of his young years on the farm. He was relaxed.

"What are you thinking, Wesley?"

He was stunned by Brent's voice. He turned around and there he was; Brent was in his hotel room. He could see his face clearly through the balcony door. He couldn't believe his eyes...he was so happy to see him.

"Brent," he cried out. "What...where have you—"

"No, Wesley, I will ask the questions. What are you doing? You are not thinking clearly. You have ordered a man's destruction: a man of God. You must stop the action you have ordered against him."

"No, Brent, I won't. You don't know about this. You've been gone; you don't know what has happened, what he's done."

"I have seen the entire picture."

"You know me, Brent. You know who I am, so you know that I can't stop this. I won't stop this."

Wesley stepped back into the hotel room. The room was dark, but Brent was illuminated and Wesley could see that Brent had wings. He was stunned. Brent was an angel.

"My mind is playin tricks on me." Wesley was in awe, and stared unbelievably at Brent.

"Your mind is not playing tricks on you!" Carlonian said.

Wesley stood staring at his earthly friend.

"Brent, you have a son, man. He's amazing."

"Yes, I know, Wesley, and I am happy that you are in his life."

"You would be so proud of him if you were around him."

"I see what a blessing he is to his mother and to you. I am around him when you are around him. I am an angel, Wes. I am your angel while you are on Earth. I have been with you throughout your entire life here, and I knew you before your birth on Earth. My name is Carlonian."

"Knew me before? Wha...This is crazy."

"Yes, there was life before this, and the reason I have revealed myself to you now, is to show you that you are wrong to do what you're doing."

"No, you're wrong Car...Brent. Angel or not, you can't really understand this. You can't understand how I feel."

Carlonian took Wesley by his shoulders and pulled him closer.

"You are the one that does not understand, Wesley. What you are doing is the way of THIS world. If you continue on this path, you will surely miss out on your heavenly blessing. Read it for yourself in the Bible, Romans 12:17–21."

"Bible! Brent, I don't read the Bible, man."

"Wesley, you need God's Word in your life. The Bible is His book, His Word. He put His Word on Earth to help His people prevail. Read it in Hebrews 4:12 and 13, and in Proverbs, chapter 3."

Wesley tried to shake Brent away from him, but Brent held him tightly. They began struggling with each other.

"I don't care about a blessing I can't see. I care about the agony my grandfather felt." Wesley shouted. He twisted and pushed until he and Brent were in full physical contact. They fell to the floor, savagely wrestling—struggling to overcome each other, while trying not to hurt each other. They rolled around the room, flipping and somersaulting, until Wesley was exhausted.

"Every blessing in your life is because of something you can't see. Your grandfather was your grandfather on Earth for a reason that only God knows. You were a blessing to each other," Carlonian calmly explained.

The room suddenly quieted. Wesley and Carlonian carefully observed each other.

"The blessing meant for all of us is paradise, Wesley, eternal paradise in the Holy City as promised in the Bible. That is the blessing we all strive toward. Even when we, as mortals, don't remember it, our souls yearn for it." He paused.

And then he added, "You wanted that once with another, the one you've been searching for during your earthly existence. You were connected to her in another world and you are still connected. She has come into your life again here on Earth. If you don't open your heart to God, you will miss the blessing that is meant for you. Come with me so you can see for yourself."

Carlonian released Wesley from his grip and they were suddenly floating above a magnificent City, perfect in every way. Then Carlonian carried Wesley through the skies to a breathtaking garden, filled with unimaginable beauty.

Wesley's soul stirred and his heart softened. He was filled with a startling sense of peace. They hovered there, enjoying the moment while being in each other's presence.

"Your grandfather is at peace, Wes," Carlonian quietly shared. "The peace that he has been blessed with is much like what you are feeling right now; but for him it is eternal."

"How do you know that?" Wesley asked, hoping more than ever that it was true.

"Because when he left Earth, he returned to the place where we all began this journey. From there, he has joined God's cloud of witnesses. He sees you, Wesley. He is watching and praying and waiting for you. His hope is that you will overcome this obstacle that the dark forces of the earth have placed before you. They are using the fire that took your grandfather's earthly shell like an albatross, to hold you from your blessing. But Wesley, you must believe that your grandfather's spirit lives."

Wesley thought about what Carlonian said as they returned to the hotel room.

"I want to believe you. I want to believe in God. I want to have faith in Him; can't you just give that to me? Can't you just take this anger from me and stop me from doin what I've set in motion?"

"No, Wesley, I cannot. God sent me to guide you, but I cannot choose for you. You must make your own decision."

"I don't know if I can do that. I really hate this man."

"Anyone who hates his brother lives in darkness," Carlonian warned.

"He is not my brother."

"Yes, Wesley, he is; and you don't hate him. You hate what has happened to you in your lifetime. The Reverend is your scapegoat. He's bearing the brunt of the anger and rage that you have felt for most of your life. Your mother took you from the farm and you feel that she deserted you. You had a hard life growing up. Time after time, you've experienced a lack of the love you've been searching for. You suffered from Claudia's heartlessness, my death, and now your grandfather's tragic passing."

"Stop, I can't think of him as my brother."

"You can't see that he is, because you are surrounding yourself with darkness. He is your brother, your brother in Christ. You knew him in another world."

"I can't remember that."

"Forgive him, Wesley. Forgive your mother, forgive this world, and allow the Holy Spirit into your heart."

"I can't forgive...I can't," he cried aloud.

Wesley fell on his knees, and then on his face. He screamed out in anguish.

Carlonian spoke gently. "Wesley, you are on a path leading to a dark place of no return, but you have not yet reached its end. A battle of good and evil is being fought within your soul as you linger in the valley of decision. Forgiveness is key. Choose this day whom you will serve."

. . . .

Wesley opened his eyes and found that he was lying on the floor of his hotel room. The balcony door was open and it was dark outside. He was alone, soaking wet with perspiration. *Had he dreamed what had just happened? He couldn't have; it was so real.* He was physically exhausted and his body was so sore that he could hardly roll over. He lay there on the floor, conflicted. When he pulled himself up, he struggled to the nightstand beside the bed to look for a Bible.

Chapter 34

ACCEPTANCE

*W*hen the sun rose, Wesley sat motionless in a chair facing the balcony while the world gradually awakened from the night. Birds chirped in the distance and the warm haze of Carolina drifted slowly into the room.

He had read the scriptures that Brent told him about first, and then delved further in the Bible. Each time that he had tried to read the Bible in the past, it had ended in frustration. This time had been different. Wesley had been touched by the scriptures to the point that his appetite for the Word was insatiable, and so he had read through the night.

As the sun cast bright yellow beams through a perfectly clear sky, Wesley's heart was warmed from within. He thought of his grandfather smiling down on this glorious morning, happy that it would be a beautiful day, because it would make the funeral less difficult for those who loved him.

Thoughts of his grandfather brought a smile to his lips. He pictured him sitting in his wheelchair, enjoying the garden at the nursing home the last time he saw him. He imagined him going through his daily routines, especially on Sundays—then the day of his death was upon Wesley again. In spite of the previous night, he didn't know how he would make it through the day ahead as the full burden of his sorrow weighed on him.

The funeral would be held at Macedonia Baptist Church in Belhaven at 2:00 that afternoon. The limousine arrived at 1:00 to take the family from the hotel to the church. When Wesley, Kailise, Julian, Liz and her family arrived at the church, they were surprised to see that the parking lot was full and a crowd stood waiting in front of the building. They quickly made their way inside.

There was no viewing or wake and the coffin would remain closed. A handsome picture of Thomas Lewis in happier times had been found, enlarged, beautifully matted and framed for display beside the casket at the front of the church. Huge floral sprays flanked the satin blanketed casket, and the altar was filled with flourishing greenery and vibrant flowers.

163

The small church was filled to capacity with standing room only, including the second floor choir loft at the rear. Liz was happy with the incredible send off for her grandfather. Wesley felt nothing.

They moved up the center aisle to the reserved pews at the front of the church. The three sisters: Lorraine, Jean and Clara, sat fanning and socializing on the front row. They were receiving the townsfolk, enjoying the attention as though they were there meeting and greeting on any given Sunday morning. Across the aisle, Aunt Etta sat tall and stoic, staring at the coffin and sniffling into her hand-embroidered handkerchief. Steven sat on the aisle beside her with Arie at her other side, offering love and support. Wesley's mood brightened a bit when he saw them, and he went directly to sit between the two ladies. Etta was grateful as Wesley placed a strong arm around her for comfort. With his other hand, he took Arie's in his, pulling her close to him.

"We'll get through this together, Aunt Etta," Wesley whispered to his grieving aunt.

She nodded and rocked to the light, rambling organ music as the church was making final preparations for the service to begin.

Wesley turned and looked into Arie's eyes. The connection he felt with her was still as intense as the day before. He hadn't dreamed it or willed more into it. It was real. He knew that without a doubt.

Kailise was horrified by Wesley's actions. *What is happening?* she thought. She followed Liz and Rick into the pew behind their mother and aunts. She was thankful that the children were all sitting together with cousins who had come, so Julian was oblivious to this. She watched Wesley with his aunt and the other woman closely. *Who was she?* She had not seen or heard of her since she arrived. Wesley was different with her, she could tell that even from across the aisle. She could see how tenderly he interacted with her. He adored her. They regarded each other with a quiet passion. Kailise was devastated. At that moment, she realized that she and Wesley would never be together, even after what had happened between them.

She swallowed hard and blinked back tears. He had been clear about keeping their relationship professional. She had pushed the issue and had taken a calculated risk when he was most vulnerable. She couldn't blame anyone but herself for what had happened between them. *Still, why didn't she know about this woman who apparently means so much to him?*

The soft music stopped, and after a few silent moments the organist began playing, "What a Friend We Have in Jesus." All who loved Thomas Lewis knew that to be a favorite hymn. Soft whimpering could be heard throughout the church. The long, difficult service had begun.

Reverend Jonas Carter was seated behind the altar. Wesley was surprised. He thought that the minister wouldn't show up, that he might run off or just stay low until the funeral was over and the family was gone. But there he was, up front, unafraid and presiding over the service. When he slowly made his way to the podium, it was obvious that he was tormented.

He began speaking to the church, recounting the fire. Wesley became rigid, stiffening as he listened to the details of how his grandfather died. Arie squeezed his hand gently for support. He looked at her; her slight smile soothed his heart, momentarily. The minister continued.

"Thomas John Lewis was a devout man, and I have been broken-hearted since that horrible, horrible day. I've blamed myself for his death," Reverend Carter calmly stated.

"I can't help but try to place the blame elsewhere, because I am a mere human being. That's what we do; we try to justify things in our minds so that our hearts can accept what has happened. How could God have let Thomas Lewis, a devout follower, die in such a tragic manner while sitting in the house of the Lord? During this past week I've prayed for an answer. And I ask you, how can we as a church family begin to explain such a morbid loss of a life, of one of God's children right here in the house of the Lord? I've been conflicted, confused and ashamed. And then I remembered…I remembered because I realized that I wasn't thinking like a man of God. I was thinking like I didn't know God, as though He wasn't my Savior. You see, it took me, the human being, to remember that I live here in this sinful world and because of that, my mind is sometimes clouded with confusion and doubt. I can't help it, just like you can't help it and Brother Lewis couldn't help it. We can't explain why Brother Lewis died the way he did, because it is not for us to explain or for us to know why."

Humph, Wesley thought.

"You see," the Reverend continued. "The world that we live in is in a state of chaos. And out of that chaos terrible things happen here every day. When these things happen we feel abandoned by God, but He has not abandoned us. He has given us everything that we need to prepare ourselves for whatever comes our way, every day. He has given us His Word. His Word! That's right, right here."

He lifted the Bible into the air, while raising his head toward the heavens, tears seeping from his closed eyes.

"Jesus never said that what would come would be easy or that we would understand why it was happening. He has a divine purpose for everything that happens in our lives and He uses every circumstance. Why did Brother Lewis die the way that he did? We will never know that. We could stay here all day, speculating and grieving and cursing that day."

The Reverend straightened. "But instead, as Christians, we must rejoice! As Christians, we are expected to rejoice today!" he shouted.

Wesley nearly felt a leap of joy inside for his Grandpap as he hung on every word the minister said.

"Brother Lewis left his earthly vessel behind, but his spirit lives. We think of Brother Lewis sitting alone, but he was not alone. He had the best company any of us could ever ask for. The Holy Spirit was there that day. And though Brother Lewis' vessel was charred, his spirit was untouched as he triumphantly left this world and made his way on to Glory to join the cloud of witnesses. His spirit soars victoriously with our Heavenly Father. He is at peace; it is only those he left behind who are tormented. And because of that, we must uplift ourselves and each other and remember our Savior's love for us: His unconditional love. We must sing praises to the Lord that our brother is no longer plagued with illness and pain and suffering. His spirit is no longer weighed down with the immobility of paralysis. He soars!"

The Reverend paused to regain his composure. Wesley silently gave thanks when he thought of his grandfather as he was years ago when he was active and fit.

"I visited Brother Lewis every week in the nursing home where he was living. He always smiled when he saw me coming. And every week he'd say, 'Thank you, Pastor, thank you for givin me flowers while I'm livin.' "

Wesley's body jerked with shock when he heard his grandfather's words from the lips of the minister. He remembered Grandpap saying that throughout his lifetime.

"Yes, Brother Lewis talked a lot about the kind and thoughtful things that people did for him. He referred to their generous acts as flowers. He'd say that those acts were the flowers he could enjoy while he was still here, unlike the flowers that would be at his funeral. Those flowers are for the family to see and to enjoy, he'd say."

The Reverend waved his arm toward the abundant flowers on the altar and continued.

"Brother Lewis shared stories about a close relative with whom he shared a special bond. A young man whose life he had followed from a little boy."

Wesley froze.

"He told me about how he lost contact with him and how he grieved for him. Years later, he was faced with a difficult decision concerning this person, who was standing at a crossroad. He agonized over how to help him. His first instinct was to rescue him and bring him to back live on his farm again. But he decided that helping him to become a man was more important, and so he forced himself to confront him face-to-face, man-to-man. When he left that confrontation, he was shattered."

Wesley was heartbroken. He had known that it was difficult for his Grandpap when he came to his boot camp, but he hadn't realized the magnitude of it. His chest felt heavy as he struggled to keep his composure.

"A few weeks ago when I went into his room, he was on his knees praying. I waited, and when he finished he gave me a sealed envelope and told me that he felt his time was near. He asked me not to open the envelope until after his death, whenever that would be, and to read it at his funeral."

Wesley sat taller and leaned forward, as did most of the family members. The Pastor took the envelope from his pocket and took a piece of paper from inside.

"These are the last known written words of Brother Thomas John Lewis..."

My time on this earth is over. I am ready! I've been blessed with a strong body for this lifetime and many years to enjoy the abundant earth, along with the loved ones that the Lord chose to place in my life. I don't know the time or the hour, and that doesn't matter to me. I don't know the how's or why's of my departure from this life. And that doesn't matter to me. But what I do know is that I am a child of God. He's sendin for me and I am honored. So when I'm gone from this place, don't mourn me. Rejoice with me, because I have fought the good fight, I have finished the race, I have kept the faith. And now, I await you.

Carlonian fluttered above Wesley. He was aware of the warm emotions that Wesley was feeling and of a shift within his being.

Grandpap's words hit Wesley like a sledgehammer. His mind and heart seemed to split wide-open and were filled with bliss. He was happy for his Grandpap. He could see him writing that letter and hear him reading it. His sadness stood still; he felt elated and happy for his grandfather's soul. He finally felt that his grandfather was okay.

Reverend Carter walked down from the altar, and when Wesley looked up he was standing before him. Their eyes met; both were filled with tears. The Reverend handed the letter to Wesley and announced:

"Brother Lewis chose the last hymn for his service. Let us rejoice with our brother as he surrendered himself to our Heavenly Father."

The final hymn, "Victory Is Mine," was sung by all with a vibrant enthusiasm.

Carlonian did somersaults in the air as all of the other angels there rejoiced and gave praise.

At the end of the service everyone left the church building and moved outside. Wesley helped Etta and Arie into the leading limousine with Liz and her family for the processional to the cemetery. He told them he'd meet everyone back at Aunt Clara's for the repast and rushed to use a church telephone. He noticed that he hadn't seen Kailise or Julian after the service; he would look for them after he made his call. He was shown to a small office, where he placed a collect call to Major Wright.

"Major, what have you done about this thing with the Reverend?"

"Hold on, now. Don't be impatient, Wes. It's in the works."

"Major, stop this thing," Wesley commanded.

"Stop it!?" The Major yelled. "What the—"

"I've got to stop it, Major. I can't explain. Somethin's changed me like I thought I could never be changed."

"Wesley, I really don't care about your newfound revelations. You've inconvenienced a lot of people, not to mention the time and money involved. I told you to be sure."

"I was sure. I was wrong: I admit that. I don't like it, but I accept it. Just stop everything, sir. Hold me fully responsible."

"Oh, believe me, I do. And I will be letting you take the responsibility for it all as soon as you get back over here. When will that be? I need you here ASAP."

"That's the other thing, sir. I am not comin back," he sternly stated.

"What are you saying, Wesley? And be careful here, son. The next thing you say could determine your existence…or the lack of it," the Major cruelly warned.

"Now it's my turn to ask, what are you sayin, Major?"

"We had a deal, Wesley, and though you are asking me to rescind an order I placed based on your request, you are still expected to live up to your end. You are my best. I will not take you walking away lightly."

"Is this a threat, Major?" he asked, heatedly.

"It could be, Wesley. When you left here, you were asking a lot of questions. I was concerned about your loyalty then. And now, you want to walk away. I don't want to be sitting in my office waiting for the other shoe to drop one day."

"Major, I'm through with Global. When I say I'm through, I mean I'm through completely. I won't work at Global. I won't think about anything concernin Global. I won't talk about Global. I will just be gone. You have nothin to worry about."

"Unfortunately, I do. Where is Kailise?" the Major asked.

"She will be leavin for Hong Kong tomorrow."

"You make sure she does," he demanded. The line went dead.

Wesley felt a chill run through his body. When he left the room, Kailise was waiting outside the door. She was noticeably angry.

"I did not know that you were in love with another woman, Wesley. Why didn't you tell me about her before?" she grumbled.

"Kailise, you will not understand this. I don't understand it myself," he said.

"What is there to understand? You are in love with someone else, I can see that. That would be alright if you had just told me. I would have understood and left you alone the other night. Why did you not go to her the other night when you were so distraught?" she demanded.

"I didn't know her then, Kailise. That is what's so hard to understand. I just met her two days ago."

Her eyes narrowed. She looked at him with disgust.

"I do not believe that. I saw the two of you today. I watched you. Why do you lie to me?"

"Until two days ago, I wouldn't have believed it was possible. But I believe that she is my soul mate, the person that my being has searched for my whole life. She is my other half. I have never felt an instant connection like that with another person. Not even with Brent."

The mere mention of Brent's name carried more weight than anything. Kailise and Wesley stood staring at each other. When Kailise spoke again, Wesley heard a person he didn't know. She was cold and filled with loathing.

"Wesley, you are a liar. Julian and I will go. I will make a flight reservation and return to Hong Kong immediately. You will never see us again."

"Kailise, please, this is what I was tryin to avoid. Please don't do this. I know you're hurt right now, but you'll see that there is someone who is meant only for you out there in the world."

"My soul mate is you, Wesley. I've waited for you to see that. You were sent into my life because that is who you are. I love you more deeply than anyone ever could," she cried.

"I am not your soul mate. If I were, we would both feel the same way. I was brought into your life for Julian, can't you see that?"

She stood glaring at him. She reached up and slapped his face as hard as she could.

"Do not use my son in this. You are a man of dishonor. With love, there can also be hatred, and with hatred anything may happen."

She turned and walked out of the church. Wesley followed, pleading with Kailise to reconsider. She had a taxi waiting, and Julian was inside waiting for her. Kailise got in, slammed the door and never looked back as the taxi sped away. Julian waved sadly from the back window.

Chapter 35

ESCAPE

esley called for a taxi, but because the town only had five, which were all in use, he had to wait for over an hour. When he reached his Aunt Clara's house, the limousines had returned from the cemetery and everyone was inside. The house was packed so full that it was difficult to move around. There was more food than could be eaten that day. The entire congregation of the The Greatest Power Baptist Church had turned out for the funeral, and it seemed that every person had brought a covered dish to the house.

The mood was festive, which was surprisingly alright with Wesley. He paused and thought of his grandfather, smiling down on everyone having a good time in memory of him. As he turned a corner, he found himself face-to-face with the Reverend Carter. Neither of them spoke. Wesley nodded his head and lightly touched the Reverend's arm before turning to walk away. Reverend Carter realized that though Wesley had not, and never would, completely forgive him, that he had found a way to deal with and move through his anguish.

When Wesley looked through the kitchen window and saw his Aunt Etta sitting in a lawn chair in the back yard, he was relieved to finally find someone in the crowd. He made his way out to her.

"Hi there, baby. Did you get your business taken care of?" she asked.

"Yes, ma'am. Are you doin okay? Can I get you anything?" he asked.

"No, honey. I'm a little tired. I want to head on home soon. Steven is meeting me back at the cottage."

"Okay, I'll find Arie, and we can all be on our way," he said, smiling, happy that the whole ordeal was nearly over.

"Okay, baby. Arie went walking with your friend, Kayley."

"What did you say, Aunt Etta?"

"You know, that lovely co-worker of yours."

"Kailise...she's here?" he stammered.

"Yes, honey. She came in and said she wanted to talk with Arie."

Wesley's face drained. He couldn't understand why Kailise would have done that, and he knew that this would not turn out well.

"Do you know where Liz and her family are?" he asked.

"Yes, they're in the house. Your mother and her sisters aren't too happy about what happened with the will, so they're arguing with Liz and Rick about it in one of the bedrooms upstairs. The children are over there." She pointed toward the trees.

"I'll be right back, Aunt Etta."

Wesley ran in the direction that Arie and Kailise had walked. He found them sitting on a bench in a small park a block from the house.

"Wesley, hello…I was telling Arie all about life in Hong Kong. She is very excited to see Hong Kong."

"No, that is not what I said, Kailise. It sounds amazing, but Wesley and I have made a different decision for our future," Arie declared.

Kailise continued as if Arie hadn't said a word. "I told her about your wonderful job there, all of the incredible work that you do. How you help so many people. The Major cannot wait to meet Arie. He hopes that the two of you will be arriving in Hong Kong soon, so there will be no need to further delay your work, which only adds complications to the system." Kailise stared coldly at Wesley.

He knew then that Kailise had spoken with Major Wright, and that he was responsible for this.

"Okay, Kailise, what do you want?" he asked, throwing his hands in the air.

"Do not sound so ominous, Wesley. The Major is being very reasonable."

"What's wrong with you?" Arie asked Kailise, as she stood and went to stand near Wesley.

"Nothing is wrong, Arie. Wesley is at another crossroad in his life. It is time for him to make a difficult choice," Kailise stated professionally.

Wesley quickly interjected. "I've informed the Major that I won't be returnin to my job. He knows that I've already made my decision."

"I think you know that it is not as simple as that. You are at risk. Never forget that," she warned.

Kailise stood up and walked past Wesley. Neither Wesley nor Arie had noticed the taxi waiting on the other side of the park. They saw Julian sleeping on the seat as Kailise opened the door and got inside. The taxi drove away.

"Okay Wesley. I know that the work you've been doing was dangerous and you're leaving it, so what does all of this today mean for us?" Arie reasoned.

"We have to leave…right away. I've made plans for somethin like this. Let's go talk to Liz and Rick," Wesley said as he watched the taxi disappear.

They walked back to the house and quickly gathered Liz, her family and Aunt Etta into one of the limousines. Their first stop was the little cottage. Liz fell in love with the place. She thought of JoJo living there someday, and that made her happy. The children ran to the water's edge, took off their shoes and socks, and frolicked in the water up to their knees. Etta and Arie packed their things. Steven arrived, and he and Etta announced that they were eloping. They were leaving immediately for Las Vegas, and then an around-the-world cruise, after a brief stop in Kansas City to settle Etta's affairs. Wesley and Rick helped Steven put Etta's things in the car while Etta and Arie said their goodbyes.

"Honey, I don't understand what happened with you and my nephew, but I am very happy for you, baby. He is a good man." Etta wrapped her arms around Arie and held her close.

Arie whispered into Ms. Etta's ear, "I found him...I found my soul mate. I don't understand it completely, but it feels so right."

Wesley walked over and wrapped his arms around them both. The three of them held each other tightly.

"Don't worry, Aunt Etta, I'll take care of her," Wesley consoled. "We'll be in touch, but for now, enjoy your new life."

"Yes, you deserve this happiness. I love you, Ms. Etta. I'll miss you." Arie hugged her again.

"Okay, okay," Etta said, wiping her eyes. "I better go before I won't be able to leave you."

Arie's things were loaded into the rental car. They locked the house and went back to the hotel. Wesley drove Aunt Etta's rental car with Arie, while Rick and Liz followed in the limousine with the kids.

When they arrived at the hotel Kailise and Julian were not there. All of their things were gone. Liz insisted that the children go to bed. After everyone was settled, Liz and Rick went to Wesley's suite to discuss what had happened.

"What do we do now?" Liz asked Wesley.

"You, Rick and the kids go home. That's what you do. Don't worry about us. Arie and I will be fine." He looked at Arie and she smiled at him.

"I just can't believe this," Liz said. "Here you are runnin around the world puttin your life on the line, doin things for your country that no one will ever even thank you for."

"Hey, man, you have my respect, you know that," Rick added. "So what's your plan, where are you headed?"

"I'll be in touch, man. I have it all worked out. I'm ready for this kind of thing. My main concern is gettin all of you out of here and back home. And that the Reverend's life is okay. Once that's done, Arie and I will be fine."

"Hey, this is a really good bottle of wine," Liz said, picking up a bottle. "Let's open it and make a toast to Grandpap and Aunt Etta. They sure had it together and stuck it to everybody, didn't they?" she laughed.

"Here honey, I got it," Rick said. He opened the bottle with a cork-screw and poured the wine into four glasses.

"To Grandpap and Aunt Etta," Liz announced. "Here's to you both, and—"

Just as Liz was finishing her toast and brought the glass to her lips, Wesley knocked it from her hand, spilling the wine on the carpet. Wesley suddenly remembered that he hadn't bought or ordered any wine.

"Wesley, are you crazy?" she scolded.

"Everybody stop!" he shouted. "Don't drink the wine. It may be poisoned."

Wesley called the front desk and asked about the wine. It turned out that the hotel didn't serve that brand. So it had begun. The incident put a damper on the evening. They left the room immediately. Wesley motioned for them to follow him to an empty banquet room. He explained that he and Arie had to go. Liz was worried, but Wesley assured her that he was the only one they wanted.

"If you stay here and leave in the mornin as planned, no one will suspect anything. That will give us time to get away from here before they know it."

"I know I don't have to tell you to be careful and make sure you come back," Liz softly pleaded.

"No Liz, you don't, because I will be careful and I will come back... someday." He embraced his sister and she hugged him tightly, wondering if this would be the last time she ever saw him. She turned to Arie and hugged her, too. She didn't understand the love that Wesley and Arie had. No way would she ever open her heart so quickly and without reservation to anyone. But she liked Arie and loved her for loving her brother. He had been such a lonely soul. He was happy now. She could see it. He walked lighter and smiled so much. She hoped it would last for them both.

Rick and Wesley shook hands and even hugged goodbye. They respected each other deeply.

Wesley and Arie slipped into the employee's locker room at the hotel and found uniforms to change into. They went out into the darkness through the employee's entrance with some of the hotel workers as they were leaving work. Then they walked on side streets for over an hour. Wesley borrowed an air conditioning van that was parked on a secluded parking lot. It was a far cry from Wesley's beloved Corvette, which would be towed to the cottage. He had left it for his brother JoJo, who would be up for parole the following year. Wesley and Arie spent their second night together on the run.

The next morning, they abandoned the van in a remote area of Research Triangle Park near the airport.

They stopped at a pay phone. Wesley made an anonymous call to the air conditioning company, informing them where the van could be found on their answering machine. Next, he called an agent that he trusted to check on the Reverend's life.

"Gray? Lewis." Wesley spoke quickly into the phone.

"You're hot, man," he informed Wesley.

"I know. Just gotta know about an order. Jonas Carter. Did you check it out for me?" Wesley asked.

"It's cool, man. Take it easy," Gray said.

"Thanks." Wesley hung up.

He smiled and was relieved. He took Arie's hand in his.

"Are you sure?" he asked her.

"More sure than anything I've ever done in my life."

"There will be some difficult times. I don't know what to expect. And it could be dangerous. You can still walk away, go back to Kansas City, to your life there. I would understand."

"Wesley, my life is with you. My life is you."

They left the airport in a taxi and went to the Raleigh train station. Wesley bought two tickets on the northbound train; then he and Arie walked out of the train station to the bus depot about a mile away. They caught a bus to Smithfield, North Carolina and hitchhiked south on I-95 into Georgia, where they bought a motorcycle with cash. Together, they rode to Atlanta, Georgia, looking over their shoulders all the way. In Atlanta, they spent three nights at a hotel in Buckhead. Wesley contacted an agent there who owed him a favor, and had several sets of passports made with different aliases for them both.

They rode the motorcycle to the airport and abandoned it in one of the parking lots after wiping their prints from it. Then they bought two airline tickets on Delta Airlines to Seattle under the names Darryl and Marie Gilmore, and two tickets on American Airlines to Dallas, Texas for Rob and Pat Blair. They flew to Dallas under those names and spent four nights there at two different hotels under different names. Next, they bought two tickets to Vancouver, British Columbia on Canadian Air for Rob and Pat Blair, and two tickets to Miami for Charles and Bridgette Tucker on TWA. Then they flew to Tampa on a charter, where they hitched a ride on a small boat to Nassau, Bahamas. They spent six days there at a small local hotel, blending into the island.

Feeling more secure, Wesley chartered a prop to St. Maarten, Netherland, Antilles for James and Sonia Rivers. They played the role of tourists and spent a week at a moderately-priced resort on the Dutch side of the island, and then a week at a pricey resort on the French side.

Finally, after taking every precaution that Wesley could think of, they took a ferryboat to a smaller island nearby and purchased a sailboat. They sailed the Caribbean stopping at intimate islands, avoiding the popular islands and tourist traps. Finally, they happened upon a sparsely populated tropical paradise.

Chapter 36

CONTENTMENT

A year later Liz and Rick and the kids waited in their minivan outside Attica Prison for JoJo to walk through the prison gates a free man. He had been awarded parole. Liz couldn't be happier. She and Rick had attended the hearing, and now they were there to help her brother begin building a life. Most of his 32 years had been spent in jail.

Liz was sure that JoJo didn't know how to live in the outside world. She had heard about many inmates who came out, couldn't cope, and ended up back in jail. She wasn't going to let that happen to her brother. She and Rick sold their home on Long Island. They found an enormous house halfway between Greenville, North Carolina and the cottage on the outskirts of Belhaven, where JoJo would be living. Rick had gotten a job at East Carolina University in Greenville. Small-town life would be good for their teens and the twins they were expecting. It was an exciting time. They looked forward to a blissful life.

The life awaiting JoJo in North Carolina would be an adjustment for him. Grandpap's little cottage was isolated enough that he would not be scrutinized by neighbors.

. . . .

Nearly two thousand miles away, Wesley and Arie strolled along a deserted beach on a small, sparsely populated island in the Caribbean. It was mid-morning on a glorious November day. Miles of white sand stretched in both directions, bordered by the clear, green waters of the Caribbean Sea. The fine, soft sand, moist from the night's light rain, felt especially pleasing on Arie's toes as she scrunched them deeply into the sand with each step. How she enjoyed their easy, uncomplicated life.

They reached the small hill, which overlooked a large island across the choppy waters in the distance. Wesley spread the blanket over the cozy, grassy area they had come to call their perfect place. Arie unpacked pre-made coffee, Danish pastries and fresh fruit for their breakfast picnic at the most beautiful place on the island.

They had found their way to the island after fleeing the people at Global. Though it was remarkably beautiful, the island was still remote and scantily developed. It took some getting used to, and they had come to cherish the serenity that it offered. The air, the land and the sea were unblemished. There was no airport on the island; it could only be reached by boat. Few people lived there, so everyone knew when an outsider arrived at the tiny marina.

Wesley and Arie felt safe there. They had walked the beach and come across the small grassy area, which seemed so out of place along the sand-filled shore, that they claimed it as their own: purchasing 10 acres of land, which included the small, special plot. They were married there and built a house a few yards away with an incredible view of the ocean. Grand-pap's intricately-designed peace pipe stood prominently on a pedestal in a brightly lit atrium in their beautiful home.

As they settled onto the blanket and breathed in the wonderment of their life together, they joined hands and gave thanks. Thanks for God's love and mercy, and thanks for each other.

Though they didn't fully understand the ramifications of the cycle of life, they truly believed that their souls had been joined at another time... in another place. They were thankful to have found each other while struggling their way through this phase of life called *earth*, and they were peaceful and content as they patiently awaited that which was yet to come.

About the Author

Alisa Lynn is a gifted author, socially-active entrepreneur and devoted wife, mother, grandmother and dutiful worshipper and worker in her local church. Having strong roots in the church from childhood, Alisa's passion for writing has been a personal outlet throughout her life, which has led to her most recent endeavor, the writing of this novel, *In the Shadows of Bliss.* After attending the University of Colorado at Boulder, encouraged by the promise of adventure, Alisa became a flight attendant for a major airline. Five years later, she met her soul mate and the two were married within the same year. They later moved their family to North Carolina and pursued their aspirations of attaining the "American Dream," starting a successful specialized services business. Alisa and her husband still reside in the Tar Heel State with her 91-year-old, sprightly father and their animated dog, Cody. With a near empty nest, Alisa is thankful for her extraordinary thirty-year marriage, her children, grandchildren, and the blessings of family. They enjoy spontaneous travel and the simple things in life.

· · · · · · · · · · · · · ·

For more information, or to invite Alisa to speak at your church, organization or event, write to:

Labyrinth Publishing
P.O. Box 19243
Raleigh, NC 27619

· · · · · · · · · · · · · ·

You can also connect with Alisa through her web site, www.ALWriter.org, and on Facebook and Twitter—"Alisa Lynn."